DEATH TO AMERICA

A Special Agent Dylan Kane Thriller

By
J. Robert Kennedy

James Acton Thrillers
The Protocol
Brass Monkey
Broken Dove
The Templar's Relic
Flags of Sin
The Arab Fall
The Circle of Eight
The Venice Code
Pompeii's Ghosts
Amazon Burning

Detective Shakespeare Mysteries
Depraved Difference
Tick Tock
The Redeemer

Special Agent Dylan Kane Thrillers
Rogue Operator
Containment Failure
Cold Warriors
Death to America

Zander Varga, Vampire Detective
The Turned

DEATH TO AMERICA

A Special Agent Dylan Kane Thriller

J. ROBERT KENNEDY

ISBN-10: 1502471744

ISBN-13: 978-1502471741

First Edition

10 9 8 7 6 5 4 3 2 1

For fifteen year old Aziza Hamid who showed me what true terror looks like. I hope you never feel fear again like you did that day.

DEATH TO AMERICA

A Special Agent Dylan Kane Thriller

"Every step we take towards making the State our Caretaker of our lives, by that much we move toward making the State our Master."

Dwight D. Eisenhower

"They who would give up an essential liberty for temporary security, deserve neither liberty or security."

Benjamin Franklin, November 11, 1755

PREFACE

The technologies described in this book exist. They are used on a daily basis to protect the United States and its allies from aggressors, both foreign and domestic. When dealing with those foreign threats, we are able to use all of the tools in our arsenal, however when dealing with domestic threats, the Constitution often hinders those who would protect the citizens of what many consider the freest country in the world.

What you are about to read raises an important question:

What happens when the domestic threat is so grave, that it can only be addressed by ignoring the very rights guaranteed to every American, the very tenets that built the greatest nation on Earth?

In today's day and age of constant vigilance, of constant fears over terrorism, what would happen if the fight, now centered in lands so far away many can't find them on a map, were to tomorrow suddenly appear on the streets of Detroit, New York City, or Miami? Would the average person cling to their liberties, guaranteed to them for over two centuries by successive democratically elected governments, or would they demand their government violate those freedoms, under the belief that "if you've done nothing wrong, then you've nothing to hide."

If we were faced with an evil so terrifying, just how willing would we be to let our government violate our rights to save us?

1301 Second Avenue, Seattle, Washington
Today

Peter Jackson pulled at his longish hair, slowly letting the strands slip though his fingers, the massaging action on the scalp actually a good stress reliever he had discovered in his youth.

But Marybeth does it the best.

He smiled as he remembered the first time she had sat behind him at his favorite watering hole and whispered in his ear.

"Stressed much?"

"Hmmm," he had nodded, his eyes half closed.

"Let me help."

And she had stood in the middle of the bar giving him a scalp massage which included the pulling of his hair, something he had never experienced before, and it was wonderful.

No, it was amazing!

It was almost erotic in its delivery, her large breasts looming over him every time he looked up at her, she smiling down at him. But alas, it wasn't to be. She definitely wasn't his type, some new age Goth type, he a straitlaced hi-tech wonk struggling to climb the corporate ladder. Not to mention the fact her boyfriend Mike was huge. And a friend.

I wonder whatever happened to her?

He pulled his hair some more as the phone demanded his attention. He hit the speaker, his office door closed, his latest rung climbed garnering him a life outside the cubicle.

Life is good!

"Go for Pete!"

1

"Is this Mr. Peter Jackson?"

His heart leapt in his chest then stopped, the voice almost mechanical, robotic. Like something from the movies, yet something he had never heard in real life.

And it had to be one of his friends playing a gag on him.

"Yes."

"Mr. Peter Jackson of forty-two Seventy-Eighth Lane?"

He decided to play along as a smile spread across his face. "Yes."

"You have a wife named Connie and a daughter Elizabeth?"

His eyes narrowed slightly. "Yes." The smile was gone, the creepiness factor amping up. "Who is this? Is this Dave?"

His buddy Dave Brooklyn was a practical joker, one of the funniest bastards he'd ever met, especially once he had half a dozen brewskies in his system. But bringing his wife and kid into this was starting to cross a line he didn't think even Dave would dare.

"Mr. Jackson, your identity has been confirmed. You have been drafted by the Caliphate Restoration Army of Mohammad. You are now under our command. If you want no harm to come to your wife Connie or your daughter Elizabeth, you will follow our instructions exactly."

Jackson's chest tightened as he stood, staring at the phone. "Okay, listen, whoever this is, this is no longer funny. I'm hanging up now."

He reached for the button when the monotone voice replied. "If you terminate the call, we will execute your wife and child." Suddenly the voice changed and he paled, dropping into his seat as he grabbed the phone from its cradle.

"Daddy? Is that you?"

"Yes, sweetheart, are you okay?" Tears filled his eyes as he realized this was no longer a joke, no longer a prank that had crossed the boundaries of good taste.

His daughter's voice disappeared, replaced by the mechanical monster that had kidnapped his family. "You are about to receive a package. You will sign for it without indicating to the delivery man that anything is wrong."

"When?"

"Now." There was a knock at his office door and he jumped in his seat, nearly shitting his pants. "No tricks, Mr. Jackson, we know everything you are doing. Put the phone back on speaker."

"No tricks," he repeated, activating the speaker phone and returning the handset to its cradle. He wiped his eyes dry and took a deep breath. "Come in!"

The door opened and a FedEx driver stepped inside. "Good morning, sir, I've got a package here for you." He lifted it off the dolly and placed it on the corner of Jackson's desk. Jackson took the handheld computer from the driver and signed, all the while his eyes flitting between the large package and the man, trying to get a sense of whether or not he was in on it.

But he's our regular guy!

Jackson had no idea what his name was.

Johnson. It's on his name tag, you idiot.

He knew he had seen Johnson on dozens of occasions, if not hundreds. An office like this had FedEx coming almost every day, and he was their regular deliveryman.

"Careful, it's marked fragile," said Johnson with a smile as he closed the door behind him.

Jackson stood by the box. Nothing too large, perhaps the size of a case of bottled beer. "I've got the package." His voice was subdued, broken. Everything up until the arrival of the package had made the entire experience almost surreal with the possibility it could still be a joke, one that his wife had enlisted their daughter's help in playing.

But knowing exactly to the moment when a FedEx package would arrive?

That made it real.

Unless they're in the office?

"Open the box, very carefully."

Jackson retrieved a letter opener from his top-right desk drawer and cut the tape sealing the box, all the while looking out his office's large, glass walled windows to see if he could spot someone watching him.

Nothing.

And when he folded open the lids, he realized immediately that this was no joke.

And he was in desperate trouble.

"Take off your suit jacket and put on the vest. Carefully. Whatever you do, do not press the red button on the detonator."

Jackson was shaking now, his entire body barely clinging to reality as his world threatened to collapse around him. He pushed the box away from him, stepping back as his arms stretched out, looking for something to support himself with. He felt the smooth, cool finish of his office door and pushed back against it, wedging his shoulder blades into the corner as his eyes fixated on the open box perched on the corner of his desk.

A suicide vest!

He had seen them in the movies, on TV shows, and of course on the news.

But never in person.

And never had he thought he'd ever have the opportunity.

Not in America.

Not in his home town.

This is insane!

"Remove your jacket, Mr. Jackson."

His eyes tore away from the box, settling on the phone for only a moment, then returning to the impossible, the unbelievable.

"I won't ask again, Mr. Jackson."

How can they know what I'm doing?

He pulled his left arm out of its sleeve, shrugging the jacket off his shoulders, his entire body shaking freely now. Hanging the jacket on the back of the door, he approached the box and looked inside. Suddenly his blinds all closed, sending him to the corner again. He looked at the panel on the corner of his desk, one of the coolest features of his new office. It allowed him to open and close the blinds, dim the lights, control his Bluetooth connected iPhone, it playable through the speakers in the ceiling.

And now it was being used against him.

Which meant they had full access to the corporate network somehow.

Who are these people?

"Now gently remove the vest from the box. Be careful not to touch the red trigger."

Jackson approached the box, arms outstretched as if he were a zombie and the box contained brains. He gripped the sides, his head held high so he wouldn't have to look inside, then, taking a deep breath, he looked. And again felt his chest tighten like a vise.

Reaching inside, he carefully picked up the vest, it literally that. No sleeves, open at the front. It looked like something hunters might wear as an extra layer to keep their torso warm but their arms free to shoot. Sewn into the front and back were long red tubes, taped in place, the thread securing them, and at the top of the tubes were wires all leading to a cluster and a rectangle hidden by more black tape, stitched in place. From the rectangle a single wire, rolled in tape disguising whether or not it was actually a single wire, stretched for about two feet, ending in a tube with a red button at the end.

That must be the detonator.

"Put it on, now."

He nodded, to whom he did not know, but he was certain he was on some sort of camera. With the blinds closed, it had to be something in his office.

Unless they have some sort of thermal camera!

As he eyed the room around him, looking for anything out of the ordinary, he gingerly pushed his right arm through the hole in the vest, then carefully pulled it up to his shoulder. He slowly reached for the detonator, and held it securely, making certain his thumb was nowhere near the button. Sliding his other arm into the vest, he breathed a sigh of relief, grabbing the edge of the desk for support. His knuckles white, he lowered his head and took several deep breaths.

He needed to figure a way out of this, but he was at a loss. His mind was barely processing anything now, fear gripping him completely as if he were slowly being wrapped in a roll of cellophane from chest to feet, with each layer fewer and fewer options remained for escape.

"Now remove the ski mask from the box and put it over your head."

This is really happening!

He opened his eyes and looked back in the box. A black ski mask sat face up, staring back at him, the hollow eyes seemingly peering into his very soul.

Are you really going to let them kill you? To kill others?

At this point he didn't care about himself, he only cared about his wife and daughter. He knew where this was heading. They were going to send him out into public and force him to detonate the vest. Which could kill dozens of people. Innocent people. People who had wives and daughters of their own.

You can't do this!

"Now, Mr. Jackson."

He reached in and grabbed the mask, gently letting the trigger dangle at his side as he quickly pulled the oppressive wool knitting over his face. He adjusted it so he could see and breathe through the holes provided.

But it still felt claustrophobic.

He could feel his hair, matted in place, already beginning to sweat, the beads of salty discharge trickling down his neck, then his spine. He wondered if it might short circuit the vest if he were to get too sweaty. His heart skipped a beat, wondering if that meant it just wouldn't work, or if it could go off on its own.

"Very good, Mr. Jackson. We are almost done. Now take the sign from the box, and place it around your neck."

Another look and his eyes filled with tears as he realized what exactly he was being drafted into. *What had they called themselves?* His mind raced, trying to remember the words spoken only moments before, the entire conversation a mere fog of memory. *Caliphate Restoration Army of Mohammad.* They were Islamists. That much was now clear as he retrieved the cardboard sign at the bottom, a string tied off on the top two corners through holes that looked like they had been punched through with a knife and a twist.

The text on it, three simple words, sent chills up and down his spine.

DEATH TO AMERICA.

It was a slogan he had heard a thousand times, a popular refrain from the brainwashed masses of the Muslim world as they burned American flags and effigies of whatever American president happened to be in power at the time, at whatever perceived affront their religious leaders had told them

America had committed yet again. Before 9/11 he had paid it little mind, the Iran hostage crisis before his time, the news and world politics a boring thing his dad paid attention to. But after 9/11 he had been enraged like everyone else, cheering the troops on as they exacted our country's revenge on those who would attack us so brazenly.

Then he had grown numb to it like most others. The wars dragged on, the original intentions questioned, the missions changed, and as each Islamist outrage around the world continued to be perpetrated, he tuned out unless it was on home soil.

And there had been too many of those, even if they were all home grown.

It's terrifying to think that our own citizens would want to harm our country!

And yet here he was, fitting a sign with those three hateful words around his neck. He retrieved the detonator with his right hand, and stood trembling by the desk side, wondering who they intended him to kill, and why he had been chosen. He wasn't political, he barely kept up with the news. He and his friends sometimes chit-chatted about what was wrong with the country, he taking the side sometimes that not only the country but the entire West had become too complacent, too politically correct to speak up and face the problem that it was now enveloped in. Muslim immigration wasn't compatible with the Judeo-Christian Western world. Most Muslims were perfectly nice people who wanted to live in peace with those around them, but they wanted to live in peace in a culture that matched theirs.

A reasonable aspiration, he thought. Americans love America. Why? Because it's the greatest country the world has ever known, built with the blood, sweat and tears of pioneers who left their homes, crossed an ocean, and helped create the greatest democracy and military power in history. But if our country turned to shit for some reason, and we were forced to leave, would we immigrate to other countries and live with the locals, or would we seek out other Americans, and try to set up America-Town or some equivalent. Most likely we'd try to do that if we moved to Mexico, where the culture might be too different for some. But if we moved to Canada, would we really try to set up our own communities, or just blend in with a local population so similar to ours.

He had bet on the latter, which his friends hadn't really argued with. His point had been that when Muslims were forced to leave their countries because of war or other intolerable conditions, they came to America or Canada or the United Kingdom and wanted to live in peace. But when they found the country they had moved into so dramatically different than anything they could have imagined, they moved into enclaves with other Muslims, trying to set up their own "Mini-Iran" as Axel Rose had so delicately put it years ago.

And with those enclaves, a bubble quickly formed blocking out the reality of the culture they were living within, inspiring leaders to step up demanding the West change its laws and ways to permit their backward ways of thinking if looked at from a Western perspective where we are in some cases centuries ahead. And when a new generation of youth, born into these enclaves, citizens of their new country, are preached to day in and day out that their own country, the adopted country of their parents, hated them and their ways because they refused to let women be covered head to toe, refused to allow Sharia law, refused to change zoning for a Mosque, refused to condemn Israel for defending itself, these children quickly learned to hate. To hate those different from them, to hate their own country.

He had thought it so blatantly obvious that he found it impossible to believe that his government hadn't come to the same conclusions. Western Europe certainly was noticing it, but was it too late? New citizenship tests and courses in the UK, right wing anti-Muslim parties winning more and more seats, Holland repealing multiculturalism, France banning the burqa. These countries were beginning to fight back, but was it too little too late when millions lived within your borders, many born there with the full rights of citizenship.

The discussion with his friends over beers had been prompted by the outrages of Boko Haram and the kidnapping of the several hundred girls, and had been one of the more spirited ones, all of them arguing passionately about the same thing, even their buddy in London joining in over Skype missing his morning "Tube" as he called it.

Jackson sighed. *That* was the most political he had ever gotten. And he wasn't even sure how political it was. It wasn't a Republican or Democratic thing, it wasn't Left of Right. It was preserving our way of life against an enemy determined to end it. It was Capitalism versus Communism, the good old days of the Cold War. Two fundamentally different visions for the world, determined to wipe out the other.

And now here he was, turned into a pawn of the enemy.

His cellphone rang in his pocket.

"Answer your phone."

He reached in and answered the call. "Hello?"

"Hang up the phone on your desk."

It was the same voice. He complied.

"Now listen carefully. You will walk out of your office, walk to the center of the floor, stand up on a desk, and yell 'Allahu Akbar' three times, each time thrusting your free hand into the air. Then you will press the detonator. We will then release your wife and daughter. Repeat these instructions."

Tears poured down Jackson's face as he carefully repeated the instructions, his shoulders slumping, his chin dropping to his chest as he realized he had only moments to live, and it was his friends and co-workers who he was to kill.

And those who survived would think *he* did this to them, not the madmen on the other end of the phone.

"Very good, now proceed."

He sucked in a deep breath.

"No."

"You will proceed or we will kill your wife and daughter, starting with your daughter."

"I won't do it, not until I've spoken to them. I want to say goodbye." His voice cracked on the last word, the tears blinding him, his entire world a blur as if looking through a water feature wall, rivulets of pain and anguish trickling from the top to the bottom, then escaping and burning hot salty streaks down his cheeks down to his neck and chest.

"Very well."

"Daddy?"

"Peter, is that you?"

The voices of his two most precious possessions killed him. There was no doubting they had them both, and there was no doubting if they were willing to have him kill dozens or more, they wouldn't hesitate to kill two more innocents to attain their goal. But just hearing their voices seemed to make everything okay, everything normal again for just a brief instance.

"Yes, it's me. Are you two okay?" It was everything he could do to control his voice, to portray the strength he felt he needed to as a man, as a father, as a husband. He knew they must be terrified, and it was up to him to save them.

"Just scared, honey. What's going on?"

He could hear the fear in his wife's voice, but also the forced strength as they both tried to shield their daughter from the horror around her. "Have you heard the conversation?"

"No, we're in a room. Somebody's with us and they just told us you were on the phone."

"Okay, Lizzy darling, Mommy and I have to talk about your birthday, okay, so Mommy's going to cover your ears."

"Okay Daddy!"

His heart almost broke as the excitement in her voice over the prospect of her birthday wiped away all fear that might have been in the little six year old's heart.

"Okay, go ahead."

"They're forcing me to wear a suicide bomb vest—"

"Oh my God!" His wife's voice cracked, her spirit breaking as his own control slowly lost grip.

"They want me to blow up my office or they'll kill you and Lizzy."

His wife was sobbing now and behind it he could hear the innocent gentle humming of his daughter as she tried to do her part in not hearing the conversation, a tune, a beautiful simple tune he had heard a thousand times before breaking through over the gasps and cries of his wife, finally sent him over the edge as he realized he would never hear the song again.

"I'm sorry, hon, but I can't think of anything to do, anyway out of this. I asked them for a chance to say goodbye and they agreed. Once this is over with, they're supposed to let you two go free."

"Oh, Pete, I'm so sorry! I don't know what to say! My mind is a mess!"

"Just say you love me, and you forgive me."

"Of course I love you, and forgive you for what? You haven't done anything wrong."

"Yet." His chest heaved as the tears flowed and his sinuses began to clog. "Today I'm just a normal guy, tomorrow I'll be a villain, hated by everyone. You need to make sure they know I was forced to do this."

"I promise you, Pete, they'll know. No one will ever believe you did this willingly. Not your parents, not your friends. No one."

"I love you, Connie, with all my heart."

"I love you too."

"Put Lizzy back on."

"Oh, God, Pete. Please don't let this be the end. Please!"

"I'm so sorry." He sucked in a deep breath and held it, trying to build up the strength to say goodbye to his daughter.

"Hi Daddy!"

"Hi, sweetie. Listen, Daddy has to go now, and I just wanted you to know that I love you, okay?"

"I love you too, Daddy!"

"Good. Now you listen to your mother, and you be good for her, okay?"

"Okay. What are you getting me for my birthday?"

A sob erupted from him as he pictured her sitting at the kitchen table next week, her party cancelled, her mother a mess, her life collapsing around her as the world vilified her daddy.

"It's a surprise, honey. Now Daddy's got to go, okay?"

"Okay, bye Daddy."

"Bye sweetie." His finger hovered over the trigger, part of him wanting to end his pain now, but he knew he had to follow their instructions to the letter. "Good bye, Connie. I love you. Forever."

"Good b—"

The conversation was cut off, the mechanical voice, emotionless, replacing the tortured voice of his wife. "You have said your goodbyes. Now do you remember your instructions?"

"Y-yes," he gasped. He glanced over at the clock on the wall, just his eyes, and noted it was almost noon. The floor would begin to empty out if it wasn't already, as the staff headed for lunch. If he could just delay things he might save lives. "Just give me a minute to compose myself."

"One minute."

"Thank you."

He carefully let the detonator hang by his side as he blew his nose several times, clearing his sinuses as best he could, tossing the tissues in the trash. A few draws from his bottle of Diet Pepsi moistened his rapidly drying mouth, then he suddenly dropped to his knees, ripping his face mask off as he retched into the waste basket, he watched in horror as the trigger bounced off the floor, the red button touching the carpet as it hit at an angle, the button not depressing.

He grabbed for it, securing it in his hand as he rid himself of his breakfast, then wiped his face clean.

"It is time."

He nodded. "Give me a second, I just vomited."

"No more delays."

"I'm not delaying." He took another large swig of his pop, swished it around his mouth then spit it into the garbage can. He checked himself in the mirror, confirming he had no vomit on his clothes or face, then pulled the face mask back in place as he eyed the clock roll 12:01. "I'm ready."

"Proceed."

He sucked in a few deep breaths, his hand gripping the knob of the door, then slowly opened it, peering out to see if anyone had noticed him yet, then peaked around the corners. And almost smiled. As he had hoped, the hallways were filled as people rushed out for lunch. No one paid him any mind, even those going past him, their minds in another world as they debated what to have for lunch, and where.

He walked down the aisle, following the flow, then turned toward where his old cubicle used to be, the phone still held to his ear. Suddenly his buddy Jake Davidson popped up from his chair and grinned. "Hey, is that you Pete? What's with the ski mask? I was just about to come see you, see if you wanted to go slumming. A few of us are going to Molly's for l—" Davidson's eyes bulged. "Oh my God!"

Jackson looked at his friend but said nothing, using every fiber of his being to try and convey the only message possible at that moment.

Run!

Davidson stood frozen, then finally comprehended what was happening and tore out of his office, sprinting to the far wall where he had a direct line to the stairwell.

"Run! There's a bomb!" he screamed at the top of his lungs as soon as he reached the wall, "There's a bomb!"

Screams erupted as Jackson climbed on the desk of his old cubicle, giving the others a focal point to run away from. He raised his fist in the air and shouted, "Allahu Akbar!" More screams erupted as those not paying attention jumped from their desks, realizing whatever was happening wasn't a joke. He slowly lowered his hand then pumped it in the air again, each precious second he delayed as he followed his captors' instructions to the letter, saving lives. "Allahu Akbar!"

A beep emitted from the vest, and he realized he had gone too far.

The pain was intense and instantaneous as Peter Jackson of 42 78th Lane erupted into a ball of flame and terror, the first draftee in a new army determined to fulfill the goal first chanted by crowds of believers in 1979 Tehran.

J. ROBERT KENNEDY

Death to America!

Site 10, U.S. Air Force Plant 42

Palmdale, California

The Skunk Works

Three days later

Major Jason "Ticker" Miller gave the thumbs up to the Crew Chief and pushed the throttle forward on the F-35B Lighting II, one of the world's most advanced Fifth Generation fighter aircraft. Taxying to Runway 07 he received clearance from the tower and pushed the throttle forward hard, the single engine shoving him into the back of the seat, a feeling he would never tire of, and a feeling he knew he would never experience again.

For today was the day he knew he would die.

As he cleared the runway, gaining altitude, he banked hard to the right, pushing it full throttle as he hugged the deck. Disabling his transponder, he turned off the radio, the tower already protesting and instead spoke into his mike, knowing the cockpit voice recorder would tape everything and that someday his family might hear why he was doing what he was doing.

He checked for threats but the display showed clear as he rapidly chewed up the two hundred miles to the Mexican border.

"This is Major Jason Miller, United States Air Force. This message is for my family, friends and fellow servicemen. What I do today I do not do willingly. I love my country, I love my job, and I love the American way of life. I would never do anything to hurt my country, nor anything that might lead to harming my country. But today I have no choice. My wife and two sons have been kidnapped by Islamic terrorists, and I have been coerced into stealing this aircraft. If I do not, they have assured me they will be killed in a most gruesome"—his voice cracked and he sucked in a breath, trying to keep it together—"and horrible manner."

He paused as he noticed two Raptors being scrambled toward his position. He ignored them, the border only two minutes away, and the Raptors behind him with no hope of catching him. He wished it wasn't so. To be splashed by two of his comrades, taken out of the game while he betrayed his country, would be a far more preferable way to go, but he had followed the instructions to the letter, not willing to risk his family being killed for his failure to deliver.

He just prayed the United States Air Force would be able to retrieve the aircraft before it was handed over to some foreign power like China or Russia. He had wondered why a terrorist group would want the plane. Using it would be almost impossible since it was unarmed and they would need to be trained on it. The thought had crossed his mind that they would force him to train them, but it would still be unarmed. Then, last night as he gripped his baby son's teddy bear in one hand and his Glock in the other, he had figured it out.

They were planning on selling the plane to raise funds for their cause.

He was certain the Chinese or Russians, hell, even the North Koreans or Iranians, would pay hundreds of millions for the plane. A fully functional Fifth Generation fighter jet, one of the most advanced aircraft in the world, would fast-forward any country by years, and for backwaters like Iran, decades.

If they could figure it out.

He had some doubt of that, but was also pretty certain if there was a bidding war, the Chinese would win.

And *they* could definitely figure it out.

Under any other circumstances he'd have reported the phone call he received last night, but it was his family. His wife, his sons, Jimmy Jr. not even a year old yet.

He knew he was betraying his country, and it broke his heart, he a true patriot. But he also knew his country better than most, and knew the capabilities of its military and intelligence resources. They would find the plane, they would retrieve it. Of that he had no doubt.

Which gave him a slight amount of comfort that in the end the damage to his country would be minimized.

I wonder if anyone will ever know.

Something like this would be hushed up for certain, but the way the press were nowadays, they didn't give a second thought to what was good for the country, they were merely obsessed with the scoop, the rush to be first to broadcast the latest government gaffe or tragedy.

He just hoped somebody would get this recording someday so his name might be cleared.

I just hope Dad forgives me.

He felt himself begin to choke up as his thoughts moved to his father, a proud Air Force man who had been prouder still the day his son had received his wings. And he knew he'd be torn apart by the stories that would be told of him should he not succeed in freeing his wife and children by sacrificing his own life.

They'll tell their story, then everyone will know.

"If anyone should find this recording, and is able to, please let my wife and children know that I love them, and that I did this to save them. And to my parents, I'm sorry. I hope you understand why I did this, and find it in your hearts to forgive me for what I've done. And to any American military who might hear this." He paused as he struggled to control himself, the

Mexican border whipping past, the trailing Raptors breaking off. "Avenge me."

He punched the GPS coordinates into the onboard computer and turned slightly west, toward the coast, and minutes later was over the coordinates he had been given.

And his heart sank.

He had images of some amateur-hour Islamic group with a flatbed truck. Instead what he spotted from the air was an entire convoy of transport vehicles of varying sizes, all disguised with bright advertising, everything from Coca-Cola to Old Spice about to make off with pieces of his aircraft.

Which means they'll have to hack it apart so at least it will never fly again.

This made him smile as he began a vertical landing on a clearing off the highway ringed with men and equipment, one guiding him down visually. He felt the jolt of a poorly executed landing, his nerves getting the better of him, and before he had finished powering down someone was tapping on his canopy. He finished his checklist as he opened the canopy, the shouts of a couple dozen voices quickly surrounding him as he manned up, pushing his emotions aside. Unbuckling himself, he climbed out of the aircraft and down to the ground.

Immediately he was flanked by two men, led away to the road he had spotted off the clearing. As he looked around him his mind began to reel. A couple of dozen well organized men were swarming the aircraft, tools as advanced and appropriate as any he had seen at the Skunk Works deployed, dismantling his state of the art plane, parts already being loaded into the back of a waiting truck.

But these weren't terrorists. At least not Middle Eastern terrorists.

What the hell is going on here?

"Hold this."

A gun was shoved into his hand and before he could think it was removed, the gloved man slipping it into a Ziploc bag and running toward a landing chopper, a civilian job with US registration tag on its tail. It was airborne within seconds, heading north, for what purpose he couldn't imagine.

"What's going on here?" he asked.

"Exercise," replied a man whose bearing suggested senior officer. "Major Miller, I presume."

"And you are?"

"Need to know, Major."

Miller's eyes narrowed. "You're military. American. Why would you do this? Why would you steal an F-35? Why would you kidnap my family?"

"No idea what you're talking about Major," replied the man as the first truck pulled away. Miller looked over his shoulder at the plane and his jaw dropped at how much of the fuselage had already been removed. There was no doubt these men knew exactly what they were doing, and had been trained in their task.

Which meant reassembly and deployment was entirely possible.

The man in charge pointed to a waiting car then walked away, leaving Miller to wonder what the hell was happening. He was marched to the car, placed in the back with Military Police precision, then on his way north. Two men were in the front seats, a divider between them and him preventing any conversation.

He didn't bother trying.

What is going on?

The car suddenly stopped, the two front seat occupants climbing out. His door was opened, nothing said. It was apparent they wanted him out so he obliged, looking at the driver's face, his eyes hidden behind sunglasses, his face a chiseled specimen right out of any seasoned army platoon.

With no emotion.

A gun was handed to him by the passenger. "It has one bullet. Fire it in the air."

They're going to kill me. They're going to make it look like suicide.

And he couldn't have that, he couldn't have his family thinking he had killed himself.

"What's going on here? You guys aren't Muslim terrorists. If I didn't know better, I'd say you're Special Ops. American Special Ops. You promised me you'd free my wife and sons. Where are they? I want to see them."

"Take the gun, fire the one bullet in the air."

"Not before I talk to my family."

"Follow my instructions and we'll let you talk to your family."

Miller realized he had no options here. He was going to die, of that there was no doubt. But he wasn't willing to die on their terms, or at least not completely on their terms. He reached forward with his left hand, taking the gun. A momentary debate had him trying to shoot one of them but the driver's gun was suddenly placed against his left temple from behind.

"Fire the gun, Major."

Miller sighed, then raised the weapon in the air, squeezing the trigger. The shot startled him slightly, the desert-like expanse he found himself in nearly silent otherwise. A few birds took to the air in protest, and before he had the satisfaction of getting away with his little deception of leaving the powder burns on the wrong hand, he felt the driver's gun press a little harder against his head, the slight movement as the trigger was squeezed leading him to close his eyes, and pray to God his family would be safe.

Kunlun Mountains, China
Three days later

CIA Special Agent Dylan Kane lay completely still, his breath steady as he stared through his binoculars, the digitally enhanced image giving him the best view any American had yet of the massive Kunlun complex built into the side of a mountain. It was China's Area 51, unknown to the world except to those with the highest of security clearances in both the Chinese and American spheres, including a few black ops specialists like himself.

He had been observing the top secret facility for two days now, more on a hunch than anything solid. An F-35B Lightning II prototype had been stolen three days ago, the event hushed up so barely anyone in the Pentagon knew about it, let alone the press. The plane had been flown by its pilot across the border to Mexico, then it vanished without a trace, the pilot's body found on the side of a lonely highway the next day, a single gunshot to the head.

The file had been sent to his tablet as part of the emergency flash traffic, all agents to be on the lookout for any hint as to where the priceless aircraft had been taken. The preliminary file had it a murder-suicide, the pilot's wife and children, including a ten month old baby, were found shot to death in their home with his personal weapon, his service weapon used to kill himself with after he had stolen the aircraft.

The red flags in the intelligence community were several fold. One, he was right handed, but shot himself with his left. This made no sense, so the thinking was he was trying to send a message that he hadn't done this willingly. Two, the fact he shot himself, or someone made it look like he had, meant the airplane had been landed safely. And three, the fact they

23

couldn't find the airplane anywhere near where he was found suggested someone had been waiting to take it.

Extortion.

To Kane it was clear that poor Major Miller had been the victim of extortion. *Give us the plane or we kill your family.* The question was who had done it? Russians, Chinese, North Koreans? They all had the resources and will to pull off such a heist. Iran, Islamic terrorists? He doubted it. Iran couldn't risk being caught. They'd be bombed back into the dark ages since there was little they could do to retaliate. Russians, Chinese and North Koreans could risk it because they had enough of a military deterrent to not have to worry about military retaliation, and terrorists could risk it since they had no real country, but their capabilities were limited.

When the flash had arrived, he had been "in the neighborhood" so had popped into Shanghai using his well-established cover as an insurance investigator for Shaw's of London. He quickly made his way to the Kunlun region where a supply drop was waiting for him including the ghillie suit he now wore, the custom fitted camouflage often used by snipers allowing him to blend in with his terrain.

His hunch was that if the Chinese were involved, they would take the plane here, their most secret of facilities. He was less than a hundred yards from the entrance, the terrain left to seed so as to help conceal the true nature of the installation, it allowing him to blend in easily and slowly advance upon the entrance.

There was little hiding the massive runway nearby that allowed any size aircraft to land with room to spare, however between flights camouflage netting would automatically deploy, disguising it from eyes in the sky. And the two times he had seen the runway used so far, he had noted they were timed to occur when the known eyes in the sky weren't overhead.

Unfortunately for the Chinese they weren't aware of all the birds the various intelligence organizations of the United States Government had placed over the planet.

And it also ignored the fact the latest satellites could look at extreme angles across massive distances, straight into that hangar door that Kane noticed was now opening.

Grinding of gears to his right had him turn slowly as a convoy of trucks appeared, at least twenty strong with a large military escort. He was on the edge of the road now, the sun low on the horizon, the mountain containing the Kunlun facility casting a massive shadow over his position, and he was confident this was what he had been waiting for. He stuffed his binoculars in his pocket and fired a piezoelectric transducer at the main doors of the complex, the first half of a transmitter designed to bridge data streams between opposite sides of thick steel. Holstering his weapon, he straightened himself parallel to the road, then waited as the first half dozen vehicles went by. He spotted a large eighteen wheeler.

Pulling a hook from his utility belt, he rolled quickly onto the road and under the truck, reaching up and grabbing on to the undercarriage with the hook. He was suddenly jerked along at nearly twenty miles per hour, his body bouncing on the ground as he pulled another hook from his utility belt and reached up, securing it to a part of the undercarriage near his waist. Pulling back and forth on a ratchet attached to his belt, he was slowly drawn up off the ground and was soon hugging the undercarriage as the sound of everything around him changed.

As the vehicle rolled into the complex, a complex no American had ever seen before, he swung himself 90 degrees and fired the second half of the transmitter at the door, both halves designed to decay within twelve hours, leaving nothing but a stain behind. The piezoelectric transducers would use ultrasound to transmit his data through the steel doors when they were closed, allowing his transmissions to still be received.

He pressed the inside of his watch band three times, activating extremely sensitive audio and video surveillance equipment, everything streaming to his phone then sent on a special carrier wave to transmitting equipment he had set up outside that would beam the data directly to a satellite stationary overhead. Langley would be already receiving his signal, which meant if he didn't survive, at least they'd know where he died.

The convoy rolled deeper into the complex, slowly now. He lowered himself a couple of feet so he could see out the sides. The walls were rock, the tunnel bored through years before. Along the sides lay piles of neatly stacked supplies, massive amounts of tinned food and water, as if the Chinese were expecting to have to hole up here for a while.

Do they know something we don't?

All he did know was that he had to get out of this convoy otherwise he'd be stuck in some secure area, hopelessly trapped.

He unhooked the first rope he had used, reeling it back in some, then hooked it as far to the right as he could reach. He unhooked the second line and swung over. The tunnel was dark, the Chinese obviously observing protocol while the convoy entered and the doors were open to prying eyes. Only dimmed headlights, filtered from shining up, lit the area, and fortunately for Kane they were doing a bad job of it.

Kane saw his moment ahead, a gap in the supplies. He reached up and grabbed the release on the hook. Squeezing it, he hit the ground and rolled, years of training and experience having it timed perfectly so he slid into the gap he had spotted. He remained still, listening for any shouts or change in the vehicles' speed indicating he might have been seen, but heard nothing.

Kane stripped out of the ghillie suit, hidden in the shadows. Rising, still hugging the wall, his back to the newly arriving vehicles, he straightened his

People's Liberation Army uniform he had worn under it, the rank of Lieutenant Colonel entitling him enough respect to at least make anyone junior question him with some hesitation.

He ran his fingers over his fake eyebrows, tape pulling his eyes slightly back to give them a bit of an Asiatic look, his skin already darkly tanned. If someone saw him close-up in the light of day, they'd know he was Caucasian. His job was rarely to actually try and go undercover as an Asian, it was to use his cover as an insurance investigator to gain access to an area then his trade craft to keep out of sight.

But today, an F-35 was worth risking his life for.

He pulled a collapsible briefcase from the backpack on his ghillie suit, transferred his recording and transmission equipment to it, then removed a hat, completing his uniform. Pulling it low over his eyes, he stepped out of the shadows, heading in the same direction as the convoy down a tunnel that seemed to have no end in sight.

He took a chance.

Turning, he waved at the next truck and heard the driver gear down, but before he could stop Kane jumped on the running board of the passenger side, shouting, "Keep going!" in perfect Chinese. He immediately faced away from the window and stood in place, gripping a handhold designed for just what he was doing, standing stiffly, as if he belonged there.

Nothing was said, the insignia on his shoulder enough to scare any soldier lowly enough to be driving a truck into silence.

A klaxon gave a single bleat and lights flickered on, the tunnel no longer the dark mystery, the front gates obviously closed. Kane kept his head turned away from the truck, but his peripheral vision took in everything. The tunnel was as wide as the hangar doors were, wide enough to taxi a full sized military transport aircraft the entire way should it be desired. It was essentially a runway inside the mountain. The supplies he had noticed earlier were now clearly visible, and still lining the sides, the sheer volume staggering. Ahead he saw the tunnel open into a massive chamber, well lit, where he knew he'd be spotted a little too easily.

He jumped off the truck, easily gaining his stride, his hat pulled low, his head slightly down as he continued to walk with purpose toward the chamber, all the while his eyes scanning the entire area, looking for a place to hole up and observe. Personnel in the tunnel seemed to be scant, but he could already see dozens if not more rushing around the chamber ahead.

Stepping between several tall pallets of supplies, he opened his briefcase, resting it on what looked like canned bean sprouts. With purpose he pulled out a file folder, pretending to read it carefully, instead letting the rest of the convoy pass, along with its escort.

Suddenly the tunnel was nearly silent, the only sounds the massive fans overhead and the activity echoing from the chamber ahead. Glancing around to make sure he wasn't seen, he slowly crouched, bringing the briefcase to the floor. He left his gun in the case, knowing if he needed to use it he was done for, instead opting for two knives and some wire, along with his phone, transmitting still, and several tiny body cameras and microphones.

Again making sure he was alone, he closed the briefcase, placing it against the pallet behind him, then spun the combination to 331. He felt his phone vibrate in his pocket. He stepped out of the shadows, continuing his purposeful walk toward the chamber. As he strode forward, his devices recording everything within view, he spied another spot for him to use for cover that would give him a view into the chamber with hopefully no one seeing him.

Stepping behind a large pallet of water bottles, he checked for company then dropped to a knee. Removing his glasses from his pocket, he put them on, the lenses as dark as any pair of sunglasses to the unsuspecting. Tapping a pressure sensor on the right arm three times, the integrated LCD displays kicked in, immediately enhancing his view. In the upper left corner he could see a view from behind him, tiny cameras mounted in the temple tips. His transmission status was indicated, along with his vitals such as pulse and other numbers monitored through his special t-shirt.

But he ignored all those. He stroked his finger along the pressure sensor built into the rim and immediately zoomed into the chamber, the video being sent directly to Langley. It was massive, easily the size of a football field inside. The trucks from the convoy were all lined up neatly, parked side by side, hundreds of troops unloading what looked like airplane parts.

F-35 parts.

He did another check to make sure he was alone, then spoke, quietly. "Control, if you're seeing this, I've found your missing bird. It's been stripped down to parts, no hope of retrieving. Will examine alternatives, out."

Those alternatives were few. Try to destroy the plane or leave it.

He'd prefer to escape alive, but if he died trying to destroy the plane, he might be okay with that. But he saw little opportunity for that. The parts were being placed in the center of the chamber with hundreds of troops surrounding them.

Something caught his eye.

He zoomed in on a group of men gathered near one of the engines. Using his other finger, he cranked up the volume.

"—your down payment, shall we say." The man speaking was black—African-American based upon his perfect Yankee English.

"Our government is pleased," said a General, his head bobbing as he looked around him. "We honestly didn't think you could do it."

"When the General makes a promise, it is kept. Of that, you can count on."

"As can be said of the Chinese government."

The American bowed slightly. "Of course."

"Then our deal is intact. We shall not interfere."

"Your cooperation is appreciated."

The general motioned and a vehicle pulled up, the American climbing in.

"Control, ID that man immediately, out," he whispered.

The vehicle with the American drove toward his position and he pushed himself back against the wall, into the shadows as his phone vibrated in his hand. Waiting for the vehicle to pass, he tapped his glasses and the info from Langley was displayed on his right lens.

Subject Identified: USAF Captain Martin Lewis, DECEASED Iraq, 2011-07-13.

"Control, there's a vehicle about to leave this complex with our dead Captain. See if you can track it, out."

His glasses vibrated, a message coming in from Langley.

Abort mission, return to extraction point.

Kane cursed as he looked at the F-35 only several hundred feet away, in a thousand pieces.

The Chinese win this one.

Or perhaps they hadn't. This was a delivery from an American. A dead American. This wasn't some simple terrorist organization that had got lucky. This was a well-orchestrated heist of massive proportions that seemed to be some sort of down payment for a favor from the Chinese.

"Then our deal is intact. We shall not interfere."

What did it mean? And the deceased Lewis thanking them for their cooperation? None of it made sense, but there was one thing he was certain of.

Behind the scenes, the world was about to get a lot more difficult.

A klaxon sounded three times then the lights went out as the vehicle reached the tunnel entrance. Kane could hear the doors at the far end begin to open and was about to head back to retrieve his ghillie suit when his phone vibrated a patterned warning to him.

Someone had just triggered the proximity sensor in his briefcase and was headed this way. He ducked down, removed his hat, shoved the phone in his pocket and retrieved his knife. As he pressed himself into the wall between the crates, he listened and could hear two voices approaching, one talking about his plans to visit his parents on the weekend, the other mostly listening. Their hardened soles clicked on the concrete, echoing among the crates and the concrete wall.

They were walking slowly, apparently in no hurry, enjoying the downtime provided by the darkness where no superiors could see them.

And this would be the time to kill them both and make his escape.

But then his presence here would be discovered and it was essential he escape undetected. His original intent was to destroy the aircraft in some way, the two large aviation fuel trucks against the far wall of the chamber seemed the likeliest solution, but with an abort ordered, it was essential to leave zero-residual footprint so they wouldn't know he had seen the dead American.

Something big is going on, and I need to find out what it is.

Through the night-vision setting on his glasses he could barely see the top of one man's head as they approached, now only paces away.

Just keep walking, nothing to see here.

They stopped, right in front of him, one man turning so his back was facing Kane, the other turning to face his companion.

A match was struck, the flame flaring, lighting the entire area for a brief instance and blinding him for a split second as his glasses protected him from the change by dimming to black then ramping back up.

31

The conversation continued, how the man loved his parents of course, but would rather take his girlfriend to Shanghai for the week.

"Have you told your parents about her?"

"Are you kidding? They'd kill me if they knew I was dating her."

"Do they know her?"

"Yeah, we grew up together. Her family was very poor. They would think she's beneath me."

"Love. Too much of a pain in the ass for me. My parents arranged a marriage for me. She was pretty—is pretty. We learned to get along. Someday I can even see loving her."

"Chin? The mother of your son?"

"Yes."

"Chin is fantastic! And you *might* love her someday?"

The second man laughed. "You're too young to understand. One day you'll be married to your pretty friend that you love, and then realize a marriage of love isn't sustainable, but a marriage from duty is, and it can turn into one of love as well."

"Sounds rather Orwellian to me."

"Be careful. If a political officer hears you talk like that you could find yourself in a lot of trouble."

"I know, I know. Slip of the tongue."

"Careful no one thinks it's the tongue of a serpent that slips, lest it get clipped."

The klaxon sounded and Kane was about to leap forward when the cigarette was tossed at him and the two men turned, briskly walking away, their footfalls indicating a disciplined Chinese pace, their conversation over.

The lights came on.

Trapping Kane in his position once again.

He donned his hat, rose slightly and tapped a sequence on the screen of his phone then slowly poked it out from behind the pallets. His glasses showed the bustle of activity in the chamber as the parts of the F-35 were being moved from the unloading area to whatever research labs the Chinese had under this massive mountain of rock, and with a smile he heard the diesel engines of the transports begin to fire up.

Which meant they would be leaving soon.

He waited. Not long, just a few minutes and as predicted the column of trucks began to pass, the klaxon sounding as the first approached the entrance, the lights going out. Kane jumped up, running toward his previous position. He jumped into his ghillie suit, shoved the hat and collapsible briefcase into his backpack, then rolled under one of the last semis with just seconds to spare.

And as he bounced underneath, hanging by a single strap, he wondered why a dead American soldier would be delivering an F-35 to America's enemy, calling it a down payment in return for not interfering.

Interfering with what?

George Washington Elementary-Middle School, Detroit, Michigan
The next day

"Brenda, would you please stop fidgeting?!"

Sarah McBride pointed an angry finger at her seven year old accompanied by a glare that usually had tears erupting from her daughter if held too long. Brenda froze and Sarah wiped the expression off her face, returning to unbuckling her daughter from the booster seat—with a smile.

Success!

She lifted her from the SUV and placed her on the sidewalk, grabbing her school bag and lunch box from the floor. Locking the doors, she motioned for Brenda to start walking, nervously glancing around at the heavy police presence. She had heard on the news this morning that all schools within the district were going to have police stationed at them due to the three schools that were bombed over the past few days across the country, but she hadn't expected the show of force to be so strong.

There must be dozens!

She had to admit she wanted to keep her daughter home today, but as her husband had said, and he was right, "What about tomorrow?" If she kept her home today, she'd have to keep her home every day until they caught these terrorists. And if the kids stopped going to school, then the terrorists would have won.

"Are you coming in with me today, Mommy?"

"Yes. I need to talk to your Principal." *Those morons!* Yesterday Brenda had been sent to the Principal's office in tears because she had brought an "inappropriate" lunch. The poor kid had been forced to eat packaged cheese and crackers in the outer office instead of the healthy lunch she had been sent with.

The note, a form letter with a box checked off, indicated she had sent something with peanuts.

She hadn't.

It was a peanut butter alternative that she had used many times, having informed the school, and some idiot substitute teacher, rather than believing her daughter, and apparently the entire class, had instead humiliated her, berating her for putting kids' lives at risk, then sent her to the Principal.

"I'll tear her goddamned throat out if I see her," she muttered.

"Who's goddamned throat, Mommy?"

"No one you know, dear. And don't say that word, it's bad."

"But you said it."

"I know, and Mommy was bad for saying it."

"You're not bad, Mommy. You're the best mommy in the world!"

Sarah smiled and patted Brenda on the head. *Please don't ever grow up!*

"Thank you, dear, now here's your bag and your lunch. You have fun today."

Brenda hugged her then ran off to catch up with a group of her friends.

In six years she'll be a bitchy little teenager. Enjoy it while it lasts.

A FedEx delivery man rushed past with a good size box under his arm. He held open the door for her with a smile.

"Ma'am."

"Thank you," she replied with a smile, chivalry one of the unwelcome losses due to overachieving feminism. She always enjoyed watching her mom and dad together. He would hold doors for her, including the car door if they were out on one of their dates. They'd walk arm in arm or hand

35

in hand, whatever the mood struck them, and they always greeted each other with a kiss and a hug in the morning.

She had given up on chivalry in her generation's men long ago. They sometimes made an effort until they conquered the great divide, then it was downhill from there. An ex-boyfriend had replied after one of her complaints with "your grandmother shouldn't have burned her bra then". They had argued, he saying "if you want to be treated equally then you have to accept the consequences. You can't be *more* equal!"

They hadn't lasted much longer.

Roger, her husband, was a bit in the middle. He sometimes did the chivalrous things, but usually only when he was trying to be romantic. Fortunately for her he was frequently romantic, and she counted herself among the lucky ones, especially when she heard some of the horror stories coming out of her friends.

She followed the FedEx guy to the main office as he made idle chit-chat. "Lots of security today."

She nodded as she remembered watching last night's newscast in horror. At first she had thought it was just CNN being CNN, rebroadcasting the same incident over and over to whip up a frenzy of fear so they'd have more to report on, but when her husband had set her straight, she had immediately become scared. Very scared. "I guess you can never be too safe. Especially with what's been happening."

"Too true. They're going to have to do something about it soon. Too many people are dying and we all know who's responsible."

Sarah's head bobbed in reluctant agreement. There had been almost a dozen large scale suicide bombings in the past week, not a day going by where someone didn't blow themselves up, screaming God is Great in that horrific guttural language, the incidents always caught on camera. What was worse was they all seemed to be Americans doing it, nobody even realizing they had converted to Islam. "I'm afraid we live in too politically correct a world to actually take the action that's needed."

"Amen, sister!" said the driver as he held open the main office door where two armed police officers, in full gear, were just leaving. She approached the front desk as her chivalrous man headed to the other end of it.

"Can I help you?" asked a bored, rather large woman from behind her desk.

"I'd like to see Mrs. Belle."

"Regarding?"

"An incident with my daughter, Brenda McBride."

"Oh yeah, the peanut butter eater."

Sarah's blood instantly went to boil. "It wasn't peanut butter," she said through clenched teeth.

"Looked like it to me. We can't take—"

"Did you check her file?"

"What?"

"I sent a letter to the school explaining what she would sometimes be taking, and it was okayed."

"Well, I don't have time to be looking at files everyti—"

"*You* don't have time!" Sarah's fists clenched, her eyes aflame. "You mental midgets humiliated a little girl who did nothing wrong, accused her of being a liar, and made her eat processed cheese and crackers here, instead of a perfectly safe and healthy meal with her friends. You even threw out her apple."

"Well, we couldn't exactly risk it being contaminated with the peanut butter from her sandwich, now could we?"

"You truly are a world class idiot, aren't you?"

"I beg your pardon?"

"I want to speak to the Principal, not the minion."

"There's no need to be rude."

"Apparently there's no need to be intelligent either." Sarah raised her finger before the fine example of unionized employee could respond. "Principal. *We're* done."

The FedEx guy turned and gave Sarah a smile and a wink as he walked out. The door to the Principal's office opened before the brainless mound of skin and bones could knock.

"Is there a package for me?" asked Mrs. Belle, who from all outward appearances seemed quite upset about something.

"No."

Belle's eyes narrowed. "Really? They—I was sure it would be here by now. Can you check?"

The useless turd sighed then walked over to the in basket, grumbling all the way. "There's a big box here for you," she said, looking back over her shoulder.

"Can you bring it to me, please?"

"I can't carry that! My back is already bad. If I carry that I could put my back out, then where'd you be?"

Sarah watched as eyes rolled around the office, it clear her co-workers would prefer an extended absence.

"Just bring me the goddamned box!" screamed Belle, everyone including Sarah jumping in shock. Belle sucked in a breath, a phone pressed to her ear. "I'm sorry. Please, just bring me the box."

Waste-of-space lifted the box, making a show of grunting, then marched it over to Belle's office. Belle took it and the door closed.

"If that bitch thinks she can talk to me like that, she's got another thing comin'!" The woman grabbed her purse and jacket. "I'm going to see my union rep. I'm filing a grievance!" Her voice continued to get louder with each word, hands beginning to wave in the air and fingers starting to shoot toward the closed office door like daggers as she rounded the counter. "She can go—"

"All students and staff, this is Principal Belle. There will be a student assembly in ten minutes. All students and staff are to report immediately to the gymnasium. Thank you."

Sarah sighed. *Lovely, now I'll never get to talk to her.*

"What the hell is that fool doing now?" asked the voice of reason. "That woman gone lost her head!" She yanked open the door to the office and poured herself into the hallway, masses of kids now filling the halls as they flowed to the gymnasium, smiles on their faces at not having to actually learn something.

Sarah sighed, looking for someone to make eye contact with when the door to the Principal's office opened.

And she peed her pants as all muscle control was lost.

Gripping the counter, she forced herself to remain on her feet as Mrs. Belle stepped slowly out of her office, an unmistakable suicide vest strapped to her chest. She had the trigger in one hand, a cellphone pressed to her ear with the other.

And tears rolling down her cheeks, falling onto a sign dangling around her neck that read "Death to America!".

She's a terrorist?

Several people screamed as they noticed her, followed by a stampede for the door by staff and visitors—except for Sarah. Her legs were frozen, locked in place. She slowly raised her arms, an instinctual move of surrender. The entire situation made no sense. The terrorists were bombing things all around the country. There had been a dozen attacks this week alone, including a few schools, but Mrs. Belle? She wasn't Muslim. Then again, neither were most of the other bombers. They were apparently converts. She couldn't imagine Belle being a convert. In fact, she knew she wasn't. Belle went to her church and she had seen her there this weekend.

Unless that was a cover?

But if she were a terrorist, why was she crying? And who was she on the phone with?

Shouts could be heard outside as the police were alerted to the situation. The office was empty now save for Belle and Sarah, and Sarah began to back away toward the door. She glanced behind her, through the glass walls and saw the hallway now empty. Through the window outside she could see police scrambling into position.

The assembly!

She felt bile fill her mouth as she realized what the plan was. Belle intended to blow herself up in the middle of the assembly.

She'll kill hundreds!

Sarah nearly threw up.

She'll kill Brenda!

Sarah's raised arms slowly lowered, instead extending out to her sides as she blocked the door to the hallway.

"I can't let you do it."

Belle suddenly stared at her, as if noticing her for the first time. "They have my kids," she cried, the words choked out as if spoken for the first time. "I have no choice."

Sarah shook her head. "You do have a choice. You always have a choice to do the right thing."

Belle looked at the empty hallway, then out the window. "I can't. I can't let my kids die."

Sarah took a step toward her, lowering her hands slowly, racking her brain for Belle's first name. *Norah!* "Norah, you know you can't do this. You can't kill hundreds of kids to save your own." Tears were flowing down her cheeks now, her heart slamming hard against her chest as she stalled for time. Through the window she could see the police rushing toward the left, where she knew the gymnasium was, its main entrance less than fifty feet down the hall.

Belle looked at Sarah, the phone slowly lowering from her ear, and she mouthed a single word at Sarah.

"Run!"

Sarah turned, racing for the door then yanking it open. As she turned toward the gymnasium, she looked back and saw Belle standing, her arms drooping at her sides, her eyes closed as she looked up toward Heaven.

The blast was deafening. Sarah didn't have time to register exactly what was happening as she continued to build a sprint toward the gym, but the last thing she remembered before the blast wave slammed her against a row of lockers was arguing with her husband about bringing Brenda here today, and rather than fill her last thoughts with anger over his decision, she instead prayed that Brenda and the other students were far enough from the blast to not die from it.

Like her.

Over a peanut butter sandwich.

J. ROBERT KENNEDY

The Oval Office, The White House, Washington, DC

"Mr. President, there's been another bombing."

President Johnathan Bridges looked up from his perch on the corner of one of the couches in his office, his morning briefing only just begun, the most exclusive newspaper in the world, circulation "tens", just having been received. The President's Daily Brief. He remembered the first time he had read one after being sworn in, and it had been chilling. The number of threats and crises the nation faced on a daily basis was staggering. And terrifying. But no briefing had been more terrifying than those delivered over the past week, and as the pressure continued to build on him to take action, actions he couldn't fathom, he wondered if he might reach his breaking point.

But he was the President, and he couldn't break.

Not when his country needed him the most.

And now there was another attack.

The troubled look on his National Security Advisor's face as she read a file just handed to her by one of her aide's immediately had him concerned.

When will it end?

"What is it, Susan?"

Susan Lawrence waved the folder. "They just hit an elementary school in Detroit. Luckily it looks like the bomb went off early and there was some warning."

"The kids?"

"All survived. Apparently there was a mother who helped delay the bomber according to some eye witnesses."

Bridges felt a swell of pride in his fellow Americans at the image of this hero. "Did she make it?"

Lawrence shook her head. "I'm sorry, Mr. President, she didn't. But her daughter did, as did over four hundred other children and staff. Several local law enforcement officers lost their lives, several were injured." She sighed. "Mr. President, we got lucky on this one. It could have been much worse."

"Thank God for small miracles."

"And determined mothers," added General Bradley Thorne, the Chairman of the Joint Chiefs of Staff.

"Amen," nodded President Bridges. He paused for a moment. "Ladies, gentlemen, this is the twelfth attack, if I'm not mistaken, in less than a week. The public is demanding action. Muslims are being attacked in the streets, vigilante groups are beginning to form. This has to stop."

Lawrence nodded. "We've recalled all law enforcement under Federal jurisdiction from leave, requested all state and local law enforcement to do the same. Several governors have already called up the National Guard and I suspect even more will follow if we have more attacks. We have security at every school, transit station, mall, and government facility in the country."

"Yet they still get through."

"Yes, sir. And we don't know how. And we don't know why it's happening. From all accounts the bombers were happy citizens and *not* Muslim."

"Anybody can convert nowadays," interjected General Thorne. "We've seen it before."

"True," agreed Lawrence, "but their friends and family usually know, and if not, we were able to confirm it after the fact. In all of these cases so

43

far these were peaceful people, most of whom went to church, some the very day they performed their heinous act."

"So what are you saying?" asked President Bridges. "That they're not Muslim? Okay, I can accept that. Then what's the motivation?"

"I might be able to shed some light on that, Mr. President," said Ben Wainwright, Secretary of Homeland Security. "Our preliminary investigation into the first few bombings is suggesting these people are being coerced into doing what the terrorists want."

"Coerced? I thought we had determined they were all murder-suicides?"

"That's what we assumed at first. Each person's family has been found dead when we searched their homes after identification. We've always assumed they killed them then went to set off their bombs, but so far we haven't found any trace of explosives or any bomb making equipment in their homes, and each device has been identical. But more importantly, witnesses and records indicate every bomber has been on the phone when they blow themselves up."

"On the phone?" Bridges rubbed his chin, transferring to a proper seat on the couch, the arm no longer comfortable. "With who?"

"We don't know, it always traces back to burners. But we do know that *they* didn't call anybody."

"What do you mean?"

"They all received incoming calls."

"Somebody called *them*?"

Wainwright nodded. "Yes, Mr. President. I can't prove this yet, but I'm convinced that these people are being coerced into blowing themselves up under threat of their families being killed. Then when they do what they are forced to do, the families are killed regardless to make it look like a murder-suicide."

"That's cold," observed NSA Secretary Susan Lawrence. "These people are killing themselves, thinking they're saving their families, and they're not."

"Sounds like something we might want to make public," suggested Wainwright. "If people are being coerced, if they knew their families were going to die regardless, they might not be so willing to take innocent people with them."

General Thorne cleared his throat. "I'd advise against that, Mr. President. In fact, I'd advise against making any of this public. Right now we have Americans mistrusting a segment of their population. We need to do everything to dissuade them of any aggression toward these people, the vast majority of whom are innocent, but if we tell the public that the actual bombers are apple pie eating Americans just like them, *every*one will be at risk. A guy wearing a puffy jacket, carrying an oversized briefcase." He shook his head. "It would be panic."

Lawrence bobbed her head. "I have to agree with the General. It could cause mass panic. We need to find out how they choose their victims."

"Isn't it just random?" asked President Bridges.

"I don't think so. These people's families are being held hostage and they are somehow being supplied with the suicide vests. These aren't just random phone calls. These people are picked, observed, then set-up."

Bridges squeezed his temples, gently massaging them. "So they could choose anybody, anywhere."

"As long as they had a family they could coerce."

"Is there anything out there, anything at all, no matter how weak, that might lead us to these people?"

Leif Morrison, National Clandestine Service Chief for the CIA, cleared his throat. "Mr. President, the one thing that is a bit odd is that none of the usual suspects are taking credit. In fact our monitoring of their chatter is revealing that they have no clue who is doing it, but they're cheering them on. A few nobody's are claiming responsibility, but we've confirmed they're simply taking advantage of the situation. What we need are those conversations that are happening when the bombers are on the phone."

"Which we can't get without violating the constitutional rights of Americans," added Lawrence as she looked over her shoulder at Morrison. She turned back to the President. "We would need to monitor pretty much everyone, then pull the data after the fact since we have no way of predicting who's next. Americans won't stand for it."

"I beg to disagree," said Homeland Security Secretary Wainwright. "The American public is demanding action. A temporary measure like this, that might solve the problem, I think would be tolerated. In fact, I think it might be applauded."

Bridges frowned. Since 9/11 so many laws had been passed that either overrode or went against the principles of the Constitution, America was no longer America, at least not the one he had grown up in. But he was guilty of it himself. He had continued the Termination List of his predecessors, a list few knew about. He had extended terrorist assassinations to include American citizens with the convenient caveat that they not be on American soil when it was done. He had sentenced so many to death without a trial, he had lost count. And he'd justified it every time under the guise of fighting terrorism. Was it right? No, deep down he knew it wasn't. Was it necessary? That he wasn't as sure about. Most days he felt it was, others, he had doubts. All he knew was that today, if he didn't have to worry about the Constitution, he could probably end the terror gripping his nation swiftly.

He sighed.

"If we go down that road, like we've done before, it becomes slippery. Look at Guantanamo, the Patriot Act, Iraq. When we react without thinking things through, we end up with unintended consequences far too often, or overzealous individuals telling us what we want to hear. It's one thing to go to war with a country over false-intelligence, it's an entirely other thing to go to war with our own."

"But we're just talking about using MYSTIC on ourselves, maybe for a week. At the rate these attacks are happening, we'd have a dozen phone calls to possibly analyze."

A dozen.

It sent shivers up and down his spine as he thought about the implications. Hundreds, even thousands more dead. The panic among the population was already palpable. One more week of this and there'd be rioting in the streets. But to implement MYSTIC, a National Security Agency system capable of recording 100% of a nation's phone calls for a month, was almost unthinkable.

But it could end this!

When he became President he had no idea just how many secrets would be involved, secrets so *secret* that there were few he could talk to. It was something his predecessor, in his traditional letter to the incumbent, had mentioned.

It's the secrets that will weigh on you the most.

Because secrets meant lies. And some secrets were lies, or thought to possibly be lies. Like the Weapons of Mass Destruction from Iraq. Everyone thought they were there, then the intel turned out to be bullshit. But then why were Russian Special Forces brought in only days before the invasion? Why were they photographed leading convoys of transport vehicles into Syria? Why, when Syria's stockpiles were recently destroyed, were they more than 50% higher than estimated? Could the WMD's have been moved to Syria by the Russians? After all, most of the chemical and biological weapons that both countries had were originally supplied by the

Soviet Union. It made sense that Putin, who many Americans didn't realize had run Russia since 2000, long before the Iraq war began, wouldn't want any evidence found of the Soviet Union he still worshipped being involved lest it embarrass the country and result in sanctions against what was a fragile Russian economy at the time.

Secrets. Lies. Where does the truth lie?

"I'll think about it," he finally said. "How much time would it take to implement MYSTIC?"

"We can go live within twenty-four hours of your approval," replied Lawrence. "But I don't agree that this is a good idea. To eavesdrop on every American phone conversation? It's"—she stopped, as if searching for the words—"it's so *un*-American!"

Bridges nodded, forced to agree with her. "Countries without a constitution, without a constitution that is respected by a people's government and institutions, don't face the moral dilemmas we face on a daily basis. Would crime be lower if we didn't have to respect someone's civil rights? Absolutely. Would America's enemies tremble in fright? Absolutely. Would our economy be better if we didn't waste so much money on maintaining our constitutional way of life? Absolutely. But then we wouldn't be America, and we wouldn't be the greatest nation in the world. We'd simply be another China and not the beacon of hope that we are today." He rose, the entire room with him. "No, people, we will *not* suspend our Constitution, we will *not* suspend civil rights. We will fight our enemies under the rule of law, lest we become the shadow of our former selves that our enemies would have us be. Thank you all for coming."

A chorus of, "Thank you, Mr. President" ended the meeting and he returned to his desk, easing back in the sumptuous leather and closing his eyes.

He felt a vibration, first in his shoes then through his entire body. He jumped to his feet and pressed against the window behind his desk, a fireball in the distance rising, surrounding the Washington Monument.

And then to his horror it teetered for a second, then began to collapse, his hopes for his nation along with it.

CIA Headquarters, Langley, Virginia

"How was your meeting, sir?"

Senior Analyst Chris Leroux rose from his chair as Leif Morrison, CIA National Clandestine Service Chief entered his office, a nice walled affair made necessary by the highly classified projects Leroux found himself working on these days. His promotion hadn't taken him out of the analysis trenches, but it afforded him additional resources including a staff of eight.

Movin' on up!

And he hated it.

He never wanted the promotion. He was happy being the geek in a cubicle, hammering away at his keyboard, thinking in obtuse ways that brought unrelated data together in ways no one else might consider.

It was his gift.

And apparently my curse.

Morrison wanted to tap him to his full potential, or some other claptrap like that, but the stress having staff gave him was beginning to impact his work. He felt he had to be everyone's friend, to listen to and consider all their ideas, to try and let people down easy all the time without hurting their feelings.

If it weren't for his girlfriend, CIA Agent Sherrie White, he might have handed in his resignation and took a job in the tech industry or at a nice quiet library somewhere. He was able to dump on her when she wasn't on an op, and take out his frustrations slaying zombies on his Xbox One when she was.

Which was far too often lately.

The life of a spy's boyfriend.

His friend Dylan Kane had joked once that Leroux was "Jane Bond's bitch" and that he better get used to it. Kane was probably his best and only friend save Sherrie, and he was the one who had ultimately pushed them together—Kane knew damned well he wouldn't have had the balls to do it himself.

And it was Kane's intel he was now working on. Intel that was mind blowing.

He watched Morrison close the door and sit down, not saying anything, his finger tapping his chin as he was lost in thought. He finally jerked out of his reverie, looking at Leroux.

"Disturbing."

"Sir?"

"You asked how the meeting was. It was disturbing."

"In what way?"

"There's talk of enabling MYSTIC."

"On who, the Chinese?"

Morrison shook his head. "Us. The United States."

Leroux's jaw dropped. MYSTIC was an incredibly powerful tool, allowing you to go back as far as a month in every phone conversation held within a nation. It was a fantastic tool for hindsight driven intelligence.

But it was never meant to be used on an ally, let alone the taxpayers that funded it.

"You can't be serious!"

"The President said no. For now. Thorne and Wainwright are pressing him though, and you know how Bridges is. Weak."

Leroux glanced around, checking for uninvited ears, still not used to having soundproof walls.

"Wouldn't that be a violation of the Constitution?"

"Absolutely, but have you heard the news? People are starting to demand troops in the streets, Muslim internment camps and deportations. We're getting very close to the tipping point where Congress and the Administration just might start to take drastic action. We're up to a few major attacks a day, thousands dead, and absolutely no leads."

"Well, I'm afraid I don't have too much for you re the F-35. The photos and video Kane took have been confirmed as authentic and definitely showing our missing bird, right down to the tail number and classified camo tag on the tail. Nobody knows about those, and even if they did, they couldn't possibly know what tag was put on the test plane that morning. This *is* the missing F-35."

"Delivered by a dead American soldier to the Chinese."

"I've got a little more on that. Facial recognition and voice pattern analysis confirm it is definitely Captain Lewis. A triple check of military personal records and civilian records confirm he died in Iraq in 2011."

"Body?"

"Recovered, but badly burnt. Closed casket funeral."

"How did they identify the body?"

Leroux smiled. "I think you'll like this. They didn't need to. He was the only one involved in the IED explosion. His men said he went down an alleyway then there was an explosion. His men went after him and found his body, blown to pieces, the pieces intact wearing his uniform and dog tags. There was no doubt in their minds this was their Captain."

Morrison tapped his chin again, thinking. "So nobody actually saw him die, and a body that could have been anyone's, pre-positioned for the killing, was *presumed* to be his."

"Affirmative."

"I want that body exhumed and DNA tested against records."

"Funny you should say that, sir. I checked the records for tampering and found that not only were his fingerprint, dental and medical files updated just before he was killed, but so was his DNA profile."

"Do we have access to the old stuff?"

"No, we don't, officially. I took a peak at an old archive most people don't know about."

"You mean the Apocalypse Archive?"

Leroux nodded at the reference to one of several massive data archives spread across the country designed to preserve all information known to man, including financial transactions, land ownership, and more. They were meant to help get the country back on its feet should some sort of calamity strike resulting in the potential collapse of the government and our way of life. "The Nevada Archive has an old snapshot. The updated records? About the only thing they have in common with the originals is that he's an African American male in his early forties. That's it."

"Remarkable." Morrison glanced over his shoulder to make sure the door was closed. "And his service record, any tampering there?"

Leroux shook his head. "No, that matches line for line. In the end, he was Army Intelligence, reporting to then Major, now Colonel, Booker."

"Two promotions in that time?"

Leroux handed him the printout showing Booker's service record. "It's worse. It was done within two years."

Morrison's eyes narrowed. "I can see that during wartime when you're taking heavy casualties, but not Iraq. Vietnam? World War Two? Absolutely. But not Iraq. I can't say for certain but I don't think there's been a single battlefield promotion in Iraq." He skimmed the service record. "And these weren't that." He shook his head. "Somebody's grooming this Colonel Booker for something."

"He might just know somebody that owes him or his family a favor. It could be completely innocent."

Morrison smiled, rising. Leroux jumped to his feet, Morrison waving him down. "Sit." He put his hand on the doorknob. "Perhaps I'm just seeing conspiracies everywhere I look in my old age, but something doesn't smell right. I think a favor was done in exchange for a quick promotion to full-bird colonel. Regardless, we need to begin looking into the Captain's death."

"Do you want me to contact Homeland Security? Have them take over?"

Morrison sucked in a long, deep breath as he stared slightly up, thinking. He let it out, shaking his head. "No, let's keep this tight. I know it's not our jurisdiction, but something is going on, I can just feel it. And when dead servicemen start delivering stolen F-35's expertly broken down in perfect condition, that tells me we've got some rogue element within our military or ex-military involved." He tapped his chin then pointed at the photo of Leroux and Sherrie on the desk. "Sherrie's in town, isn't she?"

"She's at The Farm training."

"Where's this Booker?"

"Fort Myer."

"Not far. Let's keep this in the family. Report to me directly, keep your staff out of it. Brief Sherrie and have her pay a visit to Booker. Use an Army Captain cover."

"Won't it look kind of strange? I mean, her asking about a dead soldier?"

"She's vetting him for the Medal of Honor. They'll like that and it won't arouse suspicion."

Leroux smiled. "Good idea."

"Of course," winked Morrison. "Now, any luck tracing our dead Captain?"

"Negative. We're still scanning all camera footage for arrivals over the past several days but nothing. But if he's as connected as he obviously is, I'd be stunned if he arrived through any of our controlled access points."

"Agreed. Which is why you should be checking the Chinese feeds. We can't use Kane's footage of this man. But if we can find him in public somewhere, then we can start to really run with this. Especially if we can show him in China." Morrison turned the handle on the door. "Right now everything is pointing to China for that F-35. Keep focusing on that. Normally I'd say there's no connection to the terrorist attacks except for the fact the exact same MO was used."

"Couldn't they have just used that as a copycat measure to throw us off the scent?"

Morrison nodded. "Absolutely. I find it impossible to believe our own military, even a segment within it, is behind the attacks. But we need to find out what this F-35 down payment was for. What is it that they're not supposed to interfere with?"

Chris sighed. "May you live in interesting times."

"Chinese curses can sometimes be prophetic. Where's Kane?"

"A safe house in Beijing."

"Doing?"

"Hopefully no one when on duty." Leroux blushed, shocked the joke had made it past the mouth-brain barrier. "I'm so sor—"

Morrison began to laugh. He wagged a finger at him. "I knew Sherrie would be good for you."

He opened the door and stepped out into the hallway, closing the door behind him, still chuckling.

Leroux sat stunned for a second, then sent a text to Sherrie to report to Langley for a briefing.

ETA 1 hour.

He felt a spring in his loins as the thought of seeing her so soon worked its way through his system. But then he realized he had to create an entire cover for her, with no assistance, before she arrived.

May you live in interesting times.

Mandara Spa, Beijing, China

"So they came through?"

There was a splash of water and a sigh as one of the rotund generals Major Lee Fang was assigned to protect eased himself into the hot tub. These generals disgusted her, particularly her charge, General Yee Wei. Yee insisted on surrounding himself with female bodyguards, even establishing a training course for potential recruits that would choose candidates based upon ability and looks. They'd then become bodyguards for the truly depraved elite in Chinese society, and eye candy for the dirty old men that ran things. Some would even become their sexual playthings in fear of being sent to some remote prison for reprogramming, or worse.

It *really* disgusted her.

She wasn't part of that program. She was an eight year veteran of the Beijing Military Region Special Forces Unit—codenamed Arrow—China's most elite of Special Forces that made no distinction between men and women fighting. In the People's Liberation Army of Mao, men and women had fought side by side, struggled on the Long March, helping each other as equals. In China, men and women were truly equal.

Until you reached the top tier, then men had their playthings, and women their own.

I guess there's some equality in that.

But as with most societies, men dominated, and there would be no women's lib movement in China. Rallies on the street would be crushed swiftly. All women could do in China was effect change in the home and hope someday it made it outside.

But the world she lived in? She didn't worry too much about such things. Her comrades treated her as an equal since she had proven herself in battle and on missions too often for there to be any doubt she was as tough as any man.

And if they did doubt her, she'd kick their ass.

She glanced across the room at her reflection in a large floor to ceiling mirror. Her pantsuit was unflattering, though showed her slim physique. Her lithe, fitness model quality body was hidden away, and she had no doubt General Yee was hoping he'd get to see it later, especially after the alcohol began to flow.

Which it already had.

She knew men found her attractive, especially when they saw her in her workout clothes, which was why she had purposely chosen an androgynous haircut and wore little makeup, but as her mother said, she was cursed with natural beauty. Not something that fit her chosen line of business very well except when undercover. The catcalls and wolf whistles when she'd be decked out in an evening gown or worse, a two piece bikini when trying to charm the pants off some target for information, were annoying enough—it was the leers from the senior officers that were truly uncomfortable. She sometimes wondered if her career would be hindered because some men would want to keep her around to look at, and others would block her upward path if she turned down their sexual advances.

Beauty was a curse.

Maybe a good scar down my cheek?

She smiled at the thought, but realized it would make her too noticeable for ops, and she loved her job too much to be taken out of rotation. She loved her country, and she wanted to serve. She realized it wasn't perfect, but at least it wasn't decadent and uncaring like what she had been taught about the United States. To imagine a country that actively *didn't* take care of its citizens, instead insisting they help themselves by taking advantage of the exalted Capitalism they lived under was almost unthinkable as a Chinese.

She had to admit that things were getting better in China all the time, and it seemed to be attributable to the slow introduction of capitalism here, and when she thought of the stories her parents told, she realized life was simply fantastic now compared to the previous generations.

But not for everyone. Those in the cities had generally a better life, especially if they were fortunate enough to work for one of the foreign companies. The "middle-class" as they described it was burgeoning. She couldn't count herself among them, but she didn't need to. The army would take care of her, proverbial cradle to grave.

But it would be a lonely life. Her job in Special Ops along with her training and necessary demeanor in the trade meant most Chinese men went running the opposite direction. They too often wanted some demure house wife who'd cater to their every whim and replace their mothers.

She wasn't that woman.

She'd been on a good number of first dates but very few second dates.

And she couldn't remember the last time she had been laid.

There were plenty of suitors from the one-night stand category, of that there was no doubt. There probably wasn't a man in her outfit that wouldn't want to get busy with her for a few hours, but that wasn't her style.

Don't shit in your own campground.

It was a clever phrase she had heard while on a mission in the United States and it was apropos for so many situations that she found herself using it all the time, much to the surprise of her colleagues who within her business tried to keep Americanisms out of their vocabulary unless it was necessary for a cover.

She shuddered as she caught herself staring at the lonely reflection in the mirror. It was one of those moments where you forgot it was you in the reflection, and it disturbed her.

I'm so lonely.

She was snapped from her reverie as laughter from the generals and giggles from the "professionals" that had been brought in for the occasion erupted around the corner. She shook her head imperceptibly, hoping for those poor girls' sake that nothing classified was discussed, otherwise they might disappear until it was no longer considered important.

It was sad. These girls probably were told how important these men were and thought they had finally "made it". Concubine to a party official could mean a very good life.

As long as it lasted.

But those relationships rarely lasted long, and almost never ended in marriage.

"We need to discuss recent events," said General Ling. "Just for a few minutes."

"Leave us, girls. We'll call for you." It was her charge, Yee, that sent the girls on their way. They scurried around the corner, past Fang's position near the door. The conversation at the hot tub didn't resume until the sound of the door clicking was heard.

It made her wonder if they even remembered she was there.

She thought it best she remind them with at least a walk-thru, but before she could, the conversation resumed, the words she heard freezing her in place, shivers rushing up and down her spine.

"The F-35 delivery has been confirmed complete," said Yee. "I assume that's what you wanted to talk about."

Ling grunted. "What else could there be? You realize that this course of action we've undertaken will change China forever. Within ten years we will be the strongest military in the world, unchallenged."

Yee cleared his throat, Fang's familiarity with the man suggesting he had just eaten something. "Why else would I have taken the risk?"

"But to do this behind the Politburo's back! It's insanity! A death warrant if they find out," hissed General Jiang, the youngest of the four Generals gathered.

"Only if something goes wrong," admonished Yee. "The F-35 has already been delivered at no cost to us. Our scientists are already reverse engineering it. Within ten years we will have a fifth generation stealth aircraft of our own that will rival anything the Americans can field, and with our pact of mutual noninterference in upcoming events, we will have free reign over the entire hemisphere if we play our cards right."

"That's rather ambitious, don't you think? The Russians might have something to say about that," said Ling. "And I'm not so sure I trust the Americans to stay out of our business."

Yee laughed. "Have you seen what's happening over there? They've had over a dozen major terrorist attacks this week alone. Their country is crumbling in a war with the Muslims, yet they're too damned politically correct to do anything about it! Here we simply kill them. There, they try to hug those who would have them dead." Yee paused, then cleared his throat after a few moments. Fang's stomach grumbled slightly. "They are imploding, and there's only one way they can stop it."

"Bringing home the troops," said Jiang, as if he already knew of some plan. Fang wasn't sure what she was listening to. The F-35 was a stunner that could have her killed if they knew she had heard them speaking, but the rest seemed idle chit-chat. Except for the noninterference pact.

What could they be talking about?

61

"And once those troops are brought home, under new orders to quell the uprising on their home soil, and with the American public so distracted by the Muslim problem, we will be free to implement Operation Red Dragon."

Somebody smacked the surface of the water with something.

"If it doesn't succeed, we could be ruined," said Jiang, his voice low. "I see little problem taking control of the South China Sea and Taiwan. And I anticipate little reaction from the United States should we succeed within seventy-two hours as projected. But Mongolia is another beast altogether. It borders on Russia, and they won't likely be pleased with our actions."

"Russia be damned," roared Yee, another smack on the water snapping through the air. "They're too focused on their western border and the Middle East to stop us, and they don't have the military might anymore to defeat us without incredibly heavy casualties." He paused. "No, I anticipate we can take Mongolia in less than a week, secure the new borders, then simply buy off the Russians with a promise of secure access to the rare earth elements we'll gain access to."

"It's ambitious," said Ling. "But I think it's doable if the Americans keep their word."

"They have so far."

"Yes, but that's not their leader talking."

"According to the timetable I've been provided, their leader won't be talking much longer." Yee began to laugh, the others joining in. Fang looked at the door as she felt sweat run down her spine. She had to get out of here, of that there was no doubt. She had heard too much. But she couldn't abandon her detail. That would be the ultimate tipoff that she had heard something.

She made a decision.

She grabbed the door handle with purpose, pulling the door open, nodding to the two guards on either side of the door, saying nothing. She then pushed the door closed, making certain it clicked loudly.

The laughter stopped.

She strode out from behind the wall that had been hiding her and nodded to the generals. "Sorry to interrupt, Comrades. Just doing my rounds."

Concerned glances were exchanged among the four men when Yee waved them off. "Gentlemen, this is Major Lee Fang, head of my security detail for our visit. She can be trusted to keep us safe."

Fang bowed slightly at the compliment, continuing to circle the room, checking the windows. Finished, she walked toward the door and stopped, turning back to Yee. "Is there anything I can get you, General?"

"Send back the girls. And feel free to join them, if you'd like."

Fang smiled slightly. "I'll get the girls, General."

She disappeared behind the wall separating the room from the entranceway, and exited. She turned to one of the guards. "The generals would like their entertainment brought back in." The guard snapped out a salute and jogged off to the next room.

Fang barely noticed as the giggling girls bounced back into the room, the hail of greetings from the dirty old men cutting off as the door closed behind the barely eighteen year old girls.

Instead she felt her world narrowing to a tunnel as she stood guard, her mind trying to comprehend what she had just overheard.

A conversation more terrifying than any she could have imagined.

Did they just suggest the President of the United States was about to be assassinated?

Hatfield Gate, Fort Myer, Joint Base Myer-Henderson Hall (JBM-HH), Arlington, Virginia

"—four more schools were bombed today, bringing the total to sixteen since the crisis began. In an unprecedented move today, President Bridges ordered all schools closed until further notice. He vowed to bring the perpetrators to justice, and that the American way of life would not be deterred by Islamic extremists hell bent on world domination. CJXB News sources suggest however that any justice may be long in coming. Unnamed sources within the White House claim investigators are no closer today than they were a week ago in identifying the perpetrators. Governors of California, Texas and Florida have declared a state of emergency, joining—"

CIA Agent Sherrie White muted her radio, holding up her Department of Defense ID as she pulled up to the front gate of Fort Myer. Guards immediately surrounded the car, mirrors on long poles allowing them to look under the vehicle, bomb sniffing dogs making the rounds.

"Purpose of your visit, Captain?" asked the MP.

"I have a meeting with Colonel Booker."

"At what time?"

"Six." She glanced at her watch. "About fifteen minutes from now."

"One moment please."

The MP stepped away to the guard house, phoning to confirm her appointment as the search of the vehicle continued, the security presence extremely high, at least several platoons of men within sight of the main gate.

To say she was nervous would be fair. She was still new in this game, and undercover work was even newer. They were still grooming her for foreign assignments, these type of domestic missions merely practice. Screw up here and you didn't get yourself killed. Screw up in Russia, and it could be lights out for good.

The MP returned, directing her to the visitor's parking lot with instructions to immediately report inside. It ended up taking the full fifteen minutes she had available plus some before she was arriving at Colonel Booker's office.

"I apologize for being late, Colonel," she said as she stood at attention, her CIA outfitted Captain's uniform still crisp.

Booker was the stereotype for straight-laced full bird's. Short cropped silver hair, slim but powerful build, thick leathery skin from years of deployment in the deserts of Asia. He pointed to a chair, barely looking up from the file she had provided his secretary, something quickly whipped up by her sweetheart Chris Leroux. She hoped it would prove sufficient, it modeled after another case mocked up a few years ago.

Booker looked up. "You're investigating Captain Lewis for a possible Medal of Honor citation?"

"Yes, sir."

"Who nominated him?"

"I'm sorry, sir, I'm not at liberty to say. If you knew, it might taint your answers."

Booker's eyes narrowed slightly. "I can assure you, *Captain*, that my answers will always be honest and forthright."

Sherrie tried not to gulp, realizing she had already misread Booker.

By the book! Don't volunteer anything you don't need to.

"I have no doubt, sir."

Booker eyed her again for a moment. "What is it you want from me?"

"You were his commanding officer when he died." She was about to end the sentence as if it were a question, but decided to be more succinct as Booker didn't seem to tolerate much. They both already knew the answer, so why ask the question? "From your recollection of the events leading to his death, does it agree with the written description provided to us?" She nodded toward the folder.

"Yes."

Okay, very *succinct.* Too *succinct.*

Her job was to try and elicit some response. Some surprise that this particular person was being spoken of. And at no costs reveal that the CIA knew the man was actually alive. She was looking for discomfort, and she was sensing none.

Perhaps he has no idea?

"Do you see any reason why Captain Lewis should not be awarded this honor?"

Booker leaned back in his chair, saying nothing, simply staring at Sherrie. Sweat dripped down her back as she felt herself become suddenly uncomfortable. Her intuition was telling her to get out of here, and she made the conscious decision that the last question had already been asked.

"No," said Booker finally. He suddenly rose. "I have a meeting in ten minutes. Walk with me, Captain, and I'll give you my opinion on this entire situation."

Sherrie had leapt to her feet the moment Booker had risen. "I think I have all I need, Colonel. I wouldn't want to bother you any further."

"Walk with me."

It was an order, and she had to obey, otherwise her cover would be blown. Captains don't ignore Colonel's orders, even if they're not in their chain of command. Especially orders as innocuous as "Walk with me."

She fell in one step behind the Colonel and to his left, his pace brisk.

"Let me clarify my last answer," he said as they exited the building, the sun now very low on the horizon. He pointed to the passenger seat of a Humvee as he climbed into the driver seat. Sherrie immediately felt the

66

hairs on the back of her neck raise as she eyed her rental sitting nearby. "What I meant was, if the standards of the military have dropped so low that charging into an alleyway blindly, ignoring all procedure, is grounds enough for a Medal of Honor today, then I see no reason to object."

The truck surged deeper into the base as he spoke, Sherrie merely listening, her heart racing. Something was definitely wrong. She slowly reached for her watch, a simple twist of the face then click of a button on its side enough to activate a tracking beacon and distress call.

Booker's hand lunged out, grabbing her wrist, enveloping the watch in his massive hand.

"Let's keep them out of this, shall we?"

He turned a corner and raced through an open set of garage doors, doors that immediately began to close behind them. As the vehicle screeched to a halt, large overhead lights suddenly bathed them in a harsh white glow. She gasped as she saw a woman standing nearby wearing the exact same outfit as her, hair color and style to match.

"Take her watch first," Booker said to two soldiers who approached the passenger side. She was quickly stripped of the watch, satchel, shoes, and limited jewelry, including a simple necklace that Chris had given her for their first anniversary.

She nearly cried.

But she didn't. She kept her face as devoid of emotion as she could, beginning to compartmentalize herself as she prepped for what was coming.

As they took her shoes, her double stepped into them, placing the necklace around her neck, the watch on her wrist, and the satchel under her arm. Her cap was placed atop her hair and pulled low to hide her face.

Booker nodded in approval then the double climbed in the passenger side, one of the other men driving it back out the doors and into the night.

Sherrie looked at Booker, her face blank. She had her answer. Booker knew damned well that Captain Lewis was alive, and knew at a minimum that she wasn't who she claimed to be.

And whatever it was he was protecting, was big enough for him to risk pissing off the CIA.

And if she knew her trade craft handbook as well as she knew she did, her double would take her car off the base, leaving footage showing she had left unmolested, then disappeared after the fact.

She just prayed Chris would see past the subterfuge.

Mandara Spa, Beijing, China

Lee Fang knocked on the door, her outfit hastily thrown on after she had received General Yee's orders to report to his suite at once. She assumed nothing was wrong as she waited for permission to enter, the guards on either side of the door saying nothing, their demeanor suggesting nothing wrong.

"Enter!"

She opened the door and stepped into the suite. She didn't see the General at first, but it was a large room, more like a one-bedroom apartment, much bigger than anything 99% of the population lived in on a daily basis.

Decadence.

She realized it was the new way, and she even partook at times, enjoying a nice Starbucks coffee when she was in the city, but it was one of her few indulgences. And with her meagre PLA salary, she had little spare money for such luxuries, the bulk of what was left over at the end of the month sent back home to help her parents trapped on their subsistence farm.

Life in China was hard for too many.

But things were improving, she just hoped her homeland didn't turn into the United States. At least that's what she was trained to think, or rather indoctrinated to think.

And indoctrination was hard to break.

From a baby she was taught that China was the light, the West was the great darkness. She knew that wasn't entirely true, she had been on enough ops outside of the country to have been exposed to Westerners and Western culture to realize they weren't impoverished evil devils like her parents and grandparents were taught, left to wallow in their own filth and depravity by an uncaring state.

With the Internet and the opening up of political and economic ties to the outside world, the teachings had changed since it was difficult to reconcile a failed outside world with one that could create things as amazing as Coca-Cola and McDonalds. Clearly the outside world was successful, just different. And the Chinese government would have its people believe that the outside world was not one to emulate, but to exploit, in the end creating a better China that could dominate its enemies militarily, economically, and culturally if it could avoid the trappings of the Western way of life.

Indulgence in moderation.

Unless you were part of the elite.

"In the bedroom, Major."

Her chest tightened. She knew what was about to happen and she had already decided long ago that no matter who the man was, no matter how high in the food chain they were, she would do nothing she didn't want to do.

And having sex with an obese sexagenarian party insider was not on her "to do list".

But she had to follow lawful orders, and calling her into the bedroom wasn't unlawful. He could merely be changing into his uniform.

A thought that she didn't believe for a second.

She walked through the bedroom door to her left and nearly frowned at the sight. General Yee lay spread-eagle on the bed, naked, his impressively small penis between his thumb and forefinger, a martini glass in the other.

"Fang, so good of you to come."

Fang said nothing.

"I've been watching you." He took a sip of his drink, the other hand slowly taking care of business, her arrival apparently breathing life into the small appendage. "I think you could go far should you play your cards right."

Again she remained silent, standing at attention, her eyes examining the cove molding that trimmed the ceiling.

"Come, join me," he said, patting the bed, his hand quickly returning to his wagging member.

"I'm afraid I cannot, Comrade General."

"Why not?" His voice clearly indicated he was annoyed.

"I'm on duty, Comrade General. Let me go get one of the ladies from earlier." She turned to leave before he could say anything, but was surprised by how quickly he leapt from the bed.

"Stand fast, Major."

She stopped, slowly turning back toward her commanding officer.

"Look at me."

She lowered her gaze, the leer on his face turning her stomach. He came within inches of her, his large belly pushing against her toned six-pack. A hand grasped her ass, pulling her tight against him and she felt his now fully engorged member press into her stomach.

She fought the urge to break his neck, instead remaining silent, all emotion wiped from her face as she continued to follow her orders, looking at him.

"You're a clever one," he said, draining his martini glass and tossing it against the wall, the tall stem sheering off, the rest of the crystal shattering and falling atop a dresser. His freed hand cupped her small but adequate right breast, pumping it like a stress ball, his index finger flicking over her nipple repeatedly, it involuntarily hardening.

For a split second she felt shame.

"You thought I didn't know you were around the corner, listening to our conversation, didn't you?"

She clenched her teeth lest her jaw drop open.

He squeezed her tighter against him, his hips now pumping against her shirt steadily as he lowered his mouth to her neck.

"I had forgotten you were there, but when you entered to do your fake rounds, I remembered that you had been there all along."

She said nothing, realizing that what she had overheard merited death in today's China.

His lips pressed against hers, his tongue seeking, demanding entrance into her mouth, yet her lips remained pressed tightly together. His hand moved from her breast to her throat. He squeezed.

"You will submit, Comrade Major." His hand let go of her throat and dropped down, suddenly tearing open her blouse revealing her bra and dark, toned skin. His fingers shoved under the top of her bra, gripping her breast, pinching her nipple between two of his dry fingers.

She reached her belt, her hand resting on her pistol, then dismissing shooting the pig as it would cause too much noise. He yanked her by the bra toward the bed, spinning her around so she was facing the door. She felt the edge of the bed press against the back of her legs.

She pulled the knife and raised it. He must have noticed as he stopped sucking on her exposed nipple and gasped. She plunged the blade in the top of his head, burying it to the hilt, scrambling his brains.

He died, instantly, silently, slowly sliding to the floor, a look of shock on his face as he hit the carpet, she controlling his descent with her free hand. She yanked the knife from his skull, wiped it clean on the bed, then pulled him back to his feet and rolled him onto the mattress in one fluid motion. She grabbed the blanket, tossing it over the bloodstain on the floor, then took the sheet and covered the general's body, leaving his lower half exposed so anyone looking in might hesitate. Retrieving several pillows from the living area of the suite, she formed the outline of a person snuggled up against him in the bed.

Should anyone glance in, they'd think the general and his concubine were asleep after an evening of exhausting sex.

She went to the bathroom and cleaned herself up, fixing the blouse, unable to do anything about the fact two buttons had popped off when he had assaulted her. She straightened her hair, there no makeup to fix, then returned to the hallway.

"Yes, Comrade General. I will see that you aren't disturbed until morning. Enjoy your evening."

She said it slightly louder than necessary, hoping that those on either side of the door outside were able to hear what was said. Opening the door swiftly, her trained eye immediately discerned the hall was empty save the two guards. She marched past them, letting the pneumatic door closer do its job.

"The general and his female guest are not to be disturbed for any reason until eight tomorrow morning," she said, tossing the order over her shoulder. "Make sure your relief is made aware."

The two soldiers snapped their heels together, and she thought she had made it when one of them cleared his throat. "Comrade Major, I thought he was alone when you went in."

She slowed almost imperceptibly before catching herself, continuing her march toward the elevator. She jabbed the button, turning back to the guards. "The General has one guest with him. A, shall we say, *special* guest. She is not to be looked at or mentioned to anyone. Understood?"

Again heel clicks as the implication of an underage prostitute was received.

The doors opened and she stepped aboard, pressing the button for her floor. As the elevator descended, her mind raced. She needed to escape the situation and go into hiding, probably permanently. Which meant she would have to leave China.

The thought at once crushed her and angered her, the fact she might need to flee her country because of some horny pig of a general.

But where to go?

The only place she could think of where she might be safe would be America. And she did have some intel that she felt they needed to know about. If she were correct, their President was about to be assassinated, and if it were to succeed, and link back to China, it could mean war and millions if not billions of deaths should it go nuclear.

Her duty was to her country, and right now, that duty meant betraying it.

She thought of the Americans she had met recently in Africa.

The doors opened on her floor and she swiftly made her way to her room. As she packed she finalized her decision, it clear there was little choice.

But she had no clue how to reach the soldiers she had met, at least not through channels.

Which left only one possibility.

And it meant taking a leap of faith she wasn't sure she was ready to make.

James Acton & Laura Palmer Residence
St. Paul's, Maryland

Archeology Professor James Acton lay in bed, naked, a smile on his face ten miles wide as his wife and lover lay draped across him, her naked flesh hot and sweaty, their love making session one for the record books.

At least his own record book.

It was love making at its best as far as he was concerned. He couldn't count the number of times he had counseled kids in his class that porn was sex, but sex was not porn. Boys today expected acrobatics from their women because that's all they thought sex was, their only exposure from an early age porn clips on the Internet. And young women were equally confused, kids not understanding that what was on the screen wasn't real, wasn't love, and if you were to believe the porn stars, especially the female ones, not fun.

What he and Laura had just taken part in was the real thing. It wasn't vanilla, definitely chocolate chip, and it was fantastic. And now that they knew what each other liked after several years of dating and now marriage, it heightened the excitement, the intimacy, the intensity.

Life is good!

Laura moaned. "God, that was great."

"You married a stallion."

"I certainly did. They should put you out to stud, but I want you all to myself."

A quick grin escaped his control for a second at the thought of being put out to stud.

"I saw that."

"Of course you did." He looked down at her as she looked up his chest at him. "A man's allowed to think about stuff, as long as he doesn't touch."

Laura's eyebrows rose slightly. "Oh yeah, maybe I'll just have to remind you just how lucky you have it here at the ranch."

She began to kiss her way down his chest, then his stomach, and what was once flagging was quickly at full mast as he closed his eyes, his head pressing back into the pillow.

"Where's your mind now?" she asked as she reached the prize.

"I can't even remember what we were talking about."

The phone rang.

He groaned. "You've *got* to be kidding me."

"Ignore it," she said, the ringing getting more distracting.

He looked at the call display. "It's long distance, I better get it."

She jumped off him, grinning. "Your choice."

He grabbed the phone, giving her the eye. "You're evil."

She winked. "Too late. We're married now."

He answered the phone. "Hello?"

"Professor Acton?" It was a woman's voice. It sounded like either they had a bad connection or she was speaking low. He pressed the phone against his ear a little tighter.

"Yes, who's this?"

"I can't say my name, someone might be listening, but we met in Eritrea several months ago."

Acton's mind raced as he sat up straight, the signal to Laura that something serious was going on. He had met several women in Eritrea when examining the old Roman shipwreck from Pompeii that had caused so much chaos and death. The head of the mission stood out, but she had a distinctive southern drawl absent here. "I met several women there. Could you be more specific?"

"Besides the head of the mission, I was the only other woman taken hostage."

Lee Fang!

His heart raced as he remembered one of the two Chinese observers, a woman who had inspired him with her courage, and in the end had helped save them all. He and the others were almost positive she was Chinese Special Forces, which posed an important question.

Why is she calling me?

"Yes, I remember you. How can I help you?"

"I'm in trouble. Listen carefully. I overheard something I wasn't supposed to, then my commanding officer tried to rape me. I killed him."

"Oh my God!"

It was Laura's voice that startled him, and apparently Fang.

"Who's that?"

"I'm sorry, it's Laura Palmer, James' wife. I'm on the extension phone."

"Oh, okay. Is there anyone else listening?"

"Not here," said Acton, and in all seriousness, added, "but I wouldn't trust that our conversation isn't being taped by someone. Things are very chaotic in the United States right now."

"I know. And I have important information about that. *Very* important information."

"What information? Perhaps I can pass it along?"

"No. I need safe passage from China to the United States. By this time tomorrow the entire country will be looking for me. Help get me out of China and I'll give your government the information I have."

"I'm not sure what you expect me to do about it," said Acton, Laura sitting beside him on the bed, the other cordless phone pressed to her ear.

"You have friends," was the reply. "Connected friends."

Acton and Laura exchanged glances. He knew she must be referring to his contacts within the Delta Force. "I know who you mean. I could call them but that call would definitely be monitored."

"That might not be good. This conspiracy runs deep and I don't know who to trust within my government or yours."

Laura was snapping her fingers beside him, trying to get his attention. She had her cellphone out, showing her contacts list, one name highlighted.

Dinner, Kraft.

Acton smiled. "I know exactly who we can both trust, but I will need to try and reach him. How can I or he reach you?"

"Take down this number."

Acton motioned to Laura who was way ahead of him, already opening the Notes app on her phone. "Go ahead," he said.

Fang gave them a number and a coded phrase. "I'll know your friend by that. The number will be good for one hour."

"I'll call him right away. I can't guarantee I'll reach him, but I'll try my best."

"That's all I can ask, but, Professor, please hurry. I don't have much time."

"I'll do my best," he repeated.

"Thank you."

The line went dead and Laura dialed the number on her phone for Dinner, Kraft, their coded entry for Acton's former student and CIA Special Agent, Dylan Kane. It was an emergency number that Kane had given them that couldn't be traced, acting like a pager. Laura entered their code number at the prompt, then hung up. She looked at Acton, all sexual thoughts gone from both their minds as they sat beside each other naked and scared. "Now let's just hope he's available to help."

Acton slowly nodded, putting the phone back in its cradle. "I wonder what she could possibly know about what's happening here."

Laura curled a leg up under her, turning toward him. "Maybe she knows nothing. She's obviously in trouble and she wants out. Maybe she just made it up to try and get our help."

"Possibly. She definitely sounded scared, something I don't think I ever heard when we were together in Africa. She's the toughest woman I've ever met. Almost emotionless."

"Well, even if the information part of her story isn't true, if the other part is, she's a woman who needs help."

Acton pursed his lips. "Then help is what she'll get."

The phone rang.

The Nation's Gun Show, Chantilly, Virginia

"Of course this is only a prototype, and is also illegal to sell, so I'm sorry boys, this is purely a demo."

Stan Reese stood among the fairly large crowd gathered around the 3D Gunnery booth as half a dozen 3D printers busily printed out weapons parts, at various stages in the process, the individual parts laid out for the world to see, along with numerous fully assembled weapons. Video played on several screens showing the weapons being successfully fired at ranges.

Including the one he was here to acquire.

A revolver capable of firing six shots.

As the fascinated group of gun aficionados groaned their disappointment at not being able to purchase one of these miracle weapons, the presentation continued.

But Reese could care less.

He wasn't here because he wanted to be, he was here because he was being forced. His parents were being held and he had been given a task by the same Muslim terrorists wreaking havoc across the country.

Purchase the very plastic revolver now being demonstrated.

"Has it been test fired?" asked someone from the crowd, clearly skeptical.

"Absolutely. If it survives the first test fire, and by that I mean some of the early ones coming off the printer would explode or fall apart due to defects—but we've fixed those problems with different materials and designs—so, if they survive that first shot, we find they're almost always good for the first six rounds. Most are good for a second six, but that's about it."

Reese's heart pounded in his ears. He was carrying a satchel over his shoulder with a quarter of a million dollars in it. And a Beretta. His *orders*—for they weren't instructions—were to buy the weapon from the man standing in front of the crowd, or take it, killing him if necessary.

"How much time do you need to leave between shots for everything to cool down?"

"You can fire three in quick succession, then I recommend letting it cool for a minute. I've managed all six, but it gets risky."

Whoever had *drafted* him into their Muslim army had made a mistake. Yes, he loved guns, knew everything there was to know about them, but he was a pacifist. There was no way he was going to shoot this man.

So you'll have to convince him to sell you the gun. Or Mom and Dad are dead.

The memory of their voices, especially his terrified mother's, broke his heart, and he felt his eyes glisten as a freshly printed piece of the weapon was passed around. He blinked his eyes clear and ran his fingers over the lightweight piece, the surface oddly bumpy. He passed it on.

"Do you sell the machine?"

"Ahh, now that's a completely different question, and the right one. Yes I do, I do indeed."

"What about the plans for the gun?"

"That too."

"How much?"

"Twenty-five hundred per. We take cash, credit, but no checks."

The frenzy lasted about twenty minutes with the booth emptied, even the demo units sold. Reese hung back, watching the young man, barely twenty-five, as he packed up the exhibit, his job done, nothing left to display. He headed toward the back and Reese followed him, the Exhibitor badge he wore, which had been delivered to him that morning along with the cash, a hotel key, the gun and a rather odd grocery list, allowing him to pass the light security without any hassle.

The young man was loading a box into the back of his van when Reese found him, the rear parking area a ghost town. "Excuse me," he said.

The young man spun around, startled, and Reese tried to force a smile on his face, raising his hands to show he wasn't a threat.

"Man, you scared the shit out of me! Can I help you?"

Reese nodded. He opened the satchel, revealing the quarter of a million in cash. "Two hundred and fifty thousand dollars. You give me the plastic six shooter, I give you the money. Tomorrow morning you call the police and say it was stolen out of your van."

"I can't do that!" exclaimed the man, but Reese noticed he couldn't tear his eyes from the cash.

"The cash is yours. Tax free, to do with as you please. No one will ever know." Reese lowered his voice. "Please, take the money."

Finally the man's eyes rose, looking Reese in the face. "But why? Why do you want it?"

Reese shook his head, knowing full well the phone in his pocket was listening to everything being said. "I'm a collector," he lied, the only thing he could think of to say. "I promise you, I won't hurt anyone with it, I just need it."

The man stood still for a moment, then finally, reluctantly, shook his head. "No, man, I just can't do it. I'm sorry."

Reese frowned then reached into the bag, pulling out the Beretta just enough for the man to see it. "I'd really hate to use this, but I don't have a choice. Please, just take the money, then call the police tomorrow. That way nobody gets hurt."

The man stepped backward, his knees hitting the bumper of his van, startling him as he fell into a seated position, his hands up. He pointed at a bag. "They're all in there."

Reese let go of the Beretta, dropping it to the bottom of the bag. "I only need the one."

The man grabbed the bag, unzipping it, and rooted through it until he pulled out a bubble wrapped package. "This is it. D-do you need ammo?"

"Apparently not."

The man's eyebrows narrowed at the curious answer, and Reese realized he had made his first gaffe. He reached out and took the package, then handed the bag with the money and the Beretta to the young man.

"Remember, call the police tomorrow, not today. If you try to call today, I will know."

He walked away quickly, the phone in his breast pocket vibrating, his entire body shaking with fear.

CIA Headquarters, Langley, Virginia

Chris Leroux looked at his watch once again, it thirty-four seconds later than the last time he had looked at it. It had been hours since his girlfriend Sherrie White had reported that she was approaching Fort Myer. And not a peep had been heard since.

There was a soft tap on his door and he spun his chair toward it, a smile on his face as he realized his worrying was for nothing. "Enter!"

It had been a carefully chosen word when he actually earned a door. It made him feel like Captain Picard. Sherrie had giggled the first time she heard it, and he had to admit it had hurt his feelings a bit, but she had made it up to him—boy had she made it up to him—and his injured fanboy ego had been soothed.

And he kept using it.

The door opened and to his surprise a solemn looking Director Morrison entered, closing the door behind him. Leroux began to rise when Morrison waved him off, instead heavily taking the seat in front of the desk.

He sighed, and Leroux felt every muscle in his body tighten as anguish fueled adrenaline gushed into his system.

"She's dead, isn't she?" His voice cracked as the words came out, and a cry escaped him as Morrison nodded.

"I'm afraid it looks that way."

Leroux gripped the desk with both hands, tight, his head lowering to his chest as he tried to picture the only woman he had ever loved, the only woman who had ever loved him, and he failed. He opened his eyes, tears pouring down his cheeks and grabbed the photo sitting on his desk of her, guilt racking his body that he had been the one to gather the intel that had sent her to her death.

"What happened?"

"It looks like a car accident."

Leroux's eyebrows narrowed and he wiped the tears away with the back of his hand, the old quickly replaced with new as his sinuses clogged. "What do you mean?"

"They found her car in the Potomac. Apparently according to witnesses she lost control and drove into the river. By the time rescuers got to her it was too late. She must have been able to get out, though, but was too weak to reach the surface."

"What do you mean?"

"There was no body. Dive teams are out now, but it's dark so they're not optimistic they'll find her body until tomorrow."

Leroux sucked in a deep breath, wiping his face dry with several tissues, then blew his nose.

"She's not dead."

Morrison leaned forward, forcing eye contact with Leroux. "Witnesses saw her in the car. They saw the car go into the river. If she survived, she would have contacted us by now. She left the base hours ago."

Leroux shook his head, refusing to let go of the single thread of hope he had.

"No, she's alive. And they have her."

Morrison sat back in his chair. "Excuse me? Who has her?"

"Colonel Booker."

"That's a pretty bold accusation. Care to back it up?"

Leroux nodded, slowly beginning to feel his old self as he kicked into analyst mode, his gift the ability to pull apparently unrelated data together and find relationships that no one thought was there.

And today he was grasping at straws.

"A man dead for years turns up being used on a top secret op probably conducted by part of our military. That means black ops of some kind. Colonel Booker was his commanding officer when he was killed, and miraculously goes from Major to full-bird Colonel in two years. He now heads the rapid response unit meant to protect the White House, and his son, a Major under his command, is married to the head of Raven Defense Services, a private security firm known to make Blackwater look like pansies."

"How did you find that out?"

"I dig, sir. It's what I do."

"Keep going."

Leroux leaned forward, excited he hadn't been dismissed already. "Let's say I'm involved in faking the death of one of my men, a man just used on a critical op, and someone comes asking questions about him. Wouldn't it raise your suspicions? Especially if you knew the dead captain's service record you'd know he wasn't the hero type and would never merit a Congressional Medal of Honor. If I were Booker, red flags would be popping up all around me."

"What do you think happened?"

"I think they took her prisoner to find out what she knows."

"But we have the car. Witnesses saw her go into the water."

"Witnesses saw *someone* driving her car that went into the water. Someone fully prepared for the staged accident, who probably as soon as she was under the water donned an oxygen mask and tank, then waited for the pressure to equalize and opened the door, safely swimming underwater downstream to be picked up by her Raven Defense buddies."

"That's pure conjecture, Chris." Morrison shook his head, his chin balanced on his steepled fingertips. "You have absolutely no evidence."

"Then let me get it."

"How?"

"Let me hack Fort Myer security and tap their feeds."

Morrison pursed his lips, his head slowly shaking. "It's against the law. We can't spy domestically."

"Sir, the country is falling apart. Maybe we need to stop obeying the law so we can save it."

Morrison stared at Leroux for a moment, his eyes revealing nothing of what was going on behind them.

Suddenly he rose, pushing the chair out with the back of his knees. "Do it. But don't get caught."

He left without saying another word, leaving Leroux to stare at the photo of Sherrie for a few more moments before turning to his computer to violate the Constitution.

Extended Stay America, Eisenhower Avenue, Washington, DC

"—today ordered a freeze on all immigration, travel visas and direct flights from a long list of countries. As well, all citizens of these countries have had their visas terminated and are being ordered out of the United States immediately. Though the White House wouldn't confirm any commonality among those countries named, it is obvious that all are predominantly Muslim nations. This action appears aimed at quieting those critics who are demanding the President solve the problem by confronting the Muslim community. As White House Spokesman Timothy Humble said today, the President is bound by the Constitution and unable to round up American citizens and imprison them merely based upon their religion.

"Eight more attacks today now seem aimed at our transportation infrastructure. With schools across the country empty, the stock markets closed for the second day in a row, and the dollar taking a beating on world markets, rail infrastructure seemed to be the target in five attacks. Fortunately casualties were light in these isolated attacks. Not so for the other three. Miami, Houston and Phoenix were hit today when individuals blew themselves up inside grocery stores, killing dozens.

"Retaliatory attacks continue with sixteen mosques burned to the ground to date, and today in Detroit, the local fire department refused to put out the flames at one mosque, instead merely making certain it didn't spread to any nearby structures. This resulted in condemnation from city officials however judging by the reaction on social media, the firefighters are supported by the vast majority. There are still no leads—"

Stan Reese shut off the television then sat at the small, round table perched in the corner of his hotel room. In front of him was a mix of mostly condiments, an exact list provided to him in the courier package from this morning. Specific brands and sizes, with the verbal instructions the mechanical voice had given him clearly indicating *no* substitutions would be acceptable.

It had taken three stores to complete the list.

He pushed the condiments to the far side of the table and carefully unwrapped the plastic gun. Instructions on how to break it down had been provided on a sheet of paper, and he began, carefully, terrified he might break a piece of what he feared was too delicate a weapon to be handled like this.

But to his surprise it stood up well to his manipulations, and as he thought of it, it made sense. After all, it was expected to be able to fire six shots without a problem, meaning it had to be strong enough to handle the recoil.

The weapon broken down, he placed each piece in a Ziploc baggie, carefully making certain each bag was sealed, the air forced out. He then took the six condiment jars, removed the tops from each, then placed the indicated piece into each jar, the instructions specific even in this manner.

Done, he removed any excess mayonnaise, ketchup, mustard or other tasty fluids then secured the lids once again. Placing everything in the box that had delivered the cash and instruction this morning, he sealed it with tape that had been sent along, then looked at his watch. He had completed his task just in time.

A knock at the door had him leaping to his feet, his heart jumping into his throat. He approached the door. "Who is it?"

"FedEx. I'm here for the pickup you ordered."

Whoever these guys are, they're good.

It was odd. He had never really thought of Islamic terrorists as organized and efficient. They seemed to bumble their way to success as opposed to earn it. But he had to admit he was assuming they were Islamist terrorists. Everything he had heard on the news was that the attacks were being committed in the name of Islam, it believed now by some that those committing these atrocities were being forced to.

Which did match his situation.

But he hadn't been ordered to blow himself up or shoot anyone.

Unlike those other poor bastards today.

He opened the door, pointing at the box on the table. "It's over there."

The driver nodded with a smile and walked over to the table. He affixed several labels then handed the signature device over. "Sign here, please."

Reese signed the pad, handing the plastic stylus back to the driver who grabbed the box and headed out the door. "Have a good one!" he tossed over his shoulder, Reese closing the door behind him.

His phone rang.

"Hello?"

"You are done for the evening, Mr. Reese. You are to talk to no one, interact with no one, except to get yourself food for this evening and tomorrow morning. Remember, we are watching you, and we have your parents. You will receive a phone call at seven a.m. tomorrow morning. Make certain you are awake and ready to leave at that time. Do you understand?"

"Yes, seven a.m."

The call ended with a click. Reese collapsed on the small bed, burying his head in the pillow. He fought back the tears of frustration, the tears of pain, as he realized more than ever how powerless he was to get out of his situation.

And he trembled at what they might have him do tomorrow.

Weihai, China

Lee Fang's phone vibrated in her hand. Her heart leapt as inwardly she battled an adrenaline surge, outwardly she appeared her usual calm self to anyone who might be looking. But no one should be. She was in Weihai, lying on the beach in a two piece bikini that she had been instructed to wear. Why, she had no idea. Large sunglasses covered much of her face, and a beach umbrella perched overhead hid her from satellites and UAV's that might be patrolling above.

As she put the phone to her ear, looking casually about for anyone who might be listening, she realized that she was getting a few unwelcome looks from young men staring at her ripped body. She wasn't by any means a bodybuilder, she found that look disgusting, but she was extremely fit. Gifted with genes that let her eat what she wanted, she needn't have relied on them, what with the intense physical fitness program she maintained with her unit.

Besides, she never over ate—she found the very concept revolting having come from a home where food was at a premium and still was for her parents and extended family.

The voice on the other end spoke perfect Chinese with a convincing Shanghai dialect. "Hi, is Ching there?"

"Sorry, you have the wrong number."

"Really? That bitch. I thought she liked me."

The call ended and she rose to her knees, brushing her light brown skin of the stray sand that had blown on it, the prep signal having been received. She packed her few possessions into her bag and was about to rise when a pair of legs stopped in front of her.

91

"Leaving so soon?" asked the voice in English.

She looked up but the sun was behind the man's head. Squinting, she stood, blocking the rays with her hand. A tall Caucasian man stood smiling at her, sunglasses hiding his eyes, a white button down shirt open, blowing in the wind, revealing an impressive physique.

Too bad I'm not into white guys.

"I have to go meet a friend."

"Boyfriend?"

"No, just a friend."

"So there's no boyfriend."

"No."

"Then let me buy you a drink. Perhaps a martini. How many olives do you prefer?"

"Five."

"Really? I had you pegged at no more than two."

She could have sworn he had just looked at her two rather small breasts. "I prefer five."

"Then five it shall be." He extended his hand and she gave him the bag. "There's a bar just down the beach, let's grab a drink there."

They began to walk, the olive count her indication that this was indeed the right person. Her message had indicated the number of the day was seven. Whatever number of olives she answered with, his reply had to make it total to seven.

And the pig had chosen two.

She mentally kicked herself since it was she that had chosen five, forcing him to say two, but she still felt a little exposed, her two piece leaving only about five percent of her body to the imagination, and this American seemed to be delighting in ogling her.

As they cleared the beach area she had been lying on, the man pointed to a nearby car. "How about I give you a lift to your hotel. I have a funny feeling they don't make a good martini here."

"I'd like that, thanks."

They both climbed in the tiny Chinese built Chery QQ3. She smiled as she saw the man had the front seat pushed all the way to the back and he was still having trouble fitting. She sat comfortably as she watched him struggle to get out of the parking lot.

"Why such a small car?"

"Joke from my damned handler, Chao. Next time I see him I'm sleeping with his wife."

Fang's eyebrows jumped.

"Just a joke," winked the man. "You should see his wife." He laughed heartily, his smile genuine and attractive, and she felt herself slowly beginning to relax as the tension of the past twenty-four hours gradually let up.

"What's your plan?" she asked as they roared toward the coast road and not toward the hotel district.

"To get you out of China."

"How?"

"Have you ever been to Korea?"

"North or South?"

"I'd prefer South. I've been North and they're not very hospitable."

She let a slight smile show. "You've been to the North?"

"I guess I shouldn't have said that. Now I'll have to kill you."

Again a wink.

Who is this man?

He wasn't the type of CIA operative she had ever imagined. He was extremely good looking, his Chinese was perfect, and he had so far kept his word, meeting her exactly where and when he had said he would, and in the manner he said he would.

"Prepare to be hit on," he had said. She had had to think about what that meant, his "wear a two piece bikini" filling in the blanks.

"You know my name, what's yours?"

"Do I know your name?" He pretended to think for a moment. "I supposed I do." He stuck out a hand. "Dylan Kane, nice to meet you Lee Fang."

She shook the hand, it dry, confident, the shake firm but not overpowering. She didn't want to let go, it somehow making her feel secure again.

She eyed the road. "Where are we going?"

"To catch a boat."

"You expect to get us to Korea in a boat?"

"It's only a couple of hundred kilometers. No problem."

She wasn't so sure about his plan, and said so.

"What did you expect? To just fly out on the next flight? You're a wanted woman. Pretty much everyone in China is looking for you."

She felt her chest tighten. She had assumed as much, but to hear it actually stated, it made her situation that much more real. "How do you know?"

"I know everything," Kane said, smiling. "Now, just trust me. Obviously there's no way to take you out by plane, train or automobile, they're watching the airports and borders too closely. I could have taken you out through some remote part of the border, but it would take too long, and if you've got intel that's as important as I think it is, then we don't have time to waste."

"Just what do you think I know?"

Kane glanced at her, his face devoid of any of the cheerfulness it had shown to this point. He looked back at the road, slowing as he turned into the parking lot of a marina. "I think you stumbled upon something that even *you* can't abide by. You're a patriot, love your country, believe in the Party, but you also believe in right and wrong, and whatever it is you have discovered, you feel is wrong. And because your entire country is looking for you, you obviously couldn't go to anyone within your security apparatus as they're involved."

"*Might* be involved," she interjected, not wanting to tarnish her country's name too much. "My entire country is after me because I killed General Yee and they don't know why."

Kane parked the car, turning to her. "True. But remember this. You came to us because you didn't know who to trust. Once we do this, there's no turning back. This is a one way street."

Fang nodded, slowly, and closed her eyes, a sudden overwhelming desire to cry threatening to embarrass her. She felt a hand on her shoulder and jumped slightly as this man she had just met, who was supposed to be someone she could trust, tried to provide her with comfort she had so desperately needed since she had walked into that hotel room last night.

Her chin dropped and her shoulders heaved once.

Then she felt the warm, familiar friend of anger swell within.

I did nothing wrong! He tried to rape me!

She looked up at Kane, his hand still on her shoulder. "I realize the gravity of my decision."

Kane gave her shoulder a final squeeze, his look one of understanding, as if he too had made decisions in his life knowing there was no going back.

Life altering decisions.

Permanent decisions.

"I have no doubt," he said gently. "Are you ready?"

She nodded. "Let's do this."

Kane smiled, the charming American tourist look once again replacing his serious visage. "Then let's go sea-doing!" Kane struggled out of the car, Fang trying not to grin. He grabbed a small bag from the trunk, pointing at a second bag. "Don't forget your bag, honey."

"Of course, dear."

So we're now in a relationship? He moves fast, even undercover.

"Why don't you put anything you might need in this bag instead of that other one?"

As she did so, transferring her gun, ID and a few pieces of clothing, she realized this meant they were never coming back to the car.

Does he mean to have us cross to Korea on a Sea-Doo?

They walked down a boardwalk toward a dock with several Sea-Doos, a sign indicating they were available for rent. A man who looked like he might be in his fifties, small and humble—and painfully Chinese—kept bowing to them. "A two-seater, my good man," said Kane, his voice strong and confident, but not too loud.

"How long, sir?" The man's English was thick with his Chinese tongue, but she sensed something a little off.

"Just an hour."

Money was exchanged and the key handed over as the man escorted them to a beautiful two-seater Sea-Doo personal watercraft. Kane climbed aboard first, straddling the powerful machine, then helped her down. They each slung their small backpacks over their shoulders, then Kane started the motor.

"Say hi to your wife for me," he said to the man, winking.

"I hope you enjoyed your rental car, you American devil," was the reply from the man in perfect English.

"Hold on!" yelled Kane, and as he gunned the engine she reached forward, clasping her arms around his muscled abdomen, her own bare skin pressed against his back, the tiny two-piece and his thin shirt all that separated them.

As they shot out from the dock, Kane did a few runs up and down the beach, each one getting progressively farther from the shore. Fang had never actually been on a personal watercraft before, and she began to have a great time, Kane whooping it up, putting on a show.

Completely in character.

He's good. Very good.

She wondered what he was like in real life, but then again, in their business, what was real life? She was certain his was a much deeper cover than she had ever experienced. When she left the base at night she was herself. He probably lived a permanent cover.

He'd have to lie to his friends and family.

But he obviously had at least one person who knew what he did and was outside of the special ops world. Professor James Acton had sent him, so there was clearly some connection there. She'd have to ask him if she got the chance.

Kane cut the engine, letting them drift to a stop as they bobbed in the water, the shore quite a distance away.

"Ready?" he asked.

"Ready for what?"

He winked and jumped into the water, his bag slung over his shoulder. "Come on in, the water's great!"

She jumped in, holding her breath until she popped back to the surface. With the Sea-Doo between them and the shore, Kane opened the bag slung across his shoulders and pulled out a pair of goggles that he quickly put in place, first rinsing out the glasses and spitting in each lens to prevent fogging.

She did the same with the pair she found in her bag. Next was a mouthpiece that sealed over the mouth, snapping into the goggles, a rebreather built into it with a small air tank dangling from the side. Kane then pushed ear buds in place, motioning for her to do the same. Equipped, she gave the thumbs up.

"Good," said Kane through the ear buds that turned out to be tiny receivers. "There's enough air for about an hour. We've got two-way short-range comms. Now let's go!"

He turned away from the Sea-Doo and dove under the water. She followed and they settled in about ten feet below the surface, Kane setting a brisk pace that she struggled at first to maintain, but eventually she got her rhythm set and they made good time, toward what she had no idea.

Now he expects us to reach South Korea like this?

After about thirty minutes Kane pointed below them. She looked but couldn't make out much, the water now uncomfortably deep below them. He leaned forward, shoving his butt up, and dove deeper. Fang followed, and as she went farther, a dark shadow began to take shape below them. As they neared the shape took form and she gasped.

"Here's our ride!" said Kane. "Nice and cozy, room for two."

Fang's eyes bulged as she realized what she was looking at.

A mini-sub.

She had heard of them, but never actually seen one. As Kane opened the hatch on the bottom he explained the entry sequence. "We don't need to worry about pressure since we're not deep," he finished. "You good to go?"

Fang nodded and he lowered himself, grabbing her feet and pushing up. She rushed into a chamber built for one, Kane closing the hatch below.

98

Pressing a flashing green button on the wall a countdown began along with a hissing sound and she soon found her head free of water, then her shoulders. Within minutes Fang was dripping and shivering. An alarm sounded and the display changed. She opened a hatch to the left and climbed into the small submarine. Closing the door and resealing it, she pressed a button on the wall and watched through a tiny porthole as the chamber filled back up with water. Fang looked about and found towels on a shelf. Taking one, she dried herself off then took some clothes from her bag, quickly dressing as Kane cycled through.

A cheery Kane, no longer needing to play his role of American tourist picking up the local Chinese girl, squeezed into the cramped tube with her. She handed him a towel and he flashed her a grin as he quickly dried himself off. "Chilly in here, isn't it?"

She nodded.

"No worries," he said as he tossed the towel aside and made his way to the front of the cramped vessel. He motioned to what she assumed was the co-pilot's seat as he sat at the main controls. Flicking some switches, the vessel lit up beyond the dim stand-by lighting they had been treated to upon their arrival, and he eased the controls forward, adjusting their course almost due east. He cranked another dial and she began to feel warm air circulate through the cabin. Another flick of a switch and he turned to her, his eyes no longer on the controls or the massive expanse of water in front of them.

Her heart was still pounding in her chest as she realized the trouble and expense her enemy had gone to, all in the effort to save her.

Or capture you.

But this Dylan Kane character that had so professionally and swiftly effected her escape was so different from anyone she had met, she found herself drawn to him. She wasn't sure if it was a sexual attraction, she never having found a white man attractive before, or if it was more of a big brother-little sister attraction. Whatever it was there was some sort of connection she hoped he wasn't picking up on.

Perhaps it's just because you've been so scared and now you're feeling grateful because he saved you?

That had to be it. She was a professional and she intended to keep it that way, but as he looked into her eyes, smiling, she found her emotional walls collapsing.

"Now," he said, reaching forward and placing a hand on her shoulder. "Why don't you tell me what this important intel is that my country needs to know?"

She nodded, the warmth of his hand welcome in the still chilled cabin. And she found it created a warmth that spread throughout her.

"I think someone is going to try to assassinate your President."

Kane turned and shoved the throttle to full.

DEATH TO AMERICA

Capitally Capitol Catering, Taylor Street NE, Washington, DC

Antonio Cruz hung up the phone, his face pale, sweat beaded on his forehead. He stared down at the box of condiments that had just been delivered by courier, confused. The computer modified voice on the other end of the call had been clear—they were watching his every move, and unless he put this box of condiments in with the morning delivery, his family would be killed.

Which meant he had no choice. He knew the condiments must be poisoned, but he was also sure that everything brought into their destination would be tested.

Security will catch it for sure!

All he wanted was his family back, safe and sound. He had no doubt he had just been "drafted", as the bastard had put it, into the insanity that had been gripping his country for almost two weeks now. The death toll was approaching ten thousand, and the damned government was doing nothing about it. The solution was obvious. Lock up every damned Muslim in the country, then start deporting them back to whatever shithole they had come from originally.

He didn't care that most were innocent. Innocent people didn't sit quietly by while atrocities were committed in the name of their so called "religion of peace". If they were truly opposed to the actions of the apparent fringe, then they should be up in arms protesting their deeds. Instead they remained silent.

Conspicuously silent.

And our President still does nothing.

He looked at the condiments.

Perhaps he should *be given some of this.*

He hated himself for thinking that the death of his President might be a good thing. After all, he had been a disappointment in so many ways, and his foreign policy initiatives were an embarrassment, so much so that America was now considered indecisive enough that terrorists were willing to attack so brazenly and so openly.

They don't fear us anymore.

The radio he had been listening to before the phone call said the death toll among Muslims from vigilante attacks was now in the hundreds, and he had little sympathy for them. When he spoke of it with friends, especially those who disagreed with the reprisals, he pointed out that not a single Muslim woman or child had been targeted—only healthy, young men. Not so with their victims. Men, women, children, the elderly. All were fodder for their violence.

He rose, grabbing the box, and carried it out into the warehouse. He nodded to the driver of the refrigerated truck idling for the priority delivery. "Last minute addition," he said, showing the contents with a grin. "Somebody is jonesing for some sandwiches, me thinks."

The driver laughed, taking the box and shoving it in the back. He closed the doors and climbed in the cab as a convoy of several vehicles pulled away, a security vehicle leading the way, one trailing.

For nothing could interfere with the morning fresh food delivery to the White House.

CIA Headquarters, Langley, Virginia

Chris Leroux yawned. He took a sip from his Red Bull, his third since he had begun this all-nighter, the gray and blue mini-cans, along with a box of Krispy Kreme's fueling him, he only having given into sleep once, and that for a mere thirty minutes until his phone's alarm blared at him to wake up. He knew Sherrie would give him shit for falling off the Red Bull wagon, but he figured she'd forgive him since it was because of her that he had needed them. If she were dead, it wouldn't matter, and he'd give anything for her to give him shit for breaking his promise.

I just want to hear her voice one more time.

Tears filled his eyes and he wiped them away as he looked at the screen. A smile spread slowly across his face as he saw the status message of his attack on Fort Myer's network.

Success!

He was in. He had initiated an attack on several different Department of Defense installations, making them look like they were originating from China, meaning a fairly normal occurrence, then snuck in over the secure hard lines only government agencies shared, installing a backdoor that he could now access through the Internet. Any breach, if discovered, he hoped would be blamed on the brute force attack they had been defending against.

And now with the attacks over, their network connections were back up, and his worm had just dialed home.

He immediately began quietly hunting to see what he had access to. It took several hours and another can of Red Bull before he had catalogued their network structure and devices, finally stumbling upon a list of validated Internet Protocol addresses for internal security cameras.

103

With a grin he began to pull up the feeds to each one, showing a grid of a dozen on one of his screens while he tried to locate where the archival footage was being stored on the network.

A quarter hour had the data located as he flipped to another set of camera views.

Main gate!

The camera footage was stored in a directory structure that matched the IP addresses, then were broken down by date and hour to manage file sizes. He found the footage for when he estimated Sherrie would have been at the main gate and pulled it up, fast forwarding until almost the end before he saw a car that matched the description of her rental.

He zoomed in and matched the plate numbers.

He could barely see her face through the window as she handed over ID to one of the MP's manning the gate, he imagining he could recognize her bare wrist even from here, every inch of her body deliciously familiar to him.

Unfortunately the truth was he couldn't be sure it was her, but he had to assume it was. The date and time matched when she should have arrived, the car matched, and her general features obscured by the windshield and angle of this particular camera matched.

And he could think of no reason why anyone would try to intervene at this point regardless.

The car pulled away and out of sight. A little more searching and he found several more cameras and was able to trace her to the main headquarters, this time a camera showing her clear enough that he had no doubt it was his beloved Sherrie. As he spliced each segment of footage, moving it to his own local server, he noted the timeline of her movements. There were no cameras that he could find inside the HQ beyond the main security area that showed her being led through a door and out of sight, he assumed to Colonel Booker's office.

He forwarded through the footage and not even fifteen minutes later saw her reappear, this time with Booker in the lead, Leroux recognizing him from the file he had read earlier. They exited the building and climbed into a Humvee, the Colonel driving. Leroux searched more camera feeds and found two more showing the same Humvee heading deeper into the base then entering a large warehouse, the doors closing behind them.

Leroux's heart was already racing as he watched his girlfriend disappear.

Why had they gone there?

It made no sense. She was there to ask about a dead man under the guise of him having been nominated for a Medal of Honor. Why would she head deeper into the base and into this warehouse?

The doors began to open and the Humvee exited, the tags matching and the passenger seat occupied by Sherrie. He traced it back to the HQ where another soldier, not Booker, and Sherrie exited the vehicle, salutes were exchanged, and Sherrie took the rental vehicle to the main gate. She handed something to the MP who then saluted and ordered the gate open. The vehicle left with Sherrie at the wheel and was soon out of sight.

He hit pause, sitting back, his heart sinking.

Something twigged.

He wasn't sure what it was, all he was sure of was that there was something his subconscious had noticed that wasn't right.

Perhaps it's just wishful thinking.

No, he was certain there was something. His gut told him so, and he had learned to trust his gut over the years of doing this job. Something was wrong, he just hadn't noticed it yet. He reversed the video and watched the feeds from the warehouse to the main gate again, over and over, trying to find what it was, each time the frustration level rising as adrenaline, despair and a Red Bull infused sugar and caffeine rush competed for his attention.

He snapped his fingers, pointing at the screen, turning to the empty room as if to show someone, anyone, that he wasn't crazy.

But he was alone.

And certain that Sherrie was alive.

He downloaded the file to a memory stick and headed for Director Morrison's office with the evidence he needed to prove Sherrie was still alive, and most likely still on the base. The base that claimed she had left it hours ago.

But he knew that was a lie.

For the woman who had stuck her left hand out the window to return something to the Military Police officer had a watch on that wrist. A watch that Leroux knew his Sherrie always wore on her right wrist, and a watch that hadn't been there when she first checked in at the gate.

Sherrie was alive, and someone wanted them to think she was dead.

Unknown Location

Sherrie White woke with a start, a searing pain burning her right cheek, the aftermath of a backhand from her interrogator ringing through her body. She gasped, then sucked in air, blood and saliva mixed, going down the wrong tube causing her to cough. Recovered, she looked up at the man delivering the beating.

And spat on his shiny shoes.

"My little sister hits harder than that."

She was rewarded with a punch to her midriff that had her doubled over, her handcuffed wrists burning in protest as her body weight pulled at them.

It was worth it.

She had been trained at The Farm to withstand torture techniques, including receiving a pretty severe beating over many hours on several occasions. Sometimes when you were prepared for it; sometimes when you weren't. The worst was the first time when she had been hauled out of her bed in the middle of the night, blindfolded and taken in silence to some small room then subjected to various forms of interrogation for two days. Sleep deprivation, bright lights, loud death metal, waterboarding and a good number of punches were administered, along with a few good stun guns to the neck and chest.

But she had endured, and in the end when finally released, she had made it a point to blare death metal from her car dash every time she drove by the building where it had taken place, waving with a smile and a middle finger salute.

They had been harder on her the next time.

But it had prepared her for this.

107

Beat me all you want, bitch, you'll never break me.

"Why are you asking about Captain Lewis?"

It was Booker's voice this time. It had begun with someone else yesterday evening, and continued all through the night, but now it was the big cheese himself. The four people she had been exposed to in the small room she was held in were all dressed in black, none wearing any type of insignia, making her think private security.

At least that might mean whatever is going on here doesn't involve too many military personnel.

But Booker was a full-bird Colonel, which meant at least one member of the military was involved, and with what happened to the F-35, she had to assume more.

What are you up to?

From the intel Chris had shared it appeared no money was exchanged for the delivery, instead a favor had been asked and granted.

Not to interfere.

Interfere with what?

The only thing she was aware of was the constant terrorist attacks they were under, but that was being orchestrated by Islamic fundamentalist nutbars, not Colonel Booker and some private security.

Another smack against the face, this time the hand coming to rest on her cheek, the thumb shoved into her mouth as the man gripped the skin and pulled, her split lips crying out in protest.

She felt her eyes tear, but she didn't care. Pain was pain and you reacted to it the way you needed to. Cry out, scream, moan, it didn't matter. Whatever release you needed to get through the torture without using actual words.

"You'll tell me what I need to know sooner or later, Captain." Booker stepped into sight, the only light a large, round one glaring into her eyes.

She blinked as he cast a shadow over her face, the brief respite welcome. "But I doubt you're even in the army."

She remained silent, and for the first time noticed the camera perched up in the corner, a single red light indicating it was on.

Someone was watching, somewhere.

Maybe they'll have a conscience and put an end to this.

The White House, Washington, DC

Maxwell Logan fist bumped the delivery guy, Jim, before lifting a box of condiments from the back of the catering truck as others from the kitchen staff swarmed the rear, an efficient line formed to unload and store the massive amount of food the White House needed each day.

"How they hangin', Max?" asked the driver as he supervised the chain gang.

"Can't complain."

"Cuz' nobody'll listen, eh?"

"Not even my wife!"

Jim roared with laughter, smacking Logan on the back as he walked away with the box. "See you tomorrow, Jim."

"Same bat time, same bat channel!" Another roar of laughter from Jim.

Nice guy.

Logan had known Jim for years. The White House liked routine. They might mix up schedules and routes, but they liked to see the same faces. New guys made Secret Service agents like him nervous, but Jim was as familiar as you could get.

He turned, pushing the door open with his back, the box of condiments a curious mix of the mundane and hard to find.

Worcestershire sauce?

He had heard of Worshter sauce, or something like that, but Worcestershire? He couldn't even pronounce it.

And if I can't pronounce it, I ain't eatin' it!

He passed through the kitchen and another set of doors then approached the men's room, stopping in front of the doors and looking about for a place to put the box then shrugged at the camera at the end of the hall. Entering the bathroom he saw he was alone and went to the far handicapped stall, it the largest available.

Locking the door, he rested the box on the toilet seat and quickly opened all the jars and bottles then carefully pulled out the sealed plastic baggies inside, using his fingers like squeegees to return as much of the mayonnaise and mustard among other things into their containers. He then placed each bag on the top of the toilet tank.

He soon had all the parts he was told to look for and had made a minimal mess. Resealing the jars, he used toilet paper to clean them up then made sure the box was as he had found it. He opened each baggy then wiped his hands clean. Next he carefully removed each piece of plastic from the open bags, lining them up on the toilet tank.

He listened.

Still alone.

He took the box out and placed it on the counter, stuffing the baggies into the trash after rinsing them off as best he could. He then thoroughly washed and dried his hands, returning to the stall and locking the door once again.

It took less than two minutes to reassemble the weapon, the only piece not provided in the delivery the firing pin. He removed his weapon and upturned his holster, the spare pin he had brought from home falling out into his cupped hand. He inserted the critical piece then snapped the final few pieces together.

Amazing!

He had of course been briefed on these new printed plastic weapons, but he had never actually held one. It was remarkably light, and his trained eye knew all the essentials were in place. He just couldn't see it firing successfully, though that wasn't his job. He had his instructions, and only three things remained.

111

He removed his shoe, popped the heel out and removed six bullets, the shoes sitting on his doorstep last night when he got home. He loaded the gun, a revolver—which he found even more amazing but had been briefed on several months before after the arrest of a Japanese professor who had designed and printed one, then shared the plans.

The bathroom door opened and he felt his heart race with a surge of adrenaline. Controlling his breathing, he stuffed the gun in his pocket then quickly wiped everything down, flushing the toilet. He stepped out and saw one of the kitchen staff using the urinal.

Nods were exchanged and Logan washed his hands, drying them with a paper towel. He grabbed the box, carrying it tilted so the staff member couldn't see what was inside.

Within minutes the box was sitting in the kitchen and he was on the way to fulfil his second last instruction, the image of the man he was supposed to supply the weapon to burned into his memory.

Stan Reese.

DEATH TO AMERICA

CIA Headquarters, Langley, Virginia

It had been another all-nighter and Chris Leroux was crashing. Red Bull and snacks from the vending machine were no longer able to fuel him, and after witnessing his hand shake so badly he couldn't open the last can of his forbidden caffeine and sugar infused drink, he had pushed it aside.

And now his eyes were drooping beyond his control. If he had toothpicks he would try shoving them in place to keep his eyelids open, but he knew he had to rest, even if just for a few hours.

Yet he couldn't stop. He knew Sherrie was on the base somewhere, and he also knew they might discover his hack at any moment, locking him out perhaps permanently. He had sent the footage he had gathered to Director Morrison who had only replied with, "Keep digging." Leroux had hoped for a major invasion of the base instead, but had to settle for his boss' continued support into his technically illegal activities.

And during it all the bulletins had kept arriving in his email. Another four attacks had been carried out. An NYU campus had been targeted, its common area obliterated with hundreds dead or wounded. An oil pipeline in the mid-west was now in flames, LAX had been hit at security with hundreds in line, and a rock festival had also been hit. Four hundred dead, nearly a thousand wounded by the blast and in the panic as fifty thousand people fled.

Another thousand dead.

Muslim leaders were now demanding government protection. They were gathering in mosques and community centers, armed to protect themselves from vigilantes out for revenge. More mosques had been burned, including one in New Jersey where dozens of the hundreds taking refuge inside died from smoke inhalation. The fire departments appeared now to only be intervening when human lives were at risk, and they had fought this fire valiantly, several of their own injured in the attempt. The other mosques had been left to burn once everyone was out.

The nation was at a tipping point.

The very values America represented were being abandoned and Leroux was concerned that if things continued, his country would become like those these fundamentalists came from. A land of no law and order, no equality, no rights. Merely vigilantes roaming the streets, killing whoever they thought might have wronged them in some way, with the authorities standing by unless an "American looking" person might become a victim.

He could understand the anger. Hell, he even felt it too. His blood boiled every time he heard of a new attack. He seethed when he went to the bathroom and saw a paper towel tossed in a urinal because one of his Muslim colleagues was commanded by his teachings to not touch his penis without performing ablution afterward, and apparently didn't have the time. And he cried when he saw the victims, especially the children, in the aftermath of the actions carried out by these insane individuals.

And he questioned why the Muslim community remained so silent.

Perhaps if they marched on the streets, denouncing the violence, there might be more sympathy.

Another bulletin beeped in his Inbox.

Governor of New Jersey announces voluntary internment program.

This woke him for a moment as he scanned the brief that announced the Governor of New Jersey was offering to allow Muslims to stay in the closed schools with security provided by the National Guard.

What's the next step? Japanese internment camps?

But right now even Leroux, who considered himself a firm believer in the Constitution, had his doubts. Perhaps locking them all up for now might be the best thing to do. At least it would protect them, and if the perpetrators are among them, then the attacks would stop. And if they did, they could begin to carefully screen and release the interned until the guilty parties were identified.

It'll never happen.

And he was glad of that as it went against his ideals, and those of the country he loved.

He realized he hadn't been watching the cameras for the past ten minutes and reversed them just in case he missed something. He hadn't.

I've got to sleep!

He brought up another dozen feeds.

Just one last batch.

They began to play and as his eyes travelled over the mundane views of hallways and common areas, he stopped on the last row, his eyebrows jumping and adrenaline providing a second wind.

Sitting in a chair with her hands tied behind her back, her face bloodied, was the most important woman in his life.

And he felt rage like he had never felt before.

The Whitehouse, Washington, DC

President Bridges pulled at his hair, hair he swore was far grayer today than it was two weeks ago. The country was collapsing before his eyes and he didn't know what to do about it. Which was something he couldn't admit publicly.

Never admit to the enemy you don't have a strategy.

The attacks were continuing at a furious pace and the nation was in a panic. The stock markets had been closed for days but he had finally been forced to reopen them and they had collapsed. All educational institutions were closed, stores were empty, traffic gridlock a nightmare since mass transit was being avoided like the plague.

And preliminary reports from his staff were showing the economy was quickly imploding as the retail sector foundered.

But online sales were up.

Until they find out that every one of the bombers received a courier delivery.

"Sir, what have you decided?"

"Hmm?" He looked up at National Security Advisor Susan Lawrence, she too looking like she had aged a decade in ten days. He looked about the room. They all looked haggard, worn, scared.

All except General Thorne. He appeared unaffected.

But he's military. He's trained for this type of thing.

He thought about what Lawrence was asking. He had just met with a delegation of Imams who swore what was happening wasn't representative of true Islam and promised to turn over any information they might come across, but they were also scared. They demanded that their mosques be protected and provided the same police and fire services that any church would receive, and they demanded protection for their citizens, short of internment as they considered that to be imprisonment rather than protective custody.

What was sad was that all their demands were perfectly reasonable, and if coming from a group of Christians, not a soul in the land would deny them any and all of their demands.

But they weren't, and the situation would never be reversed.

Modern Christians, with the sad exception of recent Northern Ireland history, just don't do this type of thing.

He had thanked them, promised to consider their requests, and adjourned.

"At a minimum we must guarantee that the mosques receive the same services any church would receive. I think any reasonable person can agree with that."

Lawrence nodded, as did the room. "Of course, Mr. President."

He turned to Bill Cambridge, his speech writer. "Bill, I'm going to address the nation again tonight. I need something that will calm the anger toward Muslims. These retaliatory murders have to stop. And figure out some way to *inspire* the firefighters and police to do their jobs. There has to be some way."

"It will be a great speech, Mr. President, don't you worry."

Bridges smiled slightly. "They always are, Bill, they always are. I'm afraid before this is over, I'll be asking a lot of you."

"It's an honor, sir."

Lawrence cleared her throat. "What about the camps some states have begun setting up? This is Japanese internment all over again. You should see what CNN is reporting."

Bridges frowned. "If I had my choice I'd take them off the air. All of them. Their constant fear mongering is making the situation worse." He waved his hand in the air, dismissing the words. "I know, I know, it's just the wishful thinking of a tired citizen rather than the serious thoughts of your President."

But it would be so much easier!

It wasn't the nightly news coverage that was the problem. NBC, ABC, CBS, FOX—their regular news broadcasts were terrifying, but brief with little commentary. It was the 24-hour news channels that were whipping everything into a frenzy. Was there reason to be scared? Absolutely, the country was under attack. But the unsubstantiated rumors and conjecture of the talking heads was inexcusable. As happened so often now whether it was the Malaysian Airliner going missing or Ferguson, the press seemed to latch on to a story and try to fill 24-hours of their cycle with nothing but.

Which meant people ran out of things to say, so just made stuff up. Reporters turned into commentators and gave opinion, with people at home thinking it was news. After all, when Joe Blow tells you the top stories every night at 5pm, then is now telling you that the missing airliner might have been flown to a secret base on an island in the Indian Ocean, you believed it must be based on some reliable fact, some reliable source.

Not anymore.

The news is just opinion now.

It was a sad day for the Fifth Estate.

He pulled at his ear, then finally spoke. "I would do something about the camps if it weren't for the fact they are already full with people seeking refuge voluntarily. Entire families have moved there."

"It's sad," whispered Ben Wainwright, Secretary of Homeland Security. "My grandfather on my mother's side was interned during World War Two. And I was just in Jordan visiting the refugee camps there. To think we'd see the day when American citizens would be so scared they'd leave their homes and businesses and take refuge from their fellow citizens…" His voice drifted off, there no need to finish the thought.

Everyone in the room was just as appalled.

And it's happening under your watch.

He looked up at Wainwright. "Any progress on the investigation, no matter how small? Some ray of hope?"

Wainwright shook his head slightly. "What we do know at this point is that all of the explosives being used are C4, military grade. We believe it's all part of a large shipment lost during transport to Iraq several years ago."

"How big was this shipment? I mean, how much of it do they have left?"

Wainwright lowered his briefing notes and sucked in a deep breath. "Mr. President, they've barely scratched the surface. Our estimate is that if this is indeed the source of the C4, they could sustain this level of bombing for three more months."

"By which time there won't be an America left to save," murmured Lawrence.

"Were there any leads on the theft?"

"Negative. The convoy was hit and hit hard by Iraqi insurgents. It was lightning fast, efficient, very well executed. It was one of their more professional operations according to the investigation."

"It seems so many things are out of character," observed Chief of Clandestine Operations Leif Morrison. "We have *none* of the regular chatter, *all* of the operations are performed by non-Muslims, no credit is being taken, not a single operation has truly failed, every single person coerced into these actions seems to have been well chosen—family men or women, able-bodied, none military or civilian law enforcement. It's as if these people have all been chosen to be mentally and physically capable of carrying out their task, and manipulable enough psychologically to be counted on to go through with it. If it weren't for the 'Death to America' signs and the occasional shout of Allahu Akbar, we would be looking for domestic terrorists."

"What are you saying?" asked General Thorne.

"I'm saying something doesn't smell right. We've got US military explosives being used, *no* Muslim perpetrators, *no* Muslim claims, and a certain shall we call *classified*'—he added air quotes—"event that can't be discussed that used the same MO. Is it just me or are things not adding up?"

"I think it's just you," replied General Thorne, clearly displeased. "I find it impossible to believe Americans would do this to America. I find it *perfectly* plausible to believe that Islamic extremists would. This is merely an ingenious tactic. They don't need to waste their own people, they have an unlimited number of victims—" He stopped and threw up his hands in frustration, sucking in a deep breath. Looking from Morrison to his President, Thorne raised his hands, palms facing outward. "I'm sorry, Mr. President, Director, I'm just as frustrated as you all. My country, the country I have served all my life, is under attack. I don't care who is doing it, but they need to be stopped. And the only way I can see stopping it is by asking Congress for permission to break a few rules. We *need* to implement MYSTIC."

Bridges pursed his lips, shaking his head. "We've discussed that. I'm not willing to suspend our Constitution or civil liberties. This is a slippery slope that has already harmed the Union. I've been trying to rein in some of the laws that have been passed since nine-eleven, but the pushback from congress and many constituents is unbelievable. I'm called unpatriotic, a terrorist, soft on crime."

"Ridiculous," cried Lawrence. "I support your efforts, Mr. President. We all do! Why, my husband was pulled over by State police last week. They claimed he hadn't signaled, then began interrogating him and asked him to consent to a search for drugs. He let them. He's an innocent man with nothing to hide! They searched the car and found he had an envelope with two thousand dollars in cash that he had just got at the bank for some antiques we were going to buy last weekend. They seized it as possible drug money and told him he could contest it in court! He hasn't been charged with anything and they just took his money!"

"And it's perfectly legal," said Wainwright. "I get complaints all the time. Police have executed over sixty-thousand stops since nine-eleven and seized over 2.5 billion dollars, almost none of it ultimately found illegal. And because it costs so much to try to fight it, many people aren't bothering because it will cost them more than the money taken. They're legally stealing from average Americans because they get to keep the majority of the funds to top up their budgets."

Lawrence jabbed her finger at Wainwright, her head bobbing up and down violently. "Yes! I looked into it. Huffington Post and a lot of other news organizations are starting to report on it. And some of these police precincts are using the money to pay for luxury cars, first class plane tickets and other unnecessary things. They're living high on the hog by *stealing* money." A burst of air and a growl of frustration escaped. "Mr. President, this has to be stopped!"

Bridges chuckled slightly, a smile spreading on his face. "Susan, *when* the current crisis is over, we'll look into this entire 'Stop and Seize' abuse of powers, but until then, we need to keep our focus."

Lawrence covered her mouth for a moment, flushing with embarrassment. "Oh God, I'm so sorry, Mr. President. You are of course right."

Bridges waved off the apology. "No need to apologize. Just hearing the stories upsets me too. To think our own law enforcement are encouraged to steal money from innocent Americans—legally—is outrageous." He clapped his hands together. "But today, we keep moving forward. We continue to investigate and hopefully we can finally get a break. Tomorrow I'm shutting down all parcel and courier delivery in the country that isn't from a validated business. They must have been in business for at least two years and been regularly shipping items six months before the crisis. Anyone else can be vetted by the FBI to be added to the approved list. Perhaps this will make it a little more difficult to actually deliver these bombs."

His aide poked her head into the office. "Mr. President, it's time."

General Thorne's eyebrows popped up. "Mr. President, you're not still going to greet the tour group!"

Bridges rose, as did the rest. "You know I try to meet the morning tour every day. It takes five minutes of my time and lets me meet our fellow Americans. I *refuse* to allow those who would harm our country stop our citizens from having access to their President."

Thorne's lips spread into a thin line as he clenched his jaw shut, it clear he wanted to continue his protest.

Bridges walked up to him and placed a hand on his shoulder. "I appreciate your concern, Brad. Perhaps tomorrow we'll mix up which group I actually meet?"

Thorne relaxed slightly. "A wise precaution, Mr. President."

Bridges turned to the room. "Thank you everyone."

"Thank you, Mr. President."

He smiled and headed for the door, his step a little lighter, kissing babies and pressing flesh one of his favorite perks of being President. He loved his public, loved his country, and was determined to find some way to help save it.

Stan Reese had never done the White House tour before, despite living in the DC area his entire life. He had always wanted to be a tourist in his own town, he missing the school trip most kids did due to chicken pox, but he had always thought he would have another day. Today he knew he wouldn't. He had been instructed to go here, on this day, at this time.

From everything he had seen in the news, he knew today would be his last day on Earth, he just didn't know yet what his instructions were.

He cleared the heavy security, President Bridges having refused to cancel the tours, saying they were a symbol of American democracy at its best, and no terrorist threat would let him deny Americans access to their leadership.

He was handed a tour badge and hung it around his neck. His phone immediately vibrated in his pocket.

His chest tightened and his mouth dried.

"Hello?"

"You will be handed a gun. Shoot the President immediately, as many times as you can. If he lives, your family dies."

The call ended, the mechanical voice leaving him with chills running up and down his spine.

"We're walking! We're walking!"

Reese barely heard the tour guide, the rather thin herd of those brave enough to still come near a government facility following her like sheeple, he joining them at the rear of the pack.

Where the wolf was most likely to strike.

His mind was a jumble of confusion. He knew he was being used, he knew what they were asking was wrong, and he knew that if he didn't follow their instructions his parents would die.

And he loved his parents beyond all else.

They were close, very close. He spoke to them several times a week, sometimes almost every day, and quite often for an hour at a time. They spoke about everything, including their favorite topic, politics. He couldn't begin to tally how many hours they had spent talking about what would eventually happen with the Muslim immigration situation, and now it was happening on the streets of America exactly as they had all predicted.

He and his parents had been in favor of shutting down all non-Judeo Christian immigration immediately, of deporting any immigrant who committed a crime, regardless of religion, and doing whatever it took to make America independent of non-North American oil.

Needless to say they were huge supporters of the Keystone XL pipeline which was almost completed and a mere fraction of the nation's already existing 2.5 million miles of pipelines. If you were to believe the naysayers, things should be leaking and blowing up left, right and center every few hours. It frustrated him and his father especially when those opposed refused to answer the question of whether or not they'd rather get their oil from America's closest ally of Canada, or from Saudi Arabia, the home of Wahhabism and one of the strictest interpretations of Islam. They were the source of much of the funding for most terrorist acts around the globe, and were spreading their hateful brand of Islam worldwide thanks to Arab oil money gained from selling their product to Western democracies.

His mother couldn't believe any woman in their right mind would prefer to get their oil from a country that veiled their women, stoned them to death, executed them for witchcraft, circumcised them and let them be married off younger than ten.

"Where are the feminists in this fight?"

It was a frequent refrain of hers, to which he and his father would reply, "They're blinded by the religion of global warming".

His eyes filled with tears as he realized he was never going to have those conversations again.

"Excuse me," said a man in a dark suit after he bumped into Reese from behind.

The man walked away quickly without looking back, but Reese felt something heavy in the right hand pocket of his jacket. He nearly pissed his pants as he realized the gun had just been handed off to him. He slowly, carefully, as casually as he could, reached inside and felt the coolness of the weapon now in his pocket.

It felt odd. Bumpy. And incredibly light.

And he immediately recognized it as the weapon he had been forced to steal at the gun show.

And that today was the day his victim was supposed to tell the police.

They've framed me!

He knew now no matter what happened he was going to prison. Police reports would be hitting the wire at any minute, his ID had been scanned when entering the White House, and with the heightened level of security, news of a plastic gun being stolen in the Washington, DC area had to raise red flags with everyone.

They were going to find him at any moment.

"It's the President!" somebody gushed, causing all heads to turn to a staircase where the Commander-in-Chief and his entourage were quickly descending.

He doesn't look scared at all!

A broad, confident, reassuring smile spread across President Bridges' face as he veered off and immersed himself in the crowd, his Secret Service detail none too happy about it as he glad-handed the fans.

Reese's hand wrapped around the grip and his finger found the trigger.

Then he thought of what his father would do.

And raised the gun to his head.

"Gun!" yelled Secret Service Agent Maxwell Logan, darting into the crowd of tourists and grabbing the hand of the man he had handed the weapon off to only moments before, Stan Reese. Reese hadn't followed the instructions, instead turning the weapon on himself.

Making the right decision.

But not for him. Logan's instructions were clear. If the target doesn't follow instructions, it was up to him to intervene.

He yanked the gun hand away from Reese's temple, his expression at being stopped a mix of shock and relief. Logan's hands wrapped around Reese's as he pulled the man's arm out in front of them, cupping his own hands around the grip, trapping Reese's finger on the trigger.

As he grabbed the hand he pulled Reese through the crowd, swinging the extended arm about as if Reese were putting up more of a struggle than he was.

Suddenly the President was in front of them, two Secret Service agents grabbing his arms to hurry him away as the realization of what was happening set in.

Logan pressed against Reese's finger, squeezing the trigger, the first shot hitting the agent on the left, Reese crying out in dismay. Yanking the arm slightly to the right, Logan squeezed again and as he saw the shock on President Bridges' face, he repeatedly squeezed Reese's finger against the trigger until the gun was spent, the President's body jerking with each hit, blood quickly spreading, staining his white dress shirt from the inside as the crowd panicked.

Logan twisted Reese's arm, feeling the shoulder pop out of its socket, then kicked the feet out from under him as Logan grabbed his own service weapon. And as their eyes met, Reese's filled with horror and shock,

Logan's calm and businesslike, Logan pumped three rounds into the man's chest, then let go of his hand, the stolen plastic weapon still gripped tightly by Reese, the finger still on the trigger.

And in less than ten seconds, the President of the United States was on the floor, dying, with all evidence pointing to one Stan Reese.

And in the minds of some, dying was the best thing President Bridges could do to save his country.

USS Columbia, SSN-771, Los Angeles Class Submarine
Contiguous Zone, 14 nautical miles off the coast of China

Dylan Kane held his hand out, helping Lee Fang down the final step of the ladder leading from their mini-sub. He turned and saluted the Captain. "Permission to come aboard, sir!"

"Permission granted," said Captain Lynch, snapping back a quick salute. "I'll have you know, *Mr.* White—what is it with you covert ops guys and colors?—that this little rendezvous of yours has been quite inconvenient. And how the hell did you get a mini-sub without there being a retrieval already set up?" He looked at Fang. "And who the hell is she?"

Kane smiled. "Captain, I appreciate your curiosity, and those are all questions I'd love to answer. But right now, I can't. I *will* need however to speak to you in private, immediately."

Captain Lynch frowned. "I can assure you I trust my men."

"And I, Captain, can assure you that even you don't have the clearance for what I'm about to reveal to you."

This seemed to surprise Lynch, if only for a moment, his eyes squinting slightly for a brief second. He stared at Kane, his eyes flicking over to Fang. "Follow me."

They followed the Captain, under armed escort, to his stateroom, ducking as they entered, the door closed behind them by one of the guards. The Captain sat at his small desk, pointing to the one spare chair. Kane motioned for Fang to take it, she initially resisting until he implored her with a bulge of his eyes.

She sat.

"Captain, I can't identify myself properly, however the fact that you were sent here should be enough validation of my clearance and discretion." He motioned to Fang. "I of course cannot identify my companion either, except to say she has brought valuable intelligence to us."

"A defector?"

"No!"

Kane placed a hand on Fang's shoulder, squeezing it gently, silencing her. "No, not a defector. A patriot who stumbled upon something being done without the knowledge of her government, that ultimately affects *our* country. Not knowing who to trust, she reached out to us and I retrieved her. The intelligence she has provided in exchange for our protection is of extreme importance. I must make contact with my people immediately."

"Just what is this intel?"

"I can't say, Captain, but it is of vital importance to our national interest."

Captain Lynch pointed up. "Sir, we are diving as we speak. Your retrieval was just outside of territorial waters. We are in the contiguous zone, hours at best speed to international waters. In our current position, the Chinese won't hesitate to try and surface us if they feel it necessary, even if it does violate international law. *If* our presence was detected, *and* your friend here is as important as I think she might be, they're going to want her back. We have six Chinese naval vessels in the immediate area, and I've got that pig of a mini-sub of yours attached to my hull, screwing up my tear-drop. Every damned listening device in the Pacific will be able to hear us. There is no way I can risk going to the surface for you to send a message."

Kane frowned, realizing that Lynch was right, but only under normal circumstances. In this case a chance had to be taken, and the only way he would be able to convince the man that it was worth the risk to put his vessel in danger was to tell him what he wanted to know.

"The President is going to be assassinated."

Lynch's eyes shot open, his eyebrows shooting up his forehead.

A buzzer sounded causing Fang, obviously still on edge, to jump. Lynch hit a button on a control panel. "Bridge, Captain. Report!"

"Captain, XO. Three vessels just changed course and are converging on our pickup location. ETA seven minutes."

"Other sonar contacts?"

"Six more on their way, at least a dozen civilian ships of varying sizes. They definitely know we're here, Captain. They're at flank speed."

"Are we still at communications depth?"

"Negative. We can still float a buoy if we stop our descent."

"Do it. Flash message to command as follows. Package retrieved. Reliable intel that assassination attempt to be made on POTUS. Will deliver package to extraction point beta soonest. Got that?"

"Yes, sir. Assassination?"

"You heard me. Attach our coordinates to that, then send an open broadcast to command indicating we are in the contiguous zone, not territorial. I want the Chinese to know we've gone public. Emergency dive once sent."

"Yes, sir!"

Lynch ended the call with a jab of his forefinger on the panel, then turned to Kane.

"You two might have just got us all killed."

"And if it saves the President?"

Lynch frowned. "He's only one man."

Kane had to agree with the Captain's sentiments, even though it was their sworn duty to protect the man. "And with what's happening back home, he's more important now than ever."

Lynch blew some air through his lips. "Only if he's the right man for the job."

"That's not *our* job to determine, Captain."

Lynch rose, rubbing his hands down his shirt to smooth out any wrinkles. "You're right, of course. Just the frustration of seeing our homeland being destroyed while at the command of enough firepower to start and end a war with no target to fire at."

Kane let out a short laugh. "Captain, you and I think a lot alike. Get us to South Korea and I promise you I'll do everything I can to *not* bring those responsible to justice."

Lynch's eyes narrowed questioningly. "Meaning?"

"I intend to kill every damned last one of them."

The White House, Washington, DC

Chief of Clandestine Operations Leif Morrison stood in shock at the top of the stairs, the Presidential Briefing barely over, he still discussing something with the Secretary of Homeland Security, Ben Wainwright. He had heard the scuffle and witnessed the entire assassination. And as the chaos unfolded, he numbly listened to the screams of fleeing tourists, shouts of Secret Service agents as they locked down the situation, and smelled the gun powder, the odor familiar, but accompanied by something unusual, something he couldn't place.

Plastic?

He eyeballed the agent who had taken down the gunman as he stood with his hands up, several guns pointed at him as the Secret Service tried to determine who the bad guy was.

And as he watched, he saw the man look toward the stairs Morrison now stood on, and nod.

Almost imperceptibly.

Morrison turned his head to see who the intended recipient of the acknowledgement might be but the stairs were now occupied by at least two dozen people, including most of the cabinet from the meeting he had just left.

"It's a plastic gun!" exclaimed someone as they disarmed the now dead assassin, medics finally arriving to tend to the President, it clear it was already too late. He had been hit five times by Morrison's count, and he couldn't see him surviving though his stomach was still rising and falling.

He found himself beside his dying leader, his feet having carried him down the stairs without realizing it. Bridges' eyes suddenly locked on his as his entire body trembled. A hand raised up and Morrison realized he wanted to say something, he possibly the only familiar face the poor man could see, the rest Secret Service and medical personnel.

He quickly stepped over and dropped to his knee, taking President Bridges by the hand.

"Yes, Mr. President?"

The man's breathing was labored, blood flowing freely. He stole a glance at one of the medics, who subtly shook his head.

Hopeless.

"D-did y-you s-see it?"

Morrison's eyes narrowed. "You mean the shooting?"

"Y-yes."

His voice was barely a whisper now, and Morrison dropped to both knees, leaning forward on one hand so he could get his ear as close to Bridges' mouth as possible.

"Yes, I saw everything, Mr. President."

Bridges reached up and grabbed him by the shoulder. "N-no, y-you d-didn't." His hand leapt from Morrison's shoulder to the back of his neck, pulling him down until he could feel the dying gasps of breath on his skin. "T-trust no one."

A heart monitor linked to the President suddenly flat-lined as the hand gripping Morrison's neck let go, slipping to the floor, the President of the United States dead.

Leaving Morrison to wonder just what the man had seen.

CIA Headquarters, Langley, Virginia

"The President's dead!"

Chris Leroux jerked awake, his computer beeping at him as his face, mashed against the keyboard, pressed any number of keys, Windows finally fed-up. His phone rang as he lifted his head, ending the computer's protest. His eyebrows popped as he noticed the Secure Call Indicator flashing.

He grabbed the headset.

"Leroux."

"This is Morrison. Are we secure?"

Leroux verified the indicator. "Yes, sir."

"The President has just been shot."

Leroux's heart raced as he realized it wasn't a dream, that what he had heard shouted was real. He had been working non-stop pulling together all of the footage he could of Sherrie and anyone else who looked out of place at Fort Myer, as per Morrison's orders after he had shown him the Sherrie footage in her cell. The footage of her repeated beatings had been incredibly hard to watch, tears rolling down his cheeks as his adrenaline fueled rage slowly waned, his body finally forcing him to sleep despite his best efforts to continue his work.

But he had been successful before collapsing. He had identified several dozen personnel wearing what he would characterize as paramilitary clothing. They all seemed to be confined to the same building Sherrie had been driven into, and military personnel seemed at a minimum there compared to the rest of the base. His current count was about fifty, and they never seemed to leave the building unless there was an entrance he knew nothing about.

It's as if they're all, civilian and military, confined to the one building.

And it was a large building. From the limited views he had of it there were dozens of rooms, including dozens of cubicles set up in one large area. The building was definitely a hive of activity, but for what he hadn't been able to determine yet. All he did know was everyone was armed and strict security was observed.

And now the President was dead. He felt his chest tighten as he processed the words Morrison had just spoken. He had yet to find any link between what was happening to his country and the F-35 theft. All the evidence at this point suggested it was a completely separate incident, the timing merely coincidental.

"Our deal is intact. We shall not interfere."

It had gnawed at him since he had first watched the tapes Kane had sent. *Interfere with what?*

"Chris, are you there?"

Leroux started, realizing he had drifted back to sleep, the phone ready to slip.

"S-sorry, sir. Yes, I'm here, I think I fell asleep."

"You've been up all night again, haven't you?"

"Yes, sir. I had to."

"I understand you're motivated, and that's good. But keep off the energy drinks and caffeine. They just make you more tired in the end."

"You sound like Sherrie, sir."

Morrison chuckled. "She's a wise woman. And I won't tell her you broke your promise."

"How'd—"

"I know everything."

"Now you sound like Kane."

135

"Fine company." Suddenly his tone became serious. "Okay, I'm in my vehicle now. I'm returning to Langley immediately. I want you to drop what you're doing—"

"But, sir!"

"The President has been assassinated, finding out who's behind it is essential." He lowered his voice. "Listen, Chris, the President spoke his last words to *me*. I think he saw something during the shooting, something that I think he thought didn't fit. And I swear I saw the agent who shot the assassin exchange a nod with someone, as if something had been planned. I want you to grab an Ops Center, your team, and get every damned camera angle you can on that shooting. I've already convinced Homeland to share everything so it should start streaming into you shortly."

"Yes, sir." Leroux's voice was subdued, crushed that he wasn't going to be able to continue pursuing his girlfriend's abductors but Morrison was right that it was more important to gather intel on what was happening rather than attempt a rescue.

"She's alive for now. Let's take advantage of them not knowing we're watching."

Morrison's words still echoed, but when Leroux had challenged him, the next words had chilled him to the bone.

"She knew the risks going in. Dying is sometimes part of the job."

"Chris?"

"Yes, sir?"

"You do realize what this means?"

Leroux was at a loss, his entire thought process consumed by Sherrie and her continued plight, and now his orders not to continue working on saving her.

"No, I'm sorry, sir, I can't focus."

"If this assassination isn't what it seems, and that agent who took down the assassin did indeed nod to someone on the very stairs I was standing on, then this assassination may have been committed with the full knowledge of someone inside the White House."

Leroux's eyebrows raised slightly at the thought as his mind refocused, ideas racing as intelligence reports, news footage, agent reports and more coalesced into different patterns. His eyes popped wide.

"I see a few possibilities, sir."

He could almost hear Morrison smile. "And they are?"

"First, it was a disgruntled citizen who killed the President because of what's going on, or for some other personal reason. But I doubt that."

"Why?"

"How did he get the gun in?"

"It was plastic."

This stopped Leroux in his tracks, his geek side kicking in. "Really? How many shots were fired?"

"Six. Five hit their target, the first hit a Secret Service agent."

"Remarkable," muttered Leroux, making a mental note to update himself on 3D printer technology. He smiled.

"You said six shots, five well aimed?"

"Yes."

"How did he have time to fire that many shots without someone stopping him?"

"A Secret Service agent, the one I mentioned, jumped him and in the struggle the gun went off."

"Did he fire before or after the agent jumped him?"

"I'm not sure, I think after." There was a pause. "Yes, definitely after. I heard the shouts, saw the struggle, *then* the shots were fired."

"So a man, struggling with a highly trained Secret Service Agent managed to fire six shots, placing five of them in his intended target."

It wasn't a question, it was a statement, one laid out for Morrison to come to his own conclusions on.

For Leroux had already come to his.

Ridiculous!

"There's no way it could have happened," said Morrison, the dawn of realization clear in his voice. "What you're saying is—"

"My guess is the Secret Service Agent aimed that weapon and fired it."

"Meaning our shooter is actually a patsy, another conscript into the attacks that have been happening."

"And if our agent nodded to someone like you think he did, then that means one of two things. One, someone killed the President using the same method as the terrorist attacks as a cover, keeping in mind the same method was used on our F-35 pilot. Or two, someone killed the President using the same method as the terrorist attacks, not as a cover, but as the method of choice because it has worked for them before."

Morrison cursed. "And if someone in the White House knew, then these attacks may not be at all what we think."

"And the F-35 theft could be connected."

"*Everything* could be connected." Morrison cursed again. "You know what that means, don't you?"

"What?"

"It means we can't trust anybody."

Leroux felt his chest tighten as he looked about his empty office, suddenly feeling very vulnerable. "What are we going to do, sir?"

"We're going to figure out who that agent was nodding to, and where the shooter came from. Get on it, Chris. I'll be there shortly."

"Yes, sir!"

The White House, Washington, DC

Jacob Starling shook hands with the Chief Justice of the Supreme Court. His mind was a fog of excitement, fear, and confusion. He was now the President of the United States. The Commander-in-Chief.

The leader of a country in chaos.

A country looking to *him* for solutions.

Those in the room clapped politely, no one happy about the occasion, not even himself. To say it was his dream to become President one day after Bridges had successfully completed two terms was an understatement. He had already begun the groundwork. But to get it like this? Through the assassination of his good friend?

Never.

He had received the news from his aide who had taken the call while in the limo on the way to Capitol Hill. He had wept openly at his friend's death, at his country's plight, and a small part of him in fear of what was now expected of him.

The thought had pissed him off.

If you expected to be President one day, then you better be ready to be President today!

He had wiped those tears, instructed the driver to head to the White House, and contacted the Chief Justice and House Leaders to meet him immediately.

All of whom now looked at him expectantly.

He hadn't even had time to prepare anything, to even think of something inspirational to say, but he needed to say something, to somehow bring comfort to those surrounding him.

But his frown creased his face as he spoke.

"Thank you, Mr. Chief Justice." He opened his arms, spreading them wide, his fingers splayed open, trying to convey to those in the room a sense of inclusion. "Ladies and gentlemen, *we*, and *we* together, will solve this crisis. America is under attack. We have no idea who or why they are doing this. We are on our knees, defeat is looking down upon us, but this"—he jabbed his finger at the ground—"is America! America *never* surrenders, *never* throws in the towel! We will win this fight, and we will win it by being what we are—the greatest nation on Earth. We will use the tools and knowhow that make us that great nation, rather than standby and let ourselves be destroyed. Our citizens want action, nay they *demand* action, and action is what they shall receive.

"Mr. Speaker, I will be seeking Congressional approval to temporarily suspend Posse Comitatus. Our troops are in their barracks, raring to help, so they will. I want an immediate drawdown of our foreign forces. Every man and woman not absolutely needed in theatre is to return to secure the homeland. Make certain our allies and enemies know that any hostile action against our facilities or forces will be met with a nuclear response. We are not going to tolerate anyone trying to kick us when we are down.

"Susan, I want MYSTIC activated immediately. Record every damned phone call in this country. I want to know who our victims are talking to the next time one of them blows something up."

"Sir, that violates the Constitution," interjected the Chief Justice. "You'll be challenged."

"And by the time I'm ordered to stop, we'll have at least a day's worth of data, won't we?" He dropped his head slightly, implying an "or else".

The Chief Justice bowed slightly. "I'm *certain* it would take at least that long."

"Very well. Hopefully tomorrow we might have some intel on what's been happening." Starling smiled, holding his hands out to the room again.

"And remember, *together* we will save our nation. This is by no means the final round. We may be on our knees, but it's time to stand back up, to fight back with our entire arsenal. America *will* win this war, for it is war we are facing ladies and gentlemen. We have been invaded by an unknown force that is using our own citizens against us. Today that changes. But to effect these changes, I want no changes around here. Everyone who had a job this morning, still has the same job tomorrow. The only change will be my own, and the swearing in of a new Vice President, who will be named shortly."

He paused, looking about the room. "Where's Bill?" Bill Cambridge stepped forward from behind the imposing General Thorne, the room still crowded.

"Here, Mr. President."

"Bill, you're *my* speechwriter now. I'll be addressing the nation in sixty minutes. Make it clear that the party is over and that those who have committed these acts will be eliminated, but also make it clear to our population that it will take time and to remain hopeful, vigilant, and law abiding." He smiled. "Make me sound as wise as you did our good friend and our great President, Johnathan Bridges."

"You can count on it, Mr. President."

"Excellent." He sucked in a deep breath, his lips pressing tightly together as the Nuclear Football entered the room, handcuffed to the wrist of an Air Force Major, the sight of the metal Zero Halliburton briefcase causing his heart to leap with the reality of the situation.

You're about to have control of the most powerful arsenal mankind has ever known.

"Thank you, everyone. Please give me a few minutes alone, I have some business to take care of."

The room cleared of unnecessary personnel, and within minutes the Yankee White cleared Major had handed control of the hand of God to him.

And he trembled in fear as he was finally left alone, suddenly uncertain if he was capable of doing the job he had been forced to take.

USS Columbia, SSN-771, Los Angeles Class Submarine
Contiguous Zone, 17 Nautical miles off the coast of China

Dylan Kane grabbed a handhold as the sub shook from another depth charge, the count of how many had been dropped already lost. Lee Fang gripped the seat she was in with one hand, the wall with the other, it clear she was as scared as he was. But like him, he suspected that fear was just another emotion to use. It forced the body to produce adrenaline, which heightened the senses and allowed for quicker actions and reactions if harnessed properly, rather than giving in to the shaking, quivering mass most would under these circumstances.

"Someone really wants you."

Fang nodded. "Do you really think this is over me?"

Kane placed his hand on his chest, feigning shock. "You think it's me? I'm a likeable guy!"

Fang looked at him as if she wasn't sure what to make of him.

That's the one flaw in training spies for other cultures. They almost never get the humor down, especially sarcasm.

He winked at her. "Just kidding. But yes, I'm pretty sure they want you. And it's for more than killing a General. There's no way they'd risk war with the United States over that. If they know something about the assassination, or are somehow involved, then I can see them wanting you dead, but risking war? There must be something they think you know that they can't risk having get out."

Fang bit her lip, Kane catching it immediately.

"What?"

She frowned, looking up at him, a hint of guilt on her face. "There's more I didn't tell you."

143

"Spill."

She sighed. "Are you missing an F-35?"

Kane shook his head, his chin dropping slightly toward his chest. "Excuse me?"

"From what I overheard, I think someone involved in whatever is going on delivered an F-35 to our government and they've already determined it was intact and our scientists are looking at it now." Her eyes narrowed. "You *do* know about the missing plane, don't you?"

"No comment."

"So you do."

"And you have more."

She nodded. "They also were talking about being able to take Taiwan, Mongolia and the South China Sea without interference from the United States."

Kane's eyes flared a bit on this revelation. "And they were being serious?"

Fang nodded. "Absolutely. They had barely begun to drink, and they sent the girls away before starting the conversation."

"And this is the same conversation you told me about when they mentioned the assassination of the President?"

"Yes."

"And they didn't know you were there…" His voice drifted as he began to process this new information, the sub rocking again as another depth charge exploded, this one sounding and feeling much closer than the others.

He barely noticed it.

If the Chinese involved in this overheard meeting were acting outside of the purview of their government as Fang seemed to think based upon her debriefing in the mini-sub, then this rogue element had taken delivery of the

F-35 and also knew of a planned assassination of the President, which meant the two events were linked. He found it impossible to believe that events this big would coincidentally coincide with the terrorist attacks that had been happening over the past two weeks.

"What are you thinking?"

Kane's eyes returned their focus to Fang. "I think that everything that's happening back home right now is a diversion, or a means to an end."

"But what end?"

Kane shrugged his shoulders. "If China thinks they can take Taiwan, Mongolia and the South China Sea without American interference, it can't be good. Someone has carved up the world, giving China a big chunk of it in exchange for something." He looked at her, realizing how difficult it must have been for her to give up this intel considering how much benefit her country could conceivably gain if successful. He lowered his voice. "You're a good person, Fang. Most people would have kept that intel to themselves, just in case we weren't able to save the President and we decided to cut you loose."

Fang frowned. "You wouldn't do that, would you? The deal was I give you the intel about the President then you protect me."

Kane could see a hint of fear in her eyes. It was clear she knew if she were captured she was not only dead, but her death would be long and painful—China wouldn't be trying to sink an American nuclear submarine for murder. And if he were in her position, he'd have gone deep, but he had more options. This was his life, not hers. She was Military Special Ops, not Intelligence. Military was short term, Intelligence could be years—decades even.

He reached forward to try and provide some reassurance but was jostled by another explosion that sounded far too close. He settled for a verbal delivery. "Don't worry, my government might, but *I* won't. Assuming we

145

survive the day, you'll be safe, I promise you. But you'll never be going back to China."

Her eyes glistened for a moment, then she blinked. "I've already resigned myself to that fact." She pointed up. "Each of these depth charges is another nail in the coffin of my old life, as you Americans might say."

He chuckled. "You've got some of the colloquialisms down. You'll do fine in America."

She smiled, it turning into a frown as another charge went off followed by an alarm. "If we ever make it there."

"We have to. This information is too important. If there's a connection between your intel and what's happening back home, then this has nothing to do with Islamic terrorism. My government needs to know that, and quickly."

Fang rose. "Then we need to get off this boat."

Kane nodded. "Agreed." He opened the hatch and poked his head out, looking at the guard stationed at the door. "I need to speak to your Captain immediately."

Operations Center 3, CIA Headquarters, Langley, Virginia

Someone cried.

Chris Leroux didn't bother looking to see who. The image was shocking and heartbreaking. He felt his own stomach churn in the darkness of the Op Center, as he was sure they all did. They were among the first in the country to see the assassination of their President in high-definition living color.

It was gruesome.

Leroux had seen death before, even in person. As part of his job he watched videos of beheadings and mutilations, rapes and beatings. But this was different somehow. He felt a connection with his President, not those others, and to see him shot in cold blood made him sick to his stomach.

And determined to find out what this once great man had meant when he had delivered his dying words to Director Morrison.

"Wait!" Leroux jumped from his seat, rushing to the front of the room, pointing at one of the large displays showing one of the views, six different angles already available and time-synched to play together. The view was a large swath of the crime scene, the shooter on the right, the President at the base of the stairs on the left. "Back it up ten seconds and zoom in on the shooter's hands."

"Yes, sir."

One of the techs backed up the footage and zoomed in then tagged the hands in the image so the computer would keep them in the center of the screen, no matter where they went in the frame.

"Good. Now zoom out just a bit so we can see the shooter's shoulders."

The view changed slightly. "Tag his right shoulder."

A little green plus sign appeared at the center of the shoulder.

147

"Now play it back in real-time."

They watched as the man's arm was grabbed then the struggle that ensued resulting in six shots being fired, five hitting their target.

"Okay, reset it, but in slow motion. Everyone watch the shoulder before the shots."

He could sense everyone in the room leaning forward as they looked to see what he had spotted, or at least thought he had spotted. It could be completely innocent, it could be his mind creating something from nothing, but he was sure he had seen something that didn't look right.

"He pulled him toward the President!" cried Alice Michaels, the Operations Center Coordinator for the day.

"By the hand!" agreed Harold Dillard, one of Leroux's better analysts. "And look at the trigger!"

Leroux had already moved on to the rest of the looping video the moment his fears had been confirmed. He pointed at the screen. "Remove the shoulder tag and move it to the shooter's right hand."

The plus sign moved and the video restarted. It was clear the agent's hand was enveloping the shooter's, but from their angle all they could really see was the shooter's hand and the gun. He pointed at another screen with a reverse angle. "Bring that one up, same tag." The screens swapped and everyone gasped as the enhanced image made the truth crystal clear.

The agent's finger was the one pulling the trigger.

"He's even checking his aim!" exclaimed Dillard, throwing up his hands. "This is insane! He's Secret Service, isn't he?"

"Special Agent Maxwell Logan, according to the report," replied Michaels. "Six years on the job."

Leroux was squeezing the bridge of his nose absentmindedly as he watched the replay. To no one in particular, he said, "Pull up his service record. I want to know if he's ex-military or has any connections to Raven Defense Services."

"Why?" asked Dillard. "You know something?" The way he said it Leroux knew he was smiling. His team, by reputation, and since he had become their supervisor, through experience, knew his skills, and he felt had come to respect him, even though he was younger than some of them. Dillard however was a full eighteen months Leroux's junior.

"Just a hunch." It was all Leroux could offer, his orders still standing that his investigation into Sherrie's kidnapping was off the books. He rolled his hand. "Tag the agent's head then play it forward, let's see what happens."

The action was swift as the other agents quickly secured the scene, too late, but Leroux saw it immediately.

Special Agent Logan had definitely made eye contact with someone. Leroux kept it to himself, about to clear the room so he could figure it out, when Dillard made it unnecessary.

"He looked at somebody," he said, his voice subdued, almost as if in shock.

And the room fell silent as they all realized the truth.

One is a madman.

Two a conspiracy.

And if Special Agent Logan knew who to look at in the room, he was *not* being coerced by forces unknown.

He was involved.

Deep.

Capitol Hill, Washington, DC

Senator Clark Blackburn jabbed toward an approximation of where he thought the White House was from the head of the table in Conference Room 214. There were no windows so it was just a stab in the proverbial dark, but his point he was certain wouldn't be missed on the half dozen hopefully like-minded individuals gathered with him.

"That man just violated the Constitution of these United States. By activating MYSTIC, he's violating the rights of every single law-abiding American. It's intolerable! Unprecedented! Illegal!"

Representative Terri Noel's head bobbed in agreement. "It's unpresidential. And it has to be stopped. We risk starting down a slippery slope if this is allowed to continue. I move we immediately call both Houses to order and override the President's decision."

"Agreed?" asked Blackburn, happy someone else was readily siding with him.

Heads around the table bobbed as the door behind Blackburn opened. He turned, surprised at the sight of three Secret Service agents entering. "This is a private meeting. We are not to be disturbed!"

One of the agents closed the door as the other two removed their weapons, threading suppressors in place. Blackburn jumped from his seat as quickly as his old, arthritic bones would allow, turning to face the men, spreading his arms out and expanding his chest as wide as he could, stepping to the right to shield Terri Noel, the only woman in the room. Blackburn had fought in Vietnam and didn't bother crying for help as he knew it was already too late. He had survived that war, four tours in the thick of things, and had been decorated more times than he cared to remember.

And he'd be damned if any terrorist would see a hint of fear on his face, a tremble on his lip, or hear a word of pleading on his tongue.

The first shot startled him, more the sound than the feeling. He fell backward but managed to grab the edge of the table, catching himself. A searing pain began to spread through his chest as he felt Terri's hands on his back trying to hold him up as she screamed. Like a movie played in slow motion he saw the three gunmen advance, their weapons discharging with each squeeze of the trigger, the muzzle flashes brilliant as death screamed from each elongated barrel, the suppressors muffling the sounds but not silencing them like Hollywood would have you believe.

The second shot spun him around, into Terri's arms, the horror on her face as their eyes met palpable, her scream suddenly silenced as the left side of her skull was torn open by a well-aimed shot over his shoulder.

They collapsed in a heap, he on top of her, his cheek against hers, their shared warmth quickly fading as they both bled out, the first soldiers to die in the fight to save America from itself.

Yellow Sea, Contiguous Zone, 18 Nautical miles off the coast of China

"Jesus Christ, Elisa, keep your head down!"

Christopher Dunn grabbed his wife, Elisa, pulling her back down to the deck as they hid behind the gunwales, at least six ships now converged within sight, lobbing what he assumed were depth charges over their sides. Massive eruptions under the water vibrated through their Ovni 39 sailboat, occasionally drenching them in water as the shockwaves reached the surface. They had dropped their sea anchor for the night and had been enjoying a meal with a fine bottle of Australian Chalk Hill chardonnay when the first ship had roared past them, its wake tossing them like a lone apple in a dunking barrel.

He had immediately registered his protest over several public bands to no avail, and stopped when he saw several more ships on the horizon converging on their position.

That was when the first depth charge had erupted.

"We've got to get the hell out of here!" he had shouted, immediately setting to work at raising the sails, his wife momentarily frozen in panic eventually helping. It had taken time to pull in the sea anchor but they were finally underway, heading for South Korea, his binoculars telling him these were Chinese ships that were breaking international law.

"We're in the contiguous zone," he had confirmed with their GPS when they were finally moving, they can't do that!"

"Well they are!" his wife shouted.

Underway, they had kept low, it appearing the vessels were working their way east in the same direction they were going.

"They must be tracking a sub!"

"American?"

152

"Or Russian. Certainly not one of ours!"

He had actually laughed, he and his wife Canadian, its submarine fleet woefully inadequate considering its northern territorial responsibilities. Botched politics over the past few decades had made what was once the fifth largest navy in the world a mere shadow of its former self.

Elisa had said nothing, instead raising her cellphone to record what was happening as they lay flat on the deck.

"Are you kidding me?"

She had looked at him as if she had no clue what he meant. He had never understood the cellphone craze, the urge to record everything happening and to take hundreds of pictures of yourself with your arm outstretched making duck lips at a tiny camera, then posting it on the Internet for all to click Like, there no option to click "You're an idiot with no self-esteem".

Suddenly one of the closer vessels seemed to bow toward them, its entire hull, parallel to them now, appearing to bend as a fireball erupted from the opposite side, lighting the entire area, the only light before the stars and search lights pointed at the water.

And their own lights, which he had killed after the first several minutes.

Better not to let them know there are witnesses.

Alarms carried across the waves as the ship's crew reacted to their new reality, secondary explosions sending shockwaves in all directions, Dunn certain he could feel the heat from the flames as they continued to sail east, the flaming ship's zigzag pattern halted, several other of her sister ships turning to assist.

He pushed himself to his knees, the attack apparently halted for the moment, and began to check the boat for any damage. He could hear the bilge pump working overtime as it tried to rid their sturdy vessel of the water that had washed over their deck with the blasts, but other than that they seemed none the worse for wear, their sails intact and full with a light but steady easterly wind allowing them to finally put some distance between them and the action.

Something bumped against their hull causing Elisa to yelp and drop her phone into the ocean.

DEATH TO AMERICA

Yellow Sea, Contiguous Zone, 20 Nautical miles off the coast of China
4 miles from the Exclusive Economic Zone

Dylan Kane leaned forward, trying to see through the hull of the mini-sub as they approached the surface. His displays showed camera views of what was ahead and above, and from what he could see Captain Lynch had definitely given them the diversion they needed.

And perhaps started a war.

Lynch had been about to jettison the mini-sub to make his getaway when Kane had arrived, the top speed of the USS Columbia at least as good as any of the surface ships they were facing, but not with something on its back. He had been reluctant to let them go but Kane had insisted their intel was too important to wait perhaps many hours before it would be safe enough to surface and send a signal.

Lynch had quickly agreed, simply eager to get the mini-sub away. When Kane had said he needed a diversion so they couldn't be tracked, Lynch had pointed to the hatch, saying nothing, but his barked orders as Kane left the con were clear.

He was going to fire a single torpedo.

The shockwave had been tremendous when the torpedo had made impact, and each secondary explosion vibrated through the hull sending his pulse rate up a few notches each time. Lee Fang sat beside him, her knuckles white from gripping the arms of her seat, her lips pressed tightly together, saying nothing.

His instruments were showing multiple surface contacts, all but one now converging on what he assumed was the flaming wreck of one of the Chinese ships that had been trying to either destroy the USS Columbia or bring it to the surface.

He was pretty sure either outcome would have been satisfactory.

With the target hit, the depth charges had stopped almost immediately as rescue operations began, but he was certain the reprieve wouldn't last long.

He had only minutes to get his message out.

"There it is," he said, pointing at the display. There was another target on the surface, small, moving slowly east, and Kane had a hunch it was civilian. And with it making such poor speed, perhaps five knots, he was thinking sailboat.

And they'd make excellent cover.

He had no doubt that at this moment the USS Columbia was making best speed to international waters and the nearest US Seventh Fleet ships, their top speed about four to five times his.

But they'd have to do it silent and deep.

Which meant no communications.

He didn't have that kind of time.

"Here we go."

The depth gauge indicated they were about to surface, and the eerie infrared image on one of his screens showed they were about to come up right beside the vessel he was hoping was civilian and friendly.

There was a bump as their hulls tapped.

"Oops."

He rose and backed out of his seat, motioning for Fang to take over. She quickly changed seats and assumed the controls.

"Keep us alongside, just below the surface. I'll be back."

Kane cycled through the airlock and was soon in the water, underneath the mini-sub. Attached by a long cable so he wouldn't be left behind, he crawled along the hull then reached up, pulling himself out of the water, hooking his armpits over the gunwale of what did indeed turn out to be a rather nice sailboat.

With a terrified couple staring at him.

He smiled his most disarming smile, deciding to open with humor.

"Pardon me, but do you have any Grey Poupon?"

Eyeballs popped wide as eyebrows raced up foreheads and jaws dropped. The middle-aged couple clung to each other, both shocked and terrified.

But at least they appeared to be Westerners and not Chinese.

"Do you speak English."

"Canadian," said the man.

"If you're Canadian, then shouldn't you be apologizing for something? Or do you just *speak* Canadian?"

"I'm sorry, I mean, *we're* Canadian, we speak English."

Kane rolled onto the deck, staying low. "And French no doubt."

"Sorry, that's just propaganda. The vast majority of us don't."

"No igloos and dog teams either, eh?" He emphasized the 'eh'.

The man smiled. "Only in the Arctic." He paused. "Sorry, but who are you?"

Kane winked. "I could tell you, but then I'd have to kill you." The couple pushed back slightly with their feet, Kane waving them off. "Just a joke. I'm trying to break the ice."

"Sorry, but you're not succeeding," replied the woman.

Kane frowned. "Sorry about that. My sense of humor is an acquired taste." He held up a finger. "Excuse me a minute." He fished his satellite phone out of a side pocket and removed it from the sealed baggie. He entered his code of the day into the keypad, he having received it from the Numbers Station assigned to him by Leroux, one not in common use, and different from the shortwave radio station officially assigned to him before the F-35 mission had begun.

Throughout the world spy agencies operated Numbers Stations. Begun after World War II, these short wave stations were One Way Voice Links that relayed important information to operatives in nearly unbreakable code. These mysterious channels would broadcast series of numbers, sometimes alphanumerics, read either by a computer or a woman—and on rare occasions a man or child—and were sometimes a spy's only link to home.

His critical piece of information received this morning was the code he had entered. It would allow him to communicate directly with Langley, on a completely secure line, scrambled with his code. It would be impossible to break, at least not in enough time to matter.

The phone rang.

And rang.

Uh oh.

The Oval Office, The White House, Washington, DC

President Jacob Starling had never seen real fear before, at least not in old men. Most had grown up in times far tougher than these—save the last two weeks—and most had fought in wars witnessing horrors firsthand that would rival anything on today's streets.

But Speaker of the House Carney was terrified.

As were his colleagues.

"Something has to be done, Mr. President. They've infiltrated the White House *and* Capitol Hill." He threw up his hands. "They're everywhere! The government can't function because we can't get a quorum. Almost everybody immediately went on vacation after the murders." He paused, sucking in a deep breath, staring directly at Starling. "Mr. President, the nation demands action, and the people's representatives demand it."

Starling sat on the edge of his desk, his head nodding in agreement the entire time. He was just as scared as Carney and the others were, but he hid it better.

Perhaps because you have a massive security detail.

He pursed his lips as he sucked in a deep breath.

And so did your predecessor.

"What would you have me do?"

It was a simple question. He was open to suggestions. MYSTIC had been activated but yet to yield anything. The attacks had continued, but they hadn't found any cellphone traffic yet, the last two bombers having been found fit with earpieces, the terrorists apparently already not only prepared for the MYSTIC contingency, but aware it had been activated.

They are *everywhere.*

Governments were sieves of information, people taking jobs not as callings, but for paychecks. Orders were followed if asked nicely, and lips were loose because of a lack of understanding on how something that came across your desk might be interesting to you but invaluable to the enemy.

Civilians just don't get it.

Carney looked flustered, collapsing onto one of the couches. "I don't know, Mr. President. Put troops on the streets?"

"The National Guards of every state are at full alert."

"Then the Army."

"You know I can't do that."

Carney shook his head. "No, Mr. President. You're the *only one* who can do that."

His eyebrows rose slightly at the thought. "Suspend Posse Comitatus?"

"Request Congress to authorize it, and we will. I've already confirmed this with my colleagues."

Starling looked at General Thorne, the only man in the room he couldn't read. "What do you think, General?"

General Thorne stepped forward, his expression grave. "Mr. President, I think we need to take bold, unprecedented action."

Starling rose from his perch, crossing his arms as he sensed a bombshell about to land. "Such as?"

"Sir, suspending Posse Comitatus is merely a first step. Our Armed Forces will still be hamstrung by the Constitution and the civil liberties of American citizens."

Starling felt a pit begin to form in his stomach. "And you think this is a bad thing?"

Thorne's jaw squared. "Absolutely. You need to take bold steps like you did when you activated MYSTIC."

"Which hasn't yielded anything to date that is useful," interjected Homeland Security Secretary Wainwright.

Thorne ignored him. "Decisions like that will win the day."

Starling was almost afraid to ask. "Do you have any particular decisions in mind?"

"Suspend the Constitution, declare martial law."

Gasps filled the room, but to Starling's shock he found himself agreeing as faces in the room began to turn from stunned stares to nods of assent, as if everyone was relieved someone had said what they were all thinking.

Carney rose from the couch. "Mr. President, if you do this, I guarantee you the support of Congress."

Starling looked at Carney then back at General Thorne. "As Military head of our armed forces, that would make you de facto leader of the country."

"Only for as long as necessary, Mr. President. As soon as the threat is neutralized and order is restored, civilian authority would be returned immediately."

Starling frowned, looking at the Congressional leaders gathered in the room. "And I have your support on this."

"Absolutely, Mr. President."

"You'll be at the press briefing, shoulder to shoulder with me, when I make the announcement?"

"Yes, Mr. President."

Starling shook his head, sitting back on the edge of his desk. "I don't know. It's never been done before. To hand the country over to our military seems so un-American, so unfathomable, I can't even imagine what the American people will think. To be the President who goes down in history as the one who ended over two centuries of democratic rule!"

161

"You'll go down in history as the man who saved his country so that it could continue for another two hundred years under democratic rule." It was Thorne that delivered the words.

And they made sense.

The floor vibrated and everyone jumped to their feet. Someone rushed into the room along with several Secret Service agents. The agents surrounded Starling, grabbing him by the arms when Secretary Wainwright held up his hand. "Wait." He pointed to the window and they all turned to see a fireball and large plume of smoke in the distance. "They just hit the Jefferson Memorial."

Starling turned to Speaker of the House Carney. "Draw up the paperwork and I'll sign it."

"Yes, Mr. President."

Operations Center 3, CIA Headquarters, Langley, Virginia

"Let's see if we can figure out who he's looking at."

"He was looking at someone near me, on the stairs."

It was Director Morrison who made the comment as he entered the secure Operations Center. Everyone rose and he waved them off. "Tell me what we've got."

Leroux rose from his desk, approaching the main screen. "Replay the shooting."

The shooting played out, Morrison seemingly disturbed by the sight of what he had already seen. He shook his head slowly. "Unbelievable."

"Now replay it, tagging the hand, reverse angle." Leroux pointed at the screen. "Now watch this, sir."

Morrison crossed his arms, jabbing at the screen. "The agent pulled the trigger."

"All six times. I think the shooter was just another victim, coerced into this by the same people that have been attacking the country for the past two weeks."

"Show me the nod."

Leroux motioned for it to be brought up. "We were just starting our analysis to see if we could determine who he looked at."

"Then don't let me interrupt you. If they're this deep into the White House, then we've got big problems. The President is about to declare martial law and I don't think he has all the facts he needs before making that decision."

"Can he be stopped?"

Morrison shook his head. "Congress has already agreed, they're voting on it now."

Leroux's phone vibrated in his pocket. Few people had his number. His parents, Sherrie, Kane and work. They were the only people who had it besides companies telling him he had won a free cruise.

He glanced at the call display and his heart leapt. He leaned in toward Morrison and whispered. "It's Kane, sir."

"Put it on speaker."

Leroux answered the phone. "Just a second, Dylan. I've got Director Morrison here in Op Center Three. I'm going to put you on speaker." He tossed the phone to Dillard who jacked the call in.

Morrison cocked his head up. "Go ahead, Special Agent."

There was a burst of static, the connection bad. "Sir, I may only have moments. Did you get the message on the assassination attempt from the USS Columbia's Captain?"

Morrison frowned. "Yes, but too late. The President is dead."

"Shit!" There was a moment of silence. "Okay, here's what you need to know. General Yee and the others I previously mentioned were also aware of the F-35 delivery. These same men are the ones who mentioned the assassination attempt on the President. That means that the theft of the F-35 and the assassination are connected. As well, China has plans to take Taiwan, Mongolia and the South China Sea, with no expected opposition from us. Something big is happening, sir, something really big."

Leroux could tell Morrison's mind had already caught up with his own, for it was obvious what was happening to those with most of the information.

Morrison sat in a nearby chair. "Dylan, the President is about to declare martial law."

"Sir, he has to be stopped. I have reason to believe that elements within our own military are behind these attacks. The F-35 I saw was *intact*, expertly dismantled. Only military personnel could have done that. And with a dead Army Captain delivering it, I'd say our Armed Forces have been compromised."

Leroux's head was bobbing. "And we know where they're headquartered."

"Where?"

Leroux looked at Morrison who nodded, giving him the green light. "Fort Myer. They've kidnapped Sherrie and have been—" Leroux broke off, choking up, unable to say the words.

"I'm sorry, you were cut off. What's happened to Sherrie."

"She's being tortured for information," replied Morrison gently, rising and placing a hand on Leroux's shoulder.

"Jesus Christ!" exclaimed Kane. "And you're doing nothing about it?"

Morrison frowned. "There's nothing we can do. We don't know who to trust at this point. It seems Raven Defense Services is involved, along with a Colonel Booker, the former commanding officer of our walking dead Captain Lewis. As far as we can tell they have some sort of command post in a building at the Fort Myer site."

"Chris, can you hear me?"

Leroux raised his head, wiping his eyes dry. "Y-yes, Dylan."

"Get their photos and ID them. I'm going to kill every damned last one of them."

Leroux smiled. "You'll have them."

The connection was cut off, but Leroux didn't care. He knew that no matter what happened, his friend was going to avenge Sherrie, and knowing Kane, they'd die horrible deaths.

Never mess with a CIA agent's friends or family.

"Sir, I've found a link!"

Both Leroux and Morrison looked over at Dillard.

"What is it?" asked Morrison.

165

"It's the shooter, sir. I mean the real shooter, the Special Agent. His name is Maxwell Logan. He's been Secret Service for six years, Treasury for six before that. No military service whatsoever, not even National Guard."

"Then what's the connection?" asked Morrison.

"His brother, sir. His brother served with the deceased Captain Lewis in Iraq and now is fairly high up in Raven Defense Services."

Leroux grinned. "Which means he's a co-conspirator. He's not being coerced." Leroux pointed at the central screen showing a paused view of the staircase. "He's looking at someone on that staircase."

Morrison approached the display. "And he made eye contact. He nodded as if he made eye contact. He wouldn't have nodded if they were looking away."

"Show us the time-synched moment he nodded, this angle."

The frame moved forward slightly, little changing as most people had been frozen in place, in shock. Including Morrison.

Leroux stepped toward the screen, pointing at several of the people. "Remove anyone whose back is turned."

A magic wand tool appeared on the screen, bodies being circled and removed leaving black outlines where they once were, reducing the number by more than half.

"Now eliminate the Director."

"No, don't assume I'm innocent."

Leroux looked at him. "If we can't trust you, sir, then there's no point in continuing. Let's remove you from the frame, you're just a distraction."

Morrison nodded, reluctantly.

His image disappeared.

Leroux pointed at three more people. "They're all looking in the wrong direction."

Three more disappeared. The staircase was quickly thinning, only three people remaining.

Morrison pointed at Susan Lawrence. "She's too shocked to be involved. She was screaming hysterically for at least several minutes."

She disappeared.

Both Leroux and Morrison exchanged worried glances, for only two people remained.

The Chairman of the Joint Chiefs of Staff, General Thorne, and his aide.

Both of whom were looking directly forward, not a hint of shock on their faces.

The Oval Office, The White House, Washington, DC

President Jacob Starling screwed the top of the pen until it clicked, then placed the pen in his pocket, a memento he planned to turn over to his Presidential Library someday, should the orders he just signed not blow up in his face.

For he had just signed over the country to its military, something he had never dreamed might happen. Technically he and Congress could overturn the decision, but it still made him incredibly uncomfortable. He could already see two different versions of the history texts future students would read about him. One in which he saved the country by temporarily suspending the Constitution, and another where he saved the country by permanently handing it over to the military. Either way the text books would portray him as a hero, one for the right reasons, the other for the wrong.

For the Military States of America, or whatever the hell they might be called, would never say anything bad about the man that had handed them power.

Trust in them. They are, after all, Americans too.

And that was what had at least part of him thinking this wasn't a terrible idea. This was the American military. The freest of all militaries, with a volunteer army of average citizens who wanted to serve their country. How they could support any type of permanent change of power was unimaginable.

The good people of our Armed Forces will preserve our Union.

He rose, looking at General Thorne.

"General Thorne, I hereby temporarily declare martial law, and the suspension of habeas corpus and the Constitution of these United States.

This order, signed by me in cooperation with both Houses and Parties, is temporary, and can be suspended at any time by order of Congress, which will sit in thirty days to review this order."

Thorne saluted and Starling returned the salute. "Mr. President, you honor me as well as the men and women who serve under me with the confidence you have placed in us. I give you my word that we will do whatever it takes to restore order, and when the perpetrators of these heinous crimes have been captured, restore the Constitution and return power to the people."

Starling, hands clasped behind his back looked up at the slightly taller Thorne, his figure even more imposing now that he controlled the entire country with no rule of law to hamper him. It was frightening. He felt the hairs on the back of his neck rise, but he pushed the feeling of impending doom aside. "General Thorne, I trust you to do your duty and save our country from the destruction our enemies are so intent on bringing. I look forward to the day, *very* soon, when I once again sit in this office as President of these United States. God bless you, and God bless America!"

As those in the room as witnesses applauded, shouting "God bless America!", he felt his pulse pound in his ears as he went through the motions, soon leaving the Oval Office behind him and returning to the residence. He closed the door to his bedroom behind him, his wife of thirty-four years waiting, her arms outstretched. He collapsed into her arms, and wept openly for the first time in his life.

What have I done?

J. ROBERT KENNEDY

Command Center, Fort Myer, Arlington, Virginia

"Colonel, we have a problem."

Colonel Booker was watching a live feed from the Oval Office being broadcast on every channel in the country, and probably every channel in the free and not-so-free world. It was a moment he had never dreamed possible, yet here it was, unfolding before his eyes—military rule of the United States.

And it would change things forever. Peace and security without having to worry about the courts protecting the guilty by assuming their innocence. By imposing martial law, America would be secure once again, the terrorist threat eliminated. They would rid the country of the Islamic problem, and reign in the unchecked ambitions of traditional foes like China and an ever-out of control Russia.

They had a deal with China that was one of convenience until the day came when it was no longer needed.

Then we'll deal with them as well.

But first was Russia. Tens of thousands of troops would be inside the Ukraine and Baltic States within two weeks, mobilization to begin tomorrow under the guise of an already announced exercise. Russian aggression would be stopped cold. A safe supply of oil would be secured until energy independence was achieved within two years, and negotiations with Iran would be over the moment it was achieved.

Skyrocketing oil prices on the world market were no concern when the military had a secure supply at home, which it could impose price controls on if desired.

He smiled.

Everything is going according to plan.

"Sir?"

Booker looked at his subordinate. "What?"

"Sir, we have a problem."

"What kind of problem?"

"We've been hacked."

Booker's red alert alarm sounded. "Explain."

"I've found a tap on our network feeding data out over secure lines."

"The hard lines?"

"Yes, sir. It looks like they've been pulling security video."

Booker frowned. *Not good.*

"Have you traced it?"

"Yes, sir."

"And?"

"It's Langley, sir. CIA Headquarters."

Kunsan Airbase, South Korea

It hadn't made any sense until now. The Chinese ships had never reengaged, his mini-sub and the sailboat continuing unfettered for several more hours before the USS Columbia resurfaced, scaring the shit out of the Canadians. The mini-sub had been retrieved by the time they were able to rendezvous with a helicopter over international waters and the shocking news had been received.

The United States was under martial law.

And he had failed to warn the President in time.

As he and Lee Fang jumped down from the helicopter, three black SUV's pulled up, doors from all three vehicles thrown open as men in black suits stepped out almost in unison.

This isn't good.

"Special Agent Dylan Kane?" asked one of the men.

Kane frowned. "Thanks for blowing my cover, asshole."

"Major Lee Fang of the People's Liberation Army?"

Lee Fang snapped to attention, her face forward but her eyes looking over at Kane, confusion and fear on her face.

"Special Agent Kane, by order of the Military Stewardship Council of the United States, I am placing you under arrest."

"On what charge?"

"Treason."

He cocked an eyebrow as the stiff warm wind blew open his shirt, revealing his Glock. Guns were immediately pointed at him. He laughed, pulling the gun out with his thumb and forefinger, tossing it to the nearest agent. He liberated Fang's weapon from her belt, tossing it over as well.

No point dying here.

"And just how am I supposed to have betrayed my country?"

The man shook his head. "Above my pay grade, sir. I just have orders to take you both into custody."

Kane motioned with his chin toward Fang. "And what's to become of her?"

"She's to be returned to China to face charges of murder and treason."

"Interesting." Kane took Fang by the hand. "Let's go, my dear, we don't want to keep our new military overlords waiting, now do we?"

They were both patted down, their wrists ziptied behind their backs, then placed in the rear of the second SUV. Within moments they were underway. Kane watched as they turned onto Route 21. He leaned forward, lifting off the seat, poking his head between the two headrests. "Where are you taking us?"

"Sit down!" yelled the passenger, shoving him with a face palm backward. Kane lowered his wrists and felt the ziptie snap with the force of his bodyweight falling on them. It went unnoticed up front, but not to Fang who exchanged a knowing glance with him.

She leaned forward slightly, revealing her own freed wrists.

I wonder when she did that.

He could only think of one opportunity, and that was when she had first sat in the vehicle, which meant she had entered planning to escape, or die trying.

My kind of girl.

He looked out the window, the lead vehicle about a hundred yards ahead, the trailing the same distance behind. They were doing maybe forty. It wasn't a speed you wanted to jump out of a vehicle at, but it had been done on many occasions by him and had yet to result in any permanent damage.

173

But today he couldn't afford *any* damage. He glanced at Fang then motioned slightly to the front. She nodded almost imperceptibly. He leapt forward, grabbing the driver by the head, spinning it to the right then sharply back to the left, the bone crunching nicely as the neck snapped. He looked over at the passenger, Fang strangling him with the crook of her elbow against his windpipe, her arm locked in place around the headrest.

The vehicle was beginning to fishtail and Kane reached forward, putting the vehicle in neutral to take any power from the tires but before he could grab the wheel, the vehicle suddenly swerved to the right, striking the meridian. They hit with a jar that sent them both sailing forward. Kane heard Fang's head smack the dash, the passenger suddenly gasping for air as the vehicle flipped, rolling onto the roof and skidding into oncoming traffic.

Horns blared and tires squealed, somebody reacting too slowly, the SUV hit hard on the front end sending them into a dizzying spin on the roof. Kane braced himself by shoving his arms and legs out like spokes, finally stabilizing himself just as the vehicle came to a stop.

His hand darted out, crushing the windpipe of the passenger. He grabbed the man's gun and spare mags as Fang moaned.

"Are you okay?" he asked as he liberated the driver's weapon, all the while glancing through the shattered front and rear windows for the escort vehicles. Another moan. "Answer me!"

"I-I'm okay, just groggy."

"Can you shoot straight?"

"I don't think so. Not yet."

Kane stole a glance at Fang and saw a deep gash on her forehead, blood flowing a little too freely for his liking. He pulled a handkerchief from his pocket and put it in her left hand, pressing both against her forehead. "Maintain pressure, I'll look at it later." He stuffed the Glock in her right hand. "Shoot anything that isn't handsome like me."

He kicked open the driver side door and peered out to the rear. One of the escort vehicles was stopped, blocking the road, emergency lights flickering.

And four men were advancing, weapons drawn.

He squeezed off three quick rounds, the first two men dropping, the third round missing as the remaining two dove out of the way. Gunfire began to ricochet off the SUV from the front and rear. Kane ducked back inside and yanked the passenger's body from its crumpled position on the roof, now floor, and shoved him into the windshield, affording them a little bit of protection from the bullets.

A hole in the windshield gave him a limited view, four men advancing, firing steadily. He aimed through the hole and took one of them out, the other three scattering.

Three down, five to go.

"Are you okay?" he asked Fang as he poked his head into the backseat, firing off another round through the rear windshield.

Four down.

Sirens sounded heard in the distance and he had no way of knowing whether or not it was police, fire, ambulance or more bad guys on their way. All he knew was he had little time left to play.

"Answer me!"

"I'm—I'm sleepy."

"Stay awake! It sounds like you've got a concussion."

He grabbed the second Glock from Fang, making sure both weapons were fully loaded.

"I'll be back."

"Where are you going?"

"Hopefully not off to die for my country."

He rolled out the driver side, arms extended to either side, both triggers squeezing, his aim focused on the lone gunman remaining behind them. Eliminating him meant he only had to worry about being attacked from one side.

His aim was true, allowing him to continue his roll, spreading his legs out so he ended up lying on the ground, arms stretched out in front of him as both guns belched death toward the remaining three assailants.

Another went down, a shot to the shoulder spinning him twice before crumpling to the ground. Kane turned his head to the left, ducking as a bullet ricocheted off the pavement only feet away sending shards of rock into the top of his right shoulder. He winced but kept firing, looking back quickly to make sure he was aiming.

Another was down, then the final one was out of ammo, frantically trying to reload. Kane jumped to his feet, both guns aimed at the sole survivor, the man dropping his weapon, his hands slowly rising.

"Who sent you?"

"I told you, the Military Stewardship Council."

"Bullshit. You're not military. You're what, Raven?"

The man's eyes flared for a moment.

"Thought so. Who do you report to?"

"No idea what you're talking about."

The sirens were getting close now and he didn't have much time.

Kane shot him in the right thigh. The man cried out in pain, both hands grabbing at the wound as he collapsed to the ground.

"I don't have time to interrogate you properly, or legally. But then again, since we're under martial law back home, I guess we don't have to play by the rules anymore." He stepped closer. "Want to talk now?"

"Go to hell!" the man spat, the pain clearly almost overwhelming.

Kane shot him in the shoulder, the impact throwing the man onto his back, his entire body racked in pain. "Care to talk now?"

"Booker! It's Booker! Jesus Christ don't shoot me again!"

Kane straddled the man. "Colonel Booker?"

"Y-yes."

"That's what I thought."

He put a bullet through the man's head then returned to the SUV, pulling a still groggy Fang from the vehicle. Traffic in their direction was completely stopped, but the other side, the side they had originally been on, was still moving, though the looky-loos had it down to a crawl.

He slung Fang's arm over his shoulder and half-carried, half-dragged her to the meridian. He pointed his gun at the closest car, its driver slamming on the brakes, raising his hands.

"No, not that one," gasped Fang.

Kane's eyes narrowed. "Why not?"

"Look," she said, pointing at the hood ornament. Kane frowned at the leaping jaguar, flicking the gun, indicating the driver should move on, the man relieved as he hit the gas in his Jaguar XK-8 cabriolet. Fang stood up straighter, her strength apparently returning slightly. "Even in China we know shit cars when we see them."

Kane laughed and brought a Toyota to a stop, looking at Fang for her approval. She gave a thumbs up then passed out.

Hatfield Gate, Fort Myer, Joint Base Myer-Henderson Hall (JBM-HH), Arlington, Virginia

Agent Sherrie White ached all over. Even the parts of her body that hadn't been beaten were sore in sympathy with the parts that had. Her nose was broken, her lips split and she was certain several ribs were cracked, it painful to breathe.

But she persevered.

Barely.

Her will was starting to break. She had no clue how long she had been kept here, time meaningless in a closed room with no clock. She just knew from how exhausted she was it must have been at least two days, but she couldn't be sure.

How much can any one person take?

She wanted to cry, to weep, but she knew that damned camera in the corner was recording everything, and her adversaries were watching her every move. So she refused to give them the satisfaction, keeping her jaw square, her eyes clear, fixed on the lens, glaring her weakening defiance back at them.

The red light was like the eye of a beast, unblinking, unwavering, keeping its constant vigil, ensuring her torture, her pain, never ceased. If her eyes closed, someone entered the room to wake her up, if she slumped over in her chair someone would come inside and pull her head back and smack her awake.

I'm so tired.

She thought about the questions. They obviously knew she wasn't who she said she was. They had suggested she was CIA, but it was clear they didn't truly know. Why not tell them the truth? Or at least a version of the truth. She was dead anyway. There was no way they could let her go after what they had done to her. Now it was just a delaying action. The longer she was alive, the more chance there was that her colleagues could rescue her. But the fact they hadn't done so yet made her think they had no idea she was alive, her decoy obviously having fooled them.

Poor Chris!

Her heart broke as she thought of him, all alone, crying, thinking she was dead. She just prayed that he had found enough confidence in himself that he could move on and find someone else to love, who would love him just half as much as she did. A tear rolled down her cheek as she pictured him old and alone, a broken man, because he had recessed into the cocoon he had once occupied before they had met.

The door opened.

"Something upsetting you?"

It was the man who had been doing most of the beating. She had no idea what his name was, but his face was forever burned into her memory, and if she were to ever survive this ordeal, she'd kill him the first opportunity she had.

Slowly.

Painfully.

"Tears of joy."

"She speaks!" he said, throwing his arms wide and looking up at the ceiling in mock shock. "And just what are these tears of joy for?"

"I was just thinking about how I was going to kill you."

His smile broadened as he stood in front of her. "Missy, I'd love for you and me to go at it, one on one." He stepped closer, his crotch uncomfortably close to her face as he stared down at her, his finger tracing down her right cheek toward her mouth. "Ooh, how I'd love to go one on

179

one with you." He stepped back then shrugged. "But, you're to be executed for treason soon so I guess we'll never have that chance."

She smiled, her cracked lips screaming in protest. "I guess that means I win."

A stinging smack was her reward, then she was left alone again. She stared at the camera, the light blinking randomly. Her eyes narrowed slightly as she tried to focus, then her heart leapt as she realized it was blinking in a pattern.

Morse code!

I-T-S-C-H-R-I-S

W-E-A-R-E-C-O-M-I-N-G-S-O-O-N

The message repeated twice then went back to the steady red light that had kept watch over her through her torture.

A torture forgotten.

He knows I'm alive!

DEATH TO AMERICA

Mohammed Islam sat at his computer, keeping his head down as he had for the past two weeks. Cursed with a name that he would shout with pride in his birth country of Syria, here it was a curse, especially with recent events. His co-workers no longer invited him for lunch, ignored him in the hallways, and he could hear whispers behind his back. Even some people who he knew were Muslim wouldn't speak to him, their names mercifully less obviously Islamic.

He was alone.

And scared, especially now with the military in charge. He knew it was only a matter of time before he'd be rounded up. This was the Holocaust all over again. He found it ironic since so many of his fellow Muslims were Holocaust deniers, even he when he was younger calling it a hoax perpetrated by the Zionist infidel to justify their occupation of the Holy Lands, but when he had moved to America he had seen enough proof to realize it had actually happened.

And with the fury in the streets of his adopted homeland, he wondered if roundups were merely the beginning. Muslims were dying left, right and center and nobody seemed to care. He had already ordered his wife and children to stay at home and not open the door to anyone who wasn't Muslim, nor to go outside for any reason. Fortunately they had good neighbors who knew them and were not Muslim who were providing them with groceries to keep them fed. One family had even offered to let them stay with them to be safe.

It had warmed his heart as he realized not all were buying into the insanity that all Muslims were evil killers.

His wife had begged him not to go to work, but he had insisted, fearing that should he not report it might be suspicious, but it was the most terrifying decision he made every morning, and now with General Thorne taking to the airwaves every few hours announcing more and more restrictions, he was certain he had made the wrong choice.

"Fadi Hosein, please report to personnel immediately."

The announcements had been coming all morning, starting with a friend of his whose last name was Abdullah. And now they were up to 'H'. And every name announced sounded foreign. A few Middle Eastern Christians had returned from these calls along with one Muslim who had looked at him with the first expression of pure terror he had ever seen in person. The only other time he had seen terror like that was on the poor Iraqi Yazidi girl's face inside the evacuation helicopter that CNN had covered.

That was genuine fear.

He had felt it in his homeland, Assad's troops none too friendly to his Sunni village, but the fear in her eyes had brought tears to his.

And when his friend had walked by he had almost vomited, the fear quickly shared.

He knew his name could be next.

And it terrified him to his core.

He rose, locking his computer, then walked out of the cubicle jungle and into the hallway. He casually made his way to the bathroom, relieved himself, then performed his required ablutions. Taking a deep breath he stepped back into the hall and walked with purpose toward the employee entrance and the outer parking lot where his car was.

He smiled at the guards, waving his pass over the scanner, relieved to see a green light appear, then went through the bullet proof glass doors and out into the midday sun. Its warmth was welcome, the cold stares he had encountered in the few minutes away from his desk disturbing.

182

As the doors closed behind him the PA sounded again and he could just make out his name being called.

His heart nearly froze in his chest, the world slowly closing in around him. He willed himself forward, his Ford Fiesta within sight.

"If you want to fit in, buy American!"

It was something one of his friends had told him when he first arrived in America. It was good advice that he had never regretted following, choosing Ford from the beginning, never deviating. He pressed the button on his fob and the doors unlocked as he heard shouts behind him. He resisted the urge to look as someone yelled, "Hey, you! Stop!"

Climbing into his car he started the engine and pulled out, ignoring the seatbelt warning light as he put the car into drive and hit the gas. His rearview mirror was filled with half a dozen uniformed Secret Service officers chasing him and he began to cry, the tears rolling down his cheeks as he realized his life as he knew it was over, his job about to be taken away from him, his livelihood gone, his family destroyed.

All because of his religion.

And he felt a hint of guilt, a hint of the wheel coming around as he had remained silent during all the years of terror his religion had inflicted on the religious minorities of Asia and Africa, and suddenly he knew how it must feel to be a Jew surrounded by millions of people who wanted you dead.

And he vowed if he survived this to be a beacon of change.

He considered himself a moderate, part of the silent majority of Muslims in the West who wanted to live in peace, even talking at times with his friends, also moderates, that Islam needed its own Reformation, its own Enlightenment, otherwise the world was doomed to eternal war, a war which he couldn't see any side winning.

Islam needed its own Martin Luther, its own Francis Bacon.

He had no idea how it could happen though, what with there being no overarching leader within Islam. Catholicism had the Pope, and most if not all Christian offshoots had a hierarchy with an ultimate leader at the head of each Church.

But not Islam. Anyone could declare themselves an Imam; it was only limited by how many followers you could garner.

And now as he drove toward the main gate, his foot getting heavier and heavier on the gas pedal, the guards still chasing him, he realized that he had committed to a course of action there was no returning from, and as tears of self-pity flowed down his cheeks he couldn't help but wonder if his new country, in its panic, had done the same thing.

Two armed guards with submachine guns took up position in front of him as he approached the gate and he felt his heart slam against his chest, the palpitations of adrenaline fueled panic overwhelming any reason he might have.

Then he looked at the photo of his family stuck to the dash.

And he slammed on his brakes.

He was immediately surrounded, guns pointed at his head as his shaking hands turned off the car then unlocked the doors. Hands reached in, hauling him out and onto the pavement, and as he looked up at one of the guards, pleading for forgiveness, he was hit in the head with the butt of a rifle, the world quickly fading to black as he thanked Allah for giving him the strength to persevere, if only for a few more hours.

Entering US Airspace, off the coast of California

Lee Fang yawned then stretched like a Cheshire cat. She opened her eyes, sitting up quickly as she realized she had no idea where she was.

A plane?

Dylan Kane sat across from her, grinning. "Sleep well?"

She nodded and instantly regretted it, her head throbbing in protest. He motioned toward where her hand was gingerly touching.

"You took quite the blow to the head. You've been out for hours."

She looked around, careful not to turn her head too quickly. "Where are we?"

"Rendition flight, arranged by a buddy of mine. I've got some people we can trust meeting us so we should be okay."

"What's been happening?"

"You wouldn't believe it if I told you." He pointed at his laptop perched on the table between them, the Gulfstream V Turbo they were on clearly set up for comfort rather than utility. She had never seen such opulence in an airplane.

And this is a CIA plane?

She had heard of Rendition Flights before. They were a standard way governments exchanged prisoners and were legal. The problem was most governments also had Extraordinary Rendition Flights, which were illegal under international law. They were used to transport the worst of the worst in the war against terror and were silently tolerated by necessary ports of call. Guantanamo Bay at its peak held a large contingent of prisoners brought in on planes like these.

And now here she was, a pariah in her own homeland, wanted for treason by her former colleagues, heading into an America that wanted to return her to stand trial, in the company of a man who was so casual yet capable, she didn't know what to make of him.

But so far he had kept his word.

But for how long?

He spun the laptop. "General Thorne has issued a list of decrees that are being broadcast on every station in the United States."

"You don't look happy."

Kane shook his head. "We've lost our country and the people don't even know it." He motioned at the screen. "He's declared a dusk-to-dawn curfew. Violators will be arrested, and if found outside without a valid reason, imprisoned without trial. All Muslim non-citizens are to report to repatriation centers across the country. Military transports will take them to Turkey which has agreed to act as middleman—under some sort of threat, I'm sure."

"That's horrible! Most of those people are innocent."

"The vast majority are. But whoever is behind this has created panic. Polling is showing these decrees are hugely popular. And get this, all Muslims have been ordered to report to their place of worship by the end of today, where they will be locked down and compared to membership rolls. All properly identified will then be moved into school and university campus facilities under guard. Those not identified will be deported, and those missing will have warrants issued for their arrest." Kane looked at Fang. "Thorne wants every Muslim in the United States either deported or behind bars. It's incredible!"

"How many Muslims are there in your country?"

Kane shook his head. "That's not my country anymore." He sighed. "There's almost three million Muslims. I don't know how he plans on doing it in any civilized manner. When we interned the Japanese during World War Two there were barely one hundred thousand of them. We're talking thirty times that. There's only one time in history where this many have been gathered up."

"The Holocaust."

Kane froze as if the word had hit him in the stomach, hard. He looked at Fang. "For the first time in my life I'm ashamed to be an American."

Fang reached forward, placing a hand on his knee, it her turn to provide him the comfort he apparently needed so badly. "Remember, you said this wasn't your country anymore, so anything it does isn't American. Your people are scared and scared people look for leaders. That's how throughout history tyrants came to power. Now the question is whether or not this General Thorne is that tyrant, or is he just a patsy here, thinking he's doing the right thing, but behind the scenes someone else is pulling the strings."

Kane pursed his lips, patting her hand, his eyes travelling up her chiseled arm.

Fang found her heart begin to race as she was looked at as a woman for the first time in so long. She worked in a male dominated job and tried to minimize her female appearance as much as she could, meaning she usually made herself look like a man. But today, though she didn't feel like she was dressed in any way appealing, this man, this man who was so not her type, was appreciating her sexually.

And it excited her.

Maybe you've never liked white guys because they've always been the enemy?

She had to admit most of her ops were in Asia, and most of the Caucasian men she had met were Russian, and they were definitely different from Americans and other Europeans. There was a misunderstanding in the Western world that Russians were like Western Europeans. They weren't. Not at all. Much of their population lived east of the Urals, meaning they lived in Asia. Though the bulk of their population lived in geographic

Europe, and many liked to think of themselves like other Europeans, their value systems were more oriental than Western. Eurasian is how Fang would describe them, and in their briefings when dealing with Russians, they were specifically taught that these men, though Caucasian in appearance, were not like those from Western Europe and the Anglosphere they were so used to dealing with.

They couldn't be trusted.

She had thought it quite Muslim at the time. The Quran specifically states it is not permitted to lie to another Muslim except to smooth over differences, but it is perfectly acceptable to lie to the infidel—the other six billion people on the planet—to further the cause of Islam or an individual Muslim, so as to defeat the infidel. This practice extended to business dealings as well as personal relationships. In fact, the Quran also directed Muslims to not take non-believers as friends unless it is to guard themselves from them. It made her question how any true Muslim could claim to be a friend with a Christian. If they were indeed following the Quran, did it not mean they weren't truly friends, merely covers so they could try to fit into a foreign society until the day the Caliphate was restored?

She thought of all the Muslim problems her own country was quietly having, she herself fighting many battles in the western provinces to subdue ever more frequent uprisings. She couldn't understand how all the other cultures that made up China could live together in peace, but this one culture just couldn't.

Perhaps it was because it was the only culture governed by a religious text that demanded they didn't.

The world was insane.

Now here she was, alone in an aircraft with a man who was supposed to be her enemy, who was so different from any man she had ever met, that she found herself confused.

And tingling.

She felt his hand on hers, the warmth comforting, shivers racing up her spine as she caught her breath, her body giving into the sexual attraction, her mind fighting it. The only times she had been in a sexual situation with a Caucasian had been on the job, and she had been revolted every time, but not today, not here.

It's been so long.

She couldn't remember the last time she had felt a man's lips against hers, flesh pressed against sweaty flesh, the feeling of a lover inside her, filling her as the troubles of the world were forgotten if just for a brief moment. What she would give right now to have that feeling once again, perhaps one last time, her future so uncertain, for even if she were to survive the next few days, her life would be that of a recluse, keeping a low profile, avoiding the public.

And never having a relationship again out of fear of being recognized and her partner being used against her.

She pulled her hand back, looking away from Kane who had a slight smile on his face. Not one indicating he found her momentary lapse amusing, simply that he seemed to understand her loneliness, and she knew if she jumped him right then and there he would be receptive.

"What's the plan?" she asked, trying to push the lust from her mind.

"I reached Langley, people I trust, and they arranged this flight. When we land we'll be met by more people I trust. Unfortunately with the coup having already taken place, I'm not sure yet what we can do. Being Stateside however at least gets me into the thick of things. My people think the epicenter of this is at Fort Myer in DC. We'll—"

The cockpit door opened and the co-pilot walked briskly toward them, Fang not liking the look on his face. "We've got trouble," said the man, pointing out the window.

189

Fang looked through one of the small portholes and gasped. Two F-22 Raptors were on their wing. Her head spun and she saw two more on the other side.

"They're demanding we follow them in. Some private airstrip." He handed Kane a piece of paper. "You better let your people know." He returned to the cockpit, the door closing with a bang.

Kane frowned as he pulled out his phone. "They obviously know we're on board."

"But how?"

"My guess is we've got a mole somewhere."

"Inside the CIA?"

"I think the entire country's been compromised in one way or other."

"So we can't trust anyone." Fang felt her heart sink as her chest tightened.

"No, I wouldn't say that."

Operations Center 3, CIA Headquarters, Langley, Virginia

An alarm blared nearly causing Leroux to piss his pants. He was so on edge with everything going on he wasn't sure how much more he could take. He was just an analyst, an analyst thrust into a supervisory position without his consent, with a girlfriend being tortured by citizens of his own country, possibly his own military, with his best and only friend being pursued by the same rogue elements.

Only they weren't rogue anymore. They were in charge of the country, or at least that was his theory. He wasn't sure if General Thorne was involved. All they knew was that the President's assassin had nodded toward stairs that General Thorne was standing on, but other than that they had no evidence he was behind anything. He was so high in the ranks before becoming the top dog that you'd be hard pressed to find a soldier in the Army that hadn't served directly under him at one time or another, so the fact Colonel Booker had reported to him meant little.

Was Booker and his team orchestrating events for their own perceived greater good, with General Thorne merely the unintended beneficiary? Had martial law been the endgame all along? If so, and they were indeed behind the attacks, they had orchestrated it beautifully.

With military precision.

But was Thorne involved? Leroux was certain either he or his aide were, and it wouldn't be the first time in history the man pulling the strings was an underling.

"What if the nod was a blind?"

He blurted it out loud, Morrison staring at him as he held his phone to his head to find out why the sirens were sounding. He snapped his fingers at Leroux, pointing up. Leroux looked at Dillard who nodded, the sirens silenced within moments, their dull drone still audible on the other side of the nearly soundproofed room.

"What was that?" asked Morrison, finally able to hear. "You're kidding me!" He hung up his phone. "The military is surrounding this facility. They claim it's a security measure but I think we know that's bullshit."

Leroux felt faint. "They've discovered the tap."

"That's my guess." Morrison headed for the door. "Download everything you need, wipe all record of what you've been doing, then follow me."

A flurry of keyboard activity was quickly followed by chairs kicked out as Leroux's team jumped to their feet, grabbing what few personal belongings they had with them. Leroux initiated a wipe protocol, a countdown appearing on the displays showing less than two minutes to expected completion.

Morrison marched down the hallway, Leroux bringing up the rear, making sure none of his people were left behind. As they approached the elevators Leroux couldn't believe his eyes. This wasn't the CIA. This was mass panic. It was clear nobody was certain what to do. The military was surrounding the facility, that Leroux had caught several glimpses of from windows as they passed and several security feeds being shown on television screens. But the scary fact was that it was all legal under the new laws, or lack thereof.

The military was in charge. They could very well be here to secure the CIA from attack.

Or it could all be bullshit and they were here to stop the CIA from performing its illegal investigation.

His illegal investigation.

But then again what was illegal now? With the Constitution suspended, none of what he had done was illegal. However hacking a military network was probably considered treason, the penalty for which he had no doubt was death.

Morrison ordered an elevator cleared and jammed the team plus himself inside, hitting a button for the lower levels, the doors closing. As soon as they were sealed inside he swiped his security pass then entered a code, using the numbers of the elevator's operating panel as a keypad.

The lights changed from a bright white to a reddish hue as the elevator descended past the lowest level and continued, much to the shock of all those aboard. Leroux had heard rumors of a nuclear bunker below Langley but had never actually seen any evidence of it. It was simply a joke, he thought, something the guys left over from the Cold War would mention from time-to-time with a wink.

They should put the rookies in the bunker for a couple of weeks, see what it was like in the old days.

It had been overheard in his first week on the job in the cafeteria lineup. Several laughs had been the reward, all by silver haired men loading up on low-cholesterol greens.

He hadn't paid it any mind, merely smiling awkwardly at the cashier who seemed to know exactly what the inside joke meant.

The doors opened and Morrison led them out. Four armed guards were there to greet them, Morrison swiping his card and placing his hand on a scanner. Doors on the opposite wall slid open. It was then that Leroux noticed the gun ports on either side, what looked like 50 caliber barrels trained on them. Morrison looked at the guard in charge.

"Code Tango Red."

The man's eyes bulged and he nodded. "Yes, sir." The four guards immediately stepped into the elevator as Leroux's team cleared the large metal doors that had opened with Morrison's palm print. More guards were inside, readying weapons.

Leroux caught up to Morrison. "Sir, what's going on?"

"This is 'The Bunker'. I assume you've heard of it?"

Leroux nodded. "I thought it was just a joke."

Morrison shook his head as they continued down a hallway, past door upon door. "It was built during the Cold War to survive a nuclear attack. The guards will secure the elevator so that no one else can come down here using it, and should they manage to make it down the elevator shaft, there's no way they're getting through those doors without some heavy duty equipment," he said, jerking his thumb over his shoulder.

"What are all these rooms?"

"Sleeping quarters, cafeteria, entertainment, supplies, bathrooms. Everything we'll need to hunker down for months, or longer considering our small size."

"But what about the others?"

"This isn't a nuclear war. They'll be safe as long as they don't resist the regime change."

Morrison swiped his card on a panel, the door flanked by two armed guards. A large, ultra-modern operations center was revealed. Morrison stopped the herd.

"People, once we pass through these doors, there's no coming out. We will be in lockdown. Nobody from the outside can open them." He paused. "I trust all of you because I know all of you. We must trust in each other. This will be difficult, this will be challenging, this will be frustrating. Just remember that what we do here today is for our country. We may be the only people who know the truth about what is going on. It is up to us to find the proof then present it to the American people so they can do the right thing and take back their country."

He paused, his stare moving from one to the next, finally resting on a terrified Leroux.

DEATH TO AMERICA

"This is a coup d'état people. It's up to us to save our country."

Redding Jet Center, Redding, California

"Yup, we've got company."

It was déjà vu all over again as Kane watched three SUV's roll up to the plane as it finished taxying, the small private airstrip they had been ordered to not in any way associated with the government as far as Kane could see.

This is completely off the books, even in our 'new' USA.

It made him wonder what was truly going on. If the military was in complete control, then why hide the fact they were arresting them? Why not just order them to a military airbase where they would be assured of full control? Were there two elements at play here? Or three if the terrorist attacks truly weren't part of the scheme to gain power? He would like to dismiss the third element but couldn't with one hundred percent certainty. All he knew for certain was that the America he had been born into no longer existed and he was determined to take it back.

There was no doubt there was one element at play regardless of who was the source of the terrorist attacks. Someone had stolen an F-35, someone had made a deal with the Chinese, a deal that made the Chinese bold enough to attack an American nuclear submarine, and coincidentally halt the pursuit the moment martial law had been declared. It was also a deal that was long term, it taking time to invade and secure Mongolia, Taiwan and the South China Sea.

Whoever had made that deal had no intention of handing power back to civilian authority.

They were in this for the long term.

And now it was up to him to figure out who *they* were.

But first he'd have to deal with their operatives.

He snapped the clip from his pen, sticking it between his teeth and cheek, then stuffed the pen into a seat-back pouch. The door was opened by the co-pilot who stood back as two men boarded, weapons drawn.

There were no introductions this time.

Eight more men greeted them as they descended the steps to the tarmac, it not worth the effort to try and kill them all now—they might just have a chance of subduing him and Fang. Instead he'd have to reduce the numbers and improve the odds. The first was by getting into a vehicle, immediately reducing the numbers by however many didn't join them.

As he expected, metal handcuffs were clasped around their wrists, these men apparently learning from the deadly encounter their colleagues in Korea had enjoyed. Zipties were simply a joke for anything beyond crowd control. Any seriously trained individual could escape them in seconds, but metal handcuffs were different. They required a tool.

His tongue flicked over the clip in his mouth.

They were placed in the back of one of the SUV's, the scene playing out as almost a mirror image of Korea. Four men in the lead and trailing vehicles, a driver and passenger in their vehicle.

They're following the manual a little too rigidly.

If it were him, especially after what had happened in Korea, he would have split them up into two vehicles, put a man in the backseat with him, and definitely clasped his hands in front where they could be seen.

The convoy got underway and Kane turned to Fang. "One last kiss, darling?" Before she could react he leaned in and placed an open mouth kiss on her that he could tell shocked her at first, but when she seemed to get into it, he found his own sense of arousal make its presence known.

He shoved the clip in her mouth, her eyes popping open wide as she realized what the purpose of the kiss was.

"Settle down back there!"

Kane broke the kiss, turning forward. "Sorry, boss, I couldn't resist."

He turned slightly, feigning looking out his window, cupping his hands behind him. "Look at that. Beautiful country."

Fang leaned forward. "Hopefully I'll get to see it someday." Her breath was hot on the back of his neck, and as she returned to her position, he felt the clip drop into his hand. He straightened himself.

"You will. I'm sure this is all just a misunderstanding."

He jammed the clip into the teeth of the cuffs, wiggling it in past each tooth. Suddenly one wrist was freed and he quickly moved on to the other, it too open within seconds.

He slipped the clip to Fang who he hoped would be as adept at picking handcuffs as he was.

She nodded to him within seconds.

Perhaps better than me.

Something streaked from a field to their right, a plume of smoke Kane would recognize anywhere.

A rocket, most likely from a Shoulder-launched Multipurpose Assault Weapon.

He shoved Fang down as he ducked himself, keeping just high enough to see the lead vehicle take a hit to the rear, the explosion igniting the gas tank, launching the ass end of the SUV into the air, flipping it end over end. Kane whipped around as a second explosion erupted behind them, the tail car taking a hit through the driver side window, the warhead detonating inside.

Poor bastards.

Their driver slammed his brakes on as he tried to avoid the wreckage in front of him, swerving to the left then beginning to accelerate. The windshield suddenly shattered, a hole punched through the safety glass as the passenger's head disintegrated.

"Holy shit!" cried the driver as he began to swerve, his zigzag pattern obviously aimed at making him a harder target, but if Kane knew the sniper involved, it wouldn't help.

It didn't.

Another burst of blood and brain matter sprayed through the car. Kane leapt forward and put the car in neutral, letting the speed ease off as he held the steering wheel steady, then shoved the car in park with a jerk.

He opened the door slowly, looking for shooters, but saw no one. Stepping out, he held his hands up, smoke from the two flaming vehicles obscuring his view. He squinted, peering through the smoke as he saw several figures approaching.

He smiled when the lead figure emerged, an MP5 aimed directly at his chest.

"Hey, BD, 'bout time you showed up."

Command Sergeant Major Burt "Big Dog" Dawson, leader of the Delta Force's Bravo Team, strode forward, relaxing slightly as he cradled his weapon in his arms, the rest of the team spreading out, securing the area.

"Good to see you too. Next time you change the meeting location, give us a little more warning if you want prompt pick up."

Kane grinned, holding out a hand and helping Fang out of the SUV. "May I present Major Lee Fang of the People's Liberation Army. I believe you two have already met?"

Dawson nodded. "Good to see you again, Major."

"And you too, Sergeant Major. I wish it were under better circumstances."

"As do I. Our country's gone to shit, and whoever's behind it has to be brought down. I understand you've got some intel on that."

Four vehicles pulled up, all civilian, none of them black SUV's. But they were all large with luggage space and horsepower. Dawson pointed at a

Chevy Impala. Kane and Fang climbed in the rear, Dawson in the passenger seat, a grinning Sergeant Carl "Niner" Sung driving.

"Hiya Dylan, long time no see. I'd welcome you home, but I don't think that exists anymore."

"Good to see you too, Niner. Sit rep?"

Niner put the car in gear and they were quickly rolling north, the other vehicles keeping a good distance, splitting off in different directions as Dawson explained the situation. "The Colonel put us all on leave as soon as he heard the decree, *suggesting* we needed to get to the bottom of things, so we just went on vacation. A lot of Delta did as did the SEALS and Rangers, most of Spec Ops. We're not crowd control, we're killers. Rounding up civilians and setting up road blocks is not our job. Besides, a lot of us on the boards weren't so sure of what was going on, it all sounded a little too fishy. Then when I heard from you I knew we'd all been had. I've put the word out quietly, but you just don't know who you can trust." He shook his head. "If the shit hits the fan we'll have help, but it might take time to arrive. Things are moving fast though. Roadblocks are going up everywhere, anybody who even looks Muslim is being rounded up, sorted out later. The news stations have all been assigned Press Officers to monitor the broadcasts so that 'intelligence' isn't 'accidentally' leaked. Word is the Fifth Estate isn't too pleased."

Niner looked in the rearview mirror. "All that means is we don't get fifty-five minutes an hour of commentary disguised as news anymore."

"Well, there were bound to be some improvements," said Kane. "These roadblocks have me concerned. We're wanted fugitives."

"We're going to make a run for the border."

Kane pointed at the sun. "You're going the wrong way."

"Not Taco Bell dude, Tim Hortons!" said Niner, pointing at the GPS. "We're goin' to Canada, eh!"

Kane's eyebrows rose. "Canada?"

"Getting across the border should be easy since most of it is unguarded and the Canadians have taken a pretty cautious tone with everything that's been going on. Frankly I think they're terrified this new government might just turn its eyes north if they say anything."

"Makes sense. Straight shot across Canada and back down into Washington."

"Assuming that's where this is all centered."

Kane nodded. "That's what we're assuming, but I've got some good people who just might be able to confirm it for us."

"The Bunker", Under CIA Headquarters, Langley, Virginia

They were under complete lockdown. There were eight armed guards on the other side of the thick steel doors with no relief on the way. Leroux presumed they would begin shifts like the eleven of them were already doing.

"Hunker down for the long haul," were Morrison's orders.

Leroux had sent Dillard and four of his team, along with the Op Center Coordinator Alice Michaels to quarters, Leroux to act as Coordinator and Morrison Control for now. It had been almost eighteen hours since the lockdown with no evidence anyone knew they were there. According to Morrison almost no one actually knew where The Bunker was located, nor how to get into it. And his orders to go deep had come from the top.

They had everything they would need to survive long term including dozens of hard lines dug deep underground decades ago, upgraded about five years ago by private contractors who had been brought in blind, not knowing where they were doing the work, with no plans leaving the building.

Which meant they had access to everything.

CNN and Fox, along with the BBC were on three displays to the left, the press still performing their function, though with a hint of fear except for the BBC which were unabashedly leading all their broadcasts with "Crisis in America".

The Internet was abuzz with chatter, the conspiracy theorists mostly getting it right this time and websites rapidly being taken down that suggested anything untoward.

But it was pirate footage of the roundups that was the most heartbreaking, along with the zealous nature in which some of his fellow citizens were participating. Homes and apartment doors across the nation were being tagged with a scarlet 'M' if the occupants were suspected of being Muslim. News report after news report showed Arab Christians and Jews crying on the air, terrified they were going to be targeted because of their appearance.

It made him sick.

There had been more terrorist attacks of course, with General Thorne taking to the airwaves suggesting it would take time as there were millions of Muslims to round up. CNN had shown footage earlier of military bases across the country loading hundreds of deportees at a time, the flights heading for Turkey.

No one had yet to see footage of their arrival there.

God I hope they're not just tossing them out over the ocean.

He refused to believe that possible. These were still American soldiers, men and women who had honor, who had a code, and who were just following what were lawful orders. From what he had seen the roundups were always conducted with discipline, but some pirate footage was showing private security also participating.

And they seemed out of control.

They had analyzed the assassination footage and they felt they had the proof that the Secret Service Agent had pulled the trigger. They had the President's dying last words enhanced and they had the nod which proved nothing. All they could prove was that Stan Reese was not the real shooter, he was simply a patsy set-up like all the others. He had apparently been forced to steal a plastic gun at a gun show the day before, stayed at a hotel in the area, sent a package to a catering company that presumably contained the weapon, and that weapon had somehow made it into the White House.

And his parents had been found dead hours after the shooting.

Other than these few facts they could prove nothing except that CIA Special Agent Sherrie White was being tortured and imprisoned on a US Military Facility by Colonel Booker, and that a once thought dead soldier was still walking, having delivered an F-35 to the Chinese.

There was nothing they had to connect the dots.

Leroux had tapped into the government's own backbone analysis tools that DARPA used to monitor the health of the Internet and he was running an analysis now that was quickly filtering out civilian traffic. He pointed at the screen.

"Are you seeing what I'm seeing?" he asked to no one in particular.

"Washington is the hub?" suggested one of his team.

"Yes, but that's to be expected. Watch." Lines connecting Internet hubs across the country were rapidly disappearing and changing colors. His trained eye watched as the civilian traffic almost faded away leaving only the government and military traffic. "Now eliminate the civilian government traffic."

Databases of Internet Protocol addresses known to be government were immediately accessed to begin filtering them out and soon they were left with a honeycomb of lines with the epicenters of activity in Washington, DC, again, exactly as expected.

"Zoom in on Washington."

The display enlarged the DC area and Leroux smiled.

"There it is."

"What am I looking at?" asked Morrison.

Leroux approached the screen, pointing at a massive amount of lines in bright white, indicating heavy bandwidth usage. "That's the Pentagon. As you'd expect, the vast majority of military traffic should be from them." He looked back at Sonya Tong, a promising young analyst that Leroux could see going far one day. "Zoom back out and highlight the military HQ's."

The display zoomed back out, red circles appearing around smaller white clusters of lines. "These are the HQ's for the various commands. They're getting their orders from the Pentagon then disseminating them to their bases and assets around the country and world."

"As expected," said Morrison.

"Exactly." Leroux pointed at Washington. "Zoom in again, highlight Fort Myer."

The display quickly changed, a red circle appearing around another bright white cluster.

"See?"

"I see a bunch of white lines. What the hell am I looking at?"

"Sir, why would a small installation like Fort Myer, that has almost no command authority, be lit up like a Christmas tree? They're generating a shitload more traffic than they should be."

"So you're saying this is where they're running things from?"

"That's my guess. And with them holding Sherrie, it has to be. There's no possible reason that I can think of for them to be generating that much traffic."

"But how do we take out Fort Myer?" asked Tong.

"We don't," replied Morrison. "We can't." He looked at Leroux. "Is there any way to get back into their systems?"

"Already done," said Leroux, returning to his station to confirm the status with a few keystrokes. "My backup tap dialed home twelve hours after it detected the primary was shutdown. There's no evidence they know it's there, but I've left it alone until we really need it."

"Good. Who here is a YouTube expert?"

Tong raised her hand. "I've got a channel."

Morrison's eyes narrowed, Leroux noticing he was already out of his depth. "What do you usually post?" he asked.

"Movie reviews."

"Followers?"

"A few thousand."

Leroux turned to Morrison. "I assume you're suggesting we get what we know out on the web?"

"Yes, but not yet. Is a few thousand enough?"

"It is if it's juicy enough," replied Tong. "My followers will share it with their followers. It could hit millions of views within minutes if we're lucky, days if we're not."

"Or never if people are too scared to share." Leroux shook his head. "And they could just shut it down."

Morrison nodded. "They could, but if enough people see it, then it could go viral, especially outside of the United States. This is the information age and information is hard to control once it's out there." He pointed at Tong. "Start putting together the footage we've gathered, along with bullet points of the intel. I want a video ready to go out as soon as possible, just in case. And I want you to brainstorm ideas for pushing the message out wider."

"Yes, sir!"

"Sir, I've got an incoming call from Special Agent Kane."

Both Morrison and Leroux turned to look at Marc Therrien, another senior analyst on Leroux's team who was a good fifteen years his senior. "Put it on speaker," they echoed, Leroux immediately bowing out slightly as Morrison smiled.

"Yes, sirs." Therrien hit a few keys then nodded.

"Dylan, this is Morrison. Status?"

"We ran into a little roadblock, sir, but a few friends managed to help us out."

"Friends?"

"Let's just say the next time you see them you'll want to shout 'Bravo' for their good work."

Morrison chuckled as Leroux grinned. If Delta Team-Bravo was with Kane, they just might stand a chance, it no longer one lone agent fighting the conspirators.

It's still only a dozen people.

His momentary sense of optimism quickly failed.

"Are you secure?" asked Morrison.

"For the moment. Have we confirmed who's behind this yet?"

Morrison nodded to Leroux, who took over. "Right now it looks like things are centered out of Fort Myer in the DC area."

"Same place Sherrie went? I'm familiar with it, it's kind of minor. Are you sure?"

"We can't be sure about anything, but there's a lot of unusual Internet traffic coming from there, and that *is* where they're holding Sherrie."

"Sounds as good a place as any to start. My friends and I are going to try and get into Canada, shoot across the north then reenter on the east coast. It should allow us to avoid the roadblocks."

Morrison raised a finger before Leroux could respond. "Sounds good, but don't count on the border being respected. According to the Canadian news reports there's already been several incidents of border incursions while pursuing suspects."

"Lovely. We'll keep our heads down. Anything else we need to know?"

"We've got a worm in their system, or whatever the hell you kids call it, so we have access to their feeds if you need them. Intel though says Fort Myer has been reinforced. How many troops, I don't know. My guess is they want to keep a low profile."

"Who's heading this?"

Leroux jumped in. "Colonel Booker, your dead guy's former commanding officer, seems to be in charge of the base, General Thorne at the White House."

"We don't know if Thorne is involved, or just a patsy. We're leaning toward involved, but we can't be certain," added Morrison.

"Why the uncertainty?"

"The assassin nodded to someone on the stairs but it could have been at Thorne or his aide. We're just not sure."

"Okay, let's deal with Booker first and see if we can shut down their command and control. There's just a few of us right now, but I've got it on good authority from my friends here that there is a lot more support available should we need it. It will just be a matter of getting the word out."

Morrison nodded toward Tong. "We're working on that right now. Contact us should you need anything."

"Will do, Chief. And Chris?"

"Yeah?"

"Any message for Sherrie when we rescue her?"

Leroux felt a lump form in his throat. "Yeah, tell her I'm sorry for sending her on that op."

"Bullshit! Chief, you straighten him out on that. I'll just tell her you love her and that you said to give me a big sloppy kiss that I'd pass on."

Leroux actually felt a flash of jealousy for a moment, but Kane's laughter pushed it away immediately. "Careful, she's been teaching me some moves."

"I'll bet she has. Kane out!"

The line went dead as giggles were stifled around the room, Tong having the hardest time of it. Leroux was pretty sure she had a secret crush on him, but he couldn't be sure. He was so awkward with women she might be gay for all he knew.

All he knew was he didn't care one way or the other.

He was a one woman man, and Sherrie was all he could ever want.

Please Dylan, save her!

Command Center, Fort Myer, Arlington, Virginia

"How the hell did that happen?"

Colonel Booker was red, he could feel it. His cheeks burned with rage as his blood pressure, already dangerously high according to his doctor, surged. If there was one thing he couldn't abide by it was failure. Especially failure three times in a row. The first time he could excuse, it was the Chinese who had failed to recover their operative who had possibly overheard a conversation she shouldn't have. But when his people had found out about the helicopter pickup from the USS Columbia there should have been no problem recovering the Chinese woman and her CIA escort.

But they had escaped.

Fortunately for the men who had failed, they had all died. It saved him from killing them.

But this time, on American soil, they had escaped again.

"They had help, sir. There was serious firepower used here, sir. Sniper rifles and shoulder-launched weapons of some type. Our guys didn't stand a chance."

"Survivors?"

"None."

Booker snapped his fingers. "See if we have any satellite coverage of that area. They didn't leave on foot."

"Yes, sir."

One of his techs expertly brought up footage and soon they were looking at shots showing the attack in progress, two cars in flames, several figures advancing on the middle vehicle.

"Anything else?"

"Look at this, sir."

The image changed and four vehicles were shown farther down the road.

"Can you get plates on those?"

"Give me a moment, sir."

The view changed, a shot from a different angle appearing, it clear this was from when the satellite's orbit took it farther away, but with the view no longer top down the tech was quickly zooming in and enhancing the plates.

He turned with a smile as the four plates appeared on a large screen in front of them.

"Got them, sir."

"Good. Trace them. I want to know who they belong to, where they came from, and where they went. Whoever did this are traitors to their country and must be stopped."

Booker spun on his heel and headed toward the prisoner's cell. They had identified her as CIA Agent Sherrie White, apparently only on the job for a couple of years. He felt almost insulted that they'd send a junior agent to investigate him, but all it meant was that the CIA had no damned clue at the time what they had stumbled upon. But now they knew. Their tap had been discovered and according to what his techs could pull, they had been accessing footage of the interrogations as well as the entire facility.

He had managed to nip it in the bud with the isolation of Langley, all communications cut or jammed, but who had been responsible inside was unknown. But he had a hunch. According to Homeland Security files a CIA Senior Analyst named Chris Leroux was living at the same address on file for White.

He doubted they were just roommates.

Which meant he now had leverage over her.

He felt no guilt in what he was doing. What was happening was necessary. 'A necessary evil' he had called it. The country had gone astray, blinded to the enemy within by political correctness gone mad. Islam was the greatest threat to the world today and America had to purge itself before it was too late. Europe was already in crisis with murders being committed by crazed fundamentalists and they were powerless to stop the spread. Muslims had more children than Westerners and it would just be a matter of time before they outnumbered those that had fought for generations to build the freest societies history had ever known.

And he'd be damned if he let that all fall apart because some whacko civil rights activists thought discriminating against one religion was "not nice". The fact was Islam wasn't compatible with any other religion on the face of the Earth. It was the only religion that demanded it be the ultimate religion, dominant over all others. It actively encouraged forced conversion and murder of the non-believers.

Not a single other religion on Earth advocated that.

The Judeo-Christian values Western societies were based upon were fundamentally incompatible with those of Islam, which most of the West didn't realize was much more than a religion. It was also the framework for law and governance. Sharia Law was integral to Islam. There was no Islam without Sharia Law, as there was no Sharia Law without Islam. And with the Koran and the approved follow-on interpretations of its teachings advocating the creation of a Caliphate that would rule the world under the flag of Islam, it was a clear and present danger to the United States and all likeminded countries.

He had realized it long before ISIS had come on the scene. He had witnessed it in Iraq, a religion so twisted that they killed each other over a thousand year debate on who should have succeeded Mohammed after he died. Christianity had gone through this as well, but had grown up long ago.

212

Islam showed no sign of ever growing up, and he and the likeminded individuals now fixing the problem were determined to make certain their barbaric ways of thinking wouldn't harm this country.

And when we're successful, Europe will follow.

Political leaders around the world were condemning the actions now underway, but he had it on good authority that the back channels were carefully monitoring the successes and failures, just in case they needed to enact similar measures. Already there was rioting by Muslims in Toronto, London and Paris, with the non-Muslim populations of these cities demanding similar actions, though they had yet to experience the level of terror that had been orchestrated here.

He did feel bad for the victims, but sometimes the spilling of innocent blood was necessary, and every one of those who died did so paying the ultimate price to serve their country. They were patriots, whether they knew it or not. History would be written by the victors, and those "responsible" had already been identified, their arrests and executions for treason to begin in the coming weeks, but not until the scourge had been removed. Enough would "slip through" the cracks to maintain the heightened state of fear that would be necessary for America to remain vigilant, and his group would orchestrate additional attacks should the civilian regime, once it was returned to power, waver in its commitment to keep America safe.

But he was confident the American people, after a few years of feeling safe, would kick out any government that would put them at risk again.

The only question now that the plan had succeeded was how long to hang on to power. It would take years to deport everyone, properly vetting them for terrorist ties, and until that job was done power had to remain with the military. As long as martial law was in place they could proceed—it didn't matter who was at the helm, who was the figurehead. General Thorne was doing a fine job but should he be replaced with someone else, it didn't matter. The plan was being implemented quickly and the public for the moment continued to support the moves, cooperating with the authorities and cheering them as their convoys passed in the streets.

It helped that the attacks had been ratcheted down, "proving" to the public that the policies were working and that some of the guilty were among those already rounded up.

The troops were following their orders, nothing illegal being asked of them. The illegal operations were handled by Raven Defense Services personnel, thousands of them deployed across the country to act on a moment's notice should anything go awry.

And so far the only problem was from Langley, which was temporarily neutralized.

Now he just needed to find out how much they knew, and who knew it.

And Sherrie White's boyfriend, Chris Leroux, would be his means to figuring this out.

US-Canada border, north of Havre, Montana

Dylan Kane scanned the horizon but could see nothing. Civilian air traffic had been almost non-existent for days, most airlines grounding their flights after LAX and LaGuardia were bombed. It was an eerie quiet in the skies, reminiscent of 9/11 when everything was ordered grounded except for military flights. The occasional contrail in the sky belonged to military transports and fighters, but at the moment nothing was near them.

And less than a mile away lay the border with Canada, essentially unguarded.

Security had been stepped up dramatically since 9/11 on this once undefended border, but only because morons, many of them politicians and political appointees, kept operating under the false belief that some or all of the 9/11 terrorists came across the Canadian border. The fact was not a single terrorist involved in those attacks came through Canada. As confirmed by the 9/11 Commission, every single one of them had a valid US Visa when they entered the country, and all entered on flights originating from outside North America. The closest any came to Canada might have been flying over it on their way to JFK or sampling Canadian bacon while drinking alcohol and watching strippers before killing Christians for being infidels that did the same.

Kane had Canadian friends and colleagues and he knew how pissed off they got when they heard these "inaccuracies" as they put it—they were simply too polite to call it was it was—spoken by leading American politicians and commentators.

And he shared those frustrations. People needed to realize that the threat could come from anywhere under the guise of a student or tourist, from anywhere in the world.

Or from within, as he felt the American public had been made to think with recent events.

And now America was no longer America, he and his companions now the villains, the terrorists trying to cross the very border falsely blamed for contributing to the darkest moment in American history.

"Do you see anything?" asked Command Sergeant Major Burt "Big Dog" Dawson as he stood on the runner of their SUV, scanning their surroundings. They had swapped their vehicle for an SUV a few hours ago, a retired Delta Force operator happy to help his comrades. They had a hearty meal, showers, and his wife had insisted their clothes be laundered. Kane was certain Lee Fang was the most appreciative of the taste of civilization.

It had "wasted" two hours but it had been well worth it, the SUV much better than the Impala on the ground they were now covering, roads being avoided. Master Sergeant Mike "Red" Belme's vehicle had already reported road blocks along the entire Canadian border and UAV patrols. They had managed to cross two hours ago by "borrowing" an old Jeep and crossing through some farm fields. The other two teams were already across in a similar manner and were on their way to Ontario to cross the border back into the United States through the Akwesasne Reserve that straddled the border.

They were the last to cross thanks to their layover.

"No, I think we're clear," said Kane. "Let's just hope there aren't any UAV's we can't see."

Dawson nodded. "Agreed."

They climbed back in and Niner put the SUV in gear, slowly pulling toward the border.

"Keep it slow, we don't want to be throwing up too much dust," said Dawson.

"Yes'm," squeaked Niner, the Korean American comedian of the Bravo Team. Kane grinned at Fang who he was pretty sure wasn't certain what to make of Niner, his jokes non-stop during the entire time they had been together.

"Nine o'clock!" she suddenly shouted, pointing out the driver side window. All heads turned as two plumes of dust rose on the dry land. Kane raised his binoculars and looked.

"Border patrol. Punch it Chewie."

Niner did a remarkably good Chewbacca roar as he floored it, their own dust trail blossoming behind them.

"Looks like regular Border patrol, not military," observed Dawson, his head poked out the sunroof. "I doubt they'll pursue across the border."

"Agreed, but they'll definitely be radioing this in."

"Another one to our right," announced Fang.

"Jesus Christ, they're close!" yelled Niner as he stole a glance. He adjusted slightly left, still trying to make a straight run for the border which was less than half a mile away.

"Down!" shouted Dawson as he dropped back inside, Kane throwing his body over Fang, gun shots ringing out, the distinct ping of one finding their target causing them all to curse.

"Not even sixty seconds, BD!"

"They could take us out before that!" yelled Kane.

Dawson took a bead on the nearest vehicle with his MP5. "I'm not shooting guys just doing their job!"

Kane grabbed Niner's MP5 sitting in the rear then rolled his window down. "Hit the brakes on three! Three rounds in each engine block, then hit the gas!"

"Three-two-one-now!" shouted Niner, hitting the brakes, bringing them to a halt in a cloud of dust, the border only a few hundred yards away.

Kane took aim, firing three rapid shots at the first vehicle as he heard Dawson do the same. Two of his shots were true and smoke began to pour from the engine compartment. He repeated the effort on the second vehicle, it swerving after the first shots were fired, his second group taking out the vehicle from the side.

"Go!" he yelled, Niner already revving the engine in neutral. The SUV leapt forward as he put it in Drive and they were soon across the border, three border patrol vehicles left behind them, disabled, with no casualties on either side.

But as Kane watched them through his binoculars, he could see one of them on the radio, calling in their location.

This isn't over yet.

DEATH TO AMERICA

Shore Haven Apartments, Brooklyn, New York

The screeching of tires and slamming of doors had Samir jumping for the window. What he saw below from his eighth floor apartment sent his heart into his throat. Uniformed men, head to toe black with ski masks pulled over their faces were swarming out of several large cube vans, Raven Defense Services emblazoned on the sides.

And the sight of half a dozen school buses arriving crushed any doubt he had as to why they were here.

It was the purge.

Friends he had been corresponding with over the Internet and by phone were telling of large apartment complexes known to have significant Muslim populations being raided by private security. It was happening all over the country in every city in America. Most round ups that were being reported on CNN and other stations showed peaceful searches conducted by local police, but it was the ones that only made the foreign websites that troubled him and those like him.

And now they were here for him and his family.

His wife had begged him to let them go to one of the "Secure Facilities" set up by the Governor but he had refused, calling them Muslim Concentration Camps. His father in Pakistan had laughed at him when he called them that, telling him he was a fool to believe the Jewish pig's false history. Samir had hung up on him, unwilling to listen to the hatred spewed by an uneducated simpleton. He loved his father but his backward beliefs were why they were in the situation they were in today.

Samir considered himself a good Muslim, but his version of good Muslim and that of the radicals were two completely different things. He prayed, but didn't lose any sleep over missing one of the demanded sessions. He attended his mosque once a week, but no more. He felt the Quran was a guidebook, but not law. It wasn't that he felt you could necessarily pick and choose what to obey and what not to obey, it was that he felt it all needed to be put into the context of the time it was written in. The Quran for example had so many references on how to properly go to the bathroom, if they were all followed, one would be using fingers, rocks and shitting in a hole in the ground.

Much of the Quran was a product of its time and he felt could safely be ignored as being such. Including the mistrust of other religions. In the seventh century when Mohammed relayed the teachings of the archangel Gabriel to those who could actually read and write he was the leader of a small tribe, constantly under threat. With religious fervor in his heart, he conquered neighboring tribes, forcing them to submit to his new religion, or die.

Most submitted.

It was this mistrust of his neighbors that Samir felt was what caused the Quran to be so violent and mistrusting of others. And as the Quran continued to be written, more and more of it seemed to be aimed at capitalizing on that mistrust, stirring up a hatred for Jews and Christians so that newly converted Muslim populations would be more likely to turn on Mohammed's enemies, for these populations truly were his enemies. Jews and Christians fought among each other, as they did the Muslims. All were fighting to prove their version of God's word was the only word.

And like the Old Testament referred to the Egyptians and Philistines in manners unbecoming, so did the Quran of its enemies.

The difference was the Jews weren't still trying to kill the Egyptians and Philistines.

Like the Bible, much of the Quran should be treated with an historical context. At least that's how he felt, as did his Imam, considered a great moderate and therefore a target of much hatred among the Wahabists in their community.

But as the Quran painted all non-believers with the same brush, today all Muslims were being treated the same, moderate and fanatic alike.

Someone pounded on his door. His wife yelped, her hand covering her mouth as their son and daughter, neither yet five, clung to her legs, tears rolling down their cheeks, no idea of the reason for their parents' fear, but aware of it nonetheless.

He placed a finger against his lips.

"Samir! It's me, Todd! Open up!"

Samir breathed a sigh of relief. Todd and his family had been providing them with food for the past several days, it too dangerous to leave the house anymore. He opened the door and Todd stood there, motioning for them to come.

"Quickly, before it's too late!"

Doors were open up and down the hallway, neighbors he had known for years looking at each other with fear and confusion. Many were Muslim, many were not, but this a poor building, there were many Asians and Africans here, and far too often they were all labelled as Muslim despite the fact many had fled to America to escape Muslim death squads.

Samir motioned to his wife as he grabbed the two suitcases by the door, packed days ago for just such an event. They rushed out, Samir closing the door behind them, Todd leading them down the hall.

"What the hell do you think you're doing?" asked one large white woman in a nightgown that Samir had never seen her out of. "They're Muslim, ain't they?"

Todd hustled them past her. "So what if they are. You know they've done nothing wrong."

"I want them out of my goddamned country, that's all I know."

Todd stopped and turned, looking at her, then looking at everyone standing in their thresholds. "I'm sure many Germans felt the same way about the Jews when they were being rounded up." He pointed at the woman. "Would you have turned an innocent family in to the Nazis? Or would you have kept your mouth shut?" He raised his voice as he turned. "Do the right thing people! This is America, not Nazi Germany!"

Samir pushed open the door to the stairwell and urged his family through, waving for Todd to stop his political debate no matter how honorable and just it might be.

Todd ran toward him and they took the stairs, two at a time, shouts from several floors down heard as the security sweep began. They climbed two floors and exited to find much of the same on Todd's floor—neighbors looking out the hallway doors, many unsure what to do.

Fortunately Todd's apartment was the first on the left and his wife already had the door open, waiting for them. They hurried inside, Samir hoping few if any saw them.

Todd's wife Sharon ushered them into the master bedroom, their teenage son Jeff already waiting. Several large storage bags, the type Samir had seen on television that you hooked up to a vacuum cleaner to compress them had been moved out from under the queen size bed, it shoved into the corner, the furniture still being hastily rearranged by Jeffrey.

"Get under the bed, as tight into the corner as you can, and for God's sake stay quiet!"

Samir ushered his children then his wife underneath the bed, then quickly shook Todd's hand. "Thank you, my friend."

"Don't thank me. This is payback for when someone did the same for my family seventy years ago in Warsaw."

Samir nodded, immediately understanding, and once again hating his father for his twisted views. He dropped to the ground and scurried into the back corner as the large storage bags were shoved back into place, the bed skirt closing off most of the light.

"Sharon's going to pretend to be asleep so we can put the SoundSpa on. Hopefully that will provide enough background noise to hide any breathing."

They heard the bedsprings move above them then the sounds of waves crashing as the small audio device was turned on. Samir reached into his pocket and pulled his iPhone out, turning on the flashlight app so they could see underneath. Before he did so he made sure a smile was plastered on his face so his kids wouldn't be afraid.

It didn't work.

Everyone looked terrified.

"Now we're going to play a game, okay?"

Both of his children nodded, still scared.

"We're going to play the sleeping game."

"What's that?" asked his daughter.

"It's really easy. Whoever falls asleep first, wins!" They looked puzzled. "Now, just lay your heads down and get comfortable, then close your eyes and picture your favorite place. Then just breathe nice and deep, over and over, and fall asleep. Whoever falls asleep first, wins. But remember, Mommy and Daddy decide the winner, so just because you think you lost, you might not have, so keep trying."

They both nodded and immediately curled into balls, their breathing becoming deeper and more steady as they both tried to win. He looked at his wife who had a slight smile on her face, but said nothing. Laying down himself, there several pillows already positioned for them to be comfortable, his wife joined him.

Their fingers intertwined, her tears flowing, the fear again overwhelming her, he himself fighting the urge with every fiber of his being.

Pounding on the door had him jerking, his wife squeezing his hand tight. He raised a finger to his lips as he heard Todd open the front door.

Samir couldn't hear what was being said, but it sounded heated.

"Fine, I've got nothing to hide, search all you want."

Boots on parquet echoed through the small apartment. "Do you have proof you're an American citizen?" asked a booming voice.

"I'm sure I do somewhere, but as an American citizen, you have no right to ask me to produce it."

"Times have changed. I suggest you cooperate or I might just find that you're not."

"Jesus Christ, I'm not a Muslim, I'm a Jew."

"A Jew who uses the Lord's name in vain?"

"That was irony." There was a pause. "A joke. Look, my yamaka's by the door, my Menorah is in the closet on the top shelf. I'm Jewish, so's my wife, so is my son."

"Where's your wife."

"Asleep in bed, that is probably until you guys hammered on the door."

Samir could hear boots enter the bedroom.

"Who the hell are you?" cried Sharon, the springs bouncing as she apparently jumped up in the bed.

"Government authorized search, ma'am. Are you an American citizen?"

"Goddamned right I am! I was born and raised in Atlanta!"

"Do you have proof?"

"The fact I don't have a damned accent, am as white as you, and have a brother who died in Iraq should be proof enough."

"Sorry, ma'am, I'm required to ask."

More boots and the sounds of closets and doors being opened then closed were accompanied by mild protest from Todd, who seemed to be keeping up just the right level of outrage to not arouse suspicion or ire.

"Thank you for your cooperation."

A door closed then silence.

His daughter lightly snored, winning the sleeping game.

Footsteps entered the room, quiet, socked feet approaching the bed. "They've gone for now, but let's wait until they're out of the building."

Suddenly there was a terrific crash from the front of the apartment. Sharon yelped as Todd rushed out of the room.

"Hey, what's the idea?"

"One of your neighbors reported seeing a Muslim family coming in here just a few minutes ago. Where are they?"

"I don't know what you're talking about. Half my neighbors are on crack, I wouldn't believe a word they said."

"Sir, if we find them in here you're going to the same place they are, along with your wife and son." The man's voice rose. "We're going to tear this place apart and arrest these good people if you don't come out! You've got ten seconds!"

Samir stared at his wife, his eyes finally filling with the tears he had been fighting for so long. She nodded at him as they both realized what must be done

He pushed the storage bags out of the way.

Sharon wept in the bed, hugging her pillow as he crawled to his knees and looked back at her.

He helped his children out from under the bed, then his wife.

"Time's up!" yelled the man from the front.

"We're coming," said Samir, his voice cracking.

Sharon cried out, climbing out of the bed and following them, her teenage son standing in the door of his own bedroom, his eyes red as he bit down hard on the knuckle of his thumb, fighting their shared terror.

Todd sat in his chair, his head in his hands, defeat written on his face. Samir looked at the man standing in the living room, several of his henchmen behind him.

"There's no need to hurt these good people. We'll go with you." Samir turned to Todd, choosing his words carefully. "Thank you, sir, for agreeing to take us on such short notice. I shouldn't have put someone I didn't know in such an awkward position."

Todd nodded, seeming to understand why Samir was speaking the way he was. He wisely said nothing.

Todd's son brought their suitcases from wherever they had been hidden. "Can they take these?" he asked. The man nodded.

Samir smiled his thanks then followed them out of the apartment, trading one last look with Todd, who mouthed "I'm sorry" as the door closed.

His daughter tugged on his pant leg.

"Daddy, who won the sleeping game?"

Outside Moose Jaw, Saskatchewan, Canada

Burt Dawson ran alongside the CN Rail train heading east just outside of Moose Jaw, Saskatchewan. It had yet to pick up significant speed and was just rounding a slight bend to the left hiding their illegal boarding from the engineer. He pulled at the door but it wouldn't budge. He noticed a padlock and pulled out his Glock, making quick work of the lock, tossing it to the ground. Pulling the door open, gear was tossed inside by the others then he reached out with one hand and grabbed Lee Fang's wrist, yanking her up and inside the now open boxcar. He did the same with Niner and Kane then stepped inside himself to find the boxcar mostly empty, a shipment of paper filling only a third of the compartment.

"Everybody okay?" he asked, closing the door almost completely, not wanting the engineer to notice it open on his next right hand bend.

"Peachy," said Niner. "I feel like a damned hobo." He looked at Fang. "Didn't some of your ancestors build this track? Fine job they did." Fang again looked at Niner as if he were a little touched. Niner grinned. "Spend enough time with me and you'll understand my sense of humor."

Dawson shook his head. "And when you do, you know you're due for a transfer."

Kane chuckled, pulling a battery powered lamp from one of the bags. He flicked the switch and a gentle glow filled the boxcar. The others gathered around it like a campfire, it now chilly, the sun low on the horizon, the prairie landscape quick to give up its heat. It would be a long night but hopefully a safe night, the freight train having no passenger cars to attract attention. The news reports they were listening to while waiting for the right train, one that wouldn't be stopping in every small town along the way, had been bleak. Canada's CBC News had been reporting many border incursions which the Canadian government had been strongly protesting but seemed powerless to stop. The latest news report had indicated a deal had been reached where Canadian authorities agreed to arrest and return anyone caught crossing the border illegally.

Dawson felt for the Canadians. It wasn't like they had much choice. With civilian leadership, Canada could rely on the might of the American military not being used against it, but with the new military leadership, they had no such guarantees and Dawson had a feeling even they knew this wasn't a temporary situation, many of the news organizations openly calling it a bloodless coup d'état with the foreign pundits calling for economic sanctions should the military not fulfill its promise to return power to civilian authority once the situation had been contained.

But it hadn't been yet. There were still bombings, two more today, but they seemed to be much fewer in number though still deadly. Dawson suspected this was to keep the people onside, to show the "threat" still existed. If the attacks suddenly stopped, the people might demand power be returned, and those behind this coup couldn't risk that.

But he still wondered if General Thorne was the head of this, or just a patsy. He had met General Thorne in-theatre. He was a good soldier, strict but fair from what he had been told, and a patriot. The man loved his country and loved its military. A history buff, Dawson and a few of his team had been chowing down when the General had made an appearance, regaling a nearby table with stories from the American Revolution.

The theme had been why overthrowing the government at the time had been necessary. It had been entertaining, a lecture delivered with gusto and genuine zeal, the men listening hanging off every word delivered by the popular soldier.

Thorne seemed to genuinely love his troops, his job, and his country. Whether or not he might be twisted enough to orchestrate these events,

Dawson wasn't sure. If he felt the country was being threatened by the inaction of its leadership, perhaps he might. But it would be an extreme reaction. He'd be better off trying to run for President rather than replacing him at near gunpoint.

Dawson had his doubts, and as far as he could see at this point there was only one way to end this for certain. Take out all the known *and* perceived leaders, and if that meant Thorne had to die, then so be it.

America had to be saved, and if Thorne were the man Dawson thought he was, he would gladly die to save his country, especially if he were innocent in all this.

Niner cocked an ear. "What's that?"

"What's what?" asked Dawson.

"I heard something. Sounded like a prop."

"Douse that light!" ordered Dawson as he jumped for the door, opening it slightly. He scanned the sky, the sound now obvious to him too, Niner's hearing almost dog-like. "It's gotta be a UAV."

Kane was beside him, looking as well. "Sounds big, like a Reaper."

"Do you think they've found us?" asked Fang, standing at the far wall, holding onto a railing for balance.

"Border patrol definitely would have reported us then satellite might have picked us up," said Kane.

"Do you think they'd really take out a train in Canada?"

"It's a freight train," said Dawson. "Little to no Canadian casualties, eliminating a major threat like us? I don't think they'd hesitate."

"Do you think they know who we are?"

"Probably. For sure they've pulled satellite footage of your rescue, traced the plates and saw we were heading north. They might have even traced us to Duke's place. A quick check of vehicle registrations would have his SUV plates, and those would have been reported by border patrol."

"So in other words, yes," summarized Niner succinctly.

Dawson's lips pressed together tightly, then he pointed at the gear. "Niner, what have we got in there that could take out a Reaper?"

"My rifle?"

"Do you think you can try to hit it?"

Niner shrugged. "Do or do not. There is no try." His Yoda impression was spot on.

"What do you need from us?" asked Dawson as Niner quickly began to assemble his M24A2 Sniper Weapon System.

"A spotter on the roof."

"I'll do it," said Kane.

Dawson shook his head. "Negative. Your responsibility is her. If you see a missile inbound, you two jump."

"Jesus, BD, we're doing fifty or sixty miles an hour!" exclaimed Niner.

"You *won't* survive a missile strike."

"Debate over, get on the roof," said Kane, pointing. "There it is and it's coming around. Looks like an MQ-9 Reaper." Dawson followed Kane's arm and cursed as he spotted what was indeed a Reaper banking. He swung outside and climbed up a ladder placed near the door. Reaching down he pulled up Niner's SWS, Niner scrambling up after it.

"You've got maybe thirty seconds!" yelled Kane from below as Dawson lay prone on the roof of the boxcar, his binoculars propped up on his elbows.

"Got it. Target's at one-seven-zero, bearing right at approximately one thousand feet off the ground, two miles out. You see it?"

"Affirmative," said Niner beside him, already in position.

"It's going to fire any second!" yelled Kane.

"Come to Papa," whispered Niner as he carefully took aim, it impossible for Dawson to help, there no way to give him wind speed and direction, it almost irrelevant since they were travelling so fast. Niner would have to rely on his instincts.

The weapon fired, Dawson feeling the report through the metal roof underneath him.

Nothing obvious indicated a hit.

"Presumed miss," he said.

Suddenly cannons on the Reaper opened up, tearing apart the ground as the bullets neared the boxcar. "Take cover!" shouted Dawson as he split his time between the Reaper and the unexpected approaching fire, cannon equipped Reaper's only experimental when he had last been briefed. But experimental or not, the massive caliber bullets found their mark, tearing through the boxcar's thin skin, the hot lead climbing the side as it was about to reach the roof. "Roll!" yelled Dawson.

He saw Niner roll to the left out of the corner of his eye as he rolled to the right, suddenly finding himself falling over the edge, his left hand reaching out and grabbing onto the rung of a ladder just before he dropped between the two boxcars and onto the tracks. The buzz of the Reaper's prop as it passed overhead had him looking up at the massive unmanned vehicle, his view suddenly blocked by Niner's face.

"Whatcha doin'?" he asked playfully.

"Just hangin'."

Niner reached out to pull him up when Dawson waved him off. "Forget me, just take that goddamned thing out."

"Well why didn't you just say so?"

Niner's head disappeared and Dawson regained his balance, climbing back up just in time to see Niner squeeze off another round, this time in the near opposite direction as the Reaper banked sharply, exposing a rather large target.

Smoke immediately began to trail from the fuselage and the engine suddenly grew louder in protest as the seventeen million dollar vehicle dipped sharply to its right, spinning several times before slamming into the hard ground, erupting into a ball of fire.

The train jerked as the engineer hit the brakes, shoving Dawson painfully into the boxcar, Niner losing his balance slightly, his grinning celebration cut short. The train took its time coming to a halt allowing Dawson to climb around the corner and back into the boxcar entrance. "You two okay?"

Kane nodded, pointing at several holes. "It was close." Niner passed down his sniper rifle, Kane grabbing it.

"You missed one of my better shots," said Niner as he flipped head over heels from the roof and into the boxcar.

Kane's eyes narrowed as he grabbed some of the gear. "You sure? I just assumed it was a bird strike."

Niner feigned mock anguish as he broke down his weapon. "I'm genuinely hurt that you would think such a thing."

Dawson scanned the horizon for more Reapers and saw nothing. But he knew that wouldn't last long. He looked ahead as the train continued forward, now slow enough for them to safely jump. He smiled. "There's a town ahead. We'll borrow a vehicle and hopefully be far enough away before its owner knows it's gone."

They tossed their gear and Dawson jumped first, rolling with the impact, the others following suit, the train continuing forward, the brakes squealing in protest as the engineer tried to kill the inertia built up by the incredibly heavy load. Dawson walked back and grabbed some of their gear, the others joining him.

"Shit, look!" pointed Niner at the southern horizon, a contrail streaking across the sky.

Dawson grabbed his binoculars and looked. "Reconnaissance. MC-12W Liberty by the looks of it. We used them a lot in Afghanistan."

"We better hustle then," said Kane, already breaking out into a jog. Dawson brought up the rear, tossing glances over his shoulder as the plane neared. Unless they were blind, there was no way they weren't going to be seen especially with whatever town was ahead being a good mile away.

Suddenly a dull roar was heard from the north, a roar unmistakable to Dawson having heard it countless times in his life. It was the sound of jet engines on full afterburner, and with them approaching from the north they were obviously Canadian, probably CF-18's from CFB Cold Lake.

They all stopped as the planes tore overhead, closing in directly on the USAF plane, buzzing it closely, the Canadians apparently tired of the constant border challenges. Dawson watched as the CF-18's banked sharply, returning for another run as they reduced their speed, the American Liberty beginning to turn back toward the border, the Canadians tucking in alongside to escort them to American airspace.

Dawson gave a silent thanks to the pilots and just hoped this didn't turn into a shooting war with America's closest ally and friend.

The East Wing, Presidential Residence, The White House, Washington, DC

President Jacob Starling sat in a chair whose comfort was lost to him, perched on the edge of the leather cushion, leaning toward the television, his wife and children huddled on the couch nearby. He was watching CNN and FOX split screen, unable to believe what he was seeing. His own private briefings had been curtailed and for his own "safety" he had been confined to the residence. His only news now, beyond what was "approved" for the airwaves, was delivered through kitchen and cleaning staff who would whisper tidbits to him or surreptitiously deliver notes and communiques from other staff members still employed by General Thorne's people, providing him with valuable information they felt he needed to know about.

"I have your lunch here, Mr. President."

Starling looked up as Leroy Blunt entered, his dark leathery skin so deeply wrinkled Starling found him fascinating to look at. *Will I look like that when I'm his age?* Though advanced in years, Blunt was as spry as any man twenty years his junior and had a bubbly personality.

But today he looked scared as he set the table, simple sandwiches and potato salad the order of the day. Starling sat at the head of the table, his family joining him. Blunt leaned over, pouring a glass of water from a chilled stainless steel pitcher. "They've surrounded the CIA," he whispered. "No one knows why, but they're searching it now." He rose. "Will there be anything more, Mr. President?"

Starling shook his head, stunned at the revelation. "No, I think we're good, Leroy, thank you."

"Just call me when you're finished, Mr. President."

The old man left the room, pushing the cart he had brought the food on, leaving the family to eat in silence as Starling contemplated what he had just heard.

The CIA? Surrounded. And being searched.

He found his blood pressure beginning to rise. There was no way the CIA could be responsible for anything currently happening in the country, and even if they had a mole, it would be up to them to seek out the breach, not the military. Whatever was going on didn't pass the smell test.

"Are you going to eat that?" asked his wife, Melanie.

"Huh?"

She motioned toward his untouched sandwich on the plate. Despite the fresh tomatoes and lettuce, the sweet smell of the sourdough bread baked fresh daily and the seasoned chicken breast with honey mustard, it looked unreasonably unappealing.

And when he found his meals unappealing, it meant something was wrong, something was gnawing at his subconscious that needed to be dealt with.

Today there was no doubt what the something was.

General Thorne has gone too far.

He looked at the kids' plates and they were already polished clean, his wife already halfway through her meal and she was a slow, picky eater.

How long have I been sitting here?

"Kids, you're excused."

Both kicked out from the table and rushed back to the television in the next room, leaving Starling and his wife alone.

"What's wrong, Jacob?"

"They've surrounded CIA Headquarters and are apparently searching it."

Melanie's jaw dropped, her eyes opening wide in shock. "The CIA? That's insane!"

Starling sighed in agreement. "It is. This whole thing is insane. It's only been a couple of days and things are already out of control. These roundups are going way beyond anything we agreed to, they've been violating the Canadian and Mexican borders and there's even rumors of several executions. And now the CIA? I don't care what anybody says, even if someone inside the CIA is involved in the terrorist attacks it should be up to them to find out who it is, not the military." He rose from his seat, his wife looking up at him. "This has gone too far."

"Jacob, what are you going to do?"

His wife sounded nervous.

"I'm taking my job back. The question is whether or not General Thorne will give it back voluntarily, or will it require an act of Congress."

Melanie rose, taking his hand in hers. "Be careful, Jacob. This entire situation has me scared. You should read what's happening on the Internet. Muslims are being rounded up, beaten, killed, deported, and anybody who interferes is being arrested or worse. The rule of law is gone, Jacob. And this General Thorne is at the center of it."

Starling wrapped his arms around his wife, resting his chin on the top of her head. "With things this bad, America needs its President. This won't stop without me taking action."

She hugged him harder then finally let go. "I'll put your suit out for you. Go give the kids a hug."

He nodded and she suddenly turned as if to hide her face from him, and he knew what she was thinking, he feeling it himself.

I'm never going to see them again.

236

Outside Thunder Bay, Ontario, Canada

Kane woke in the backseat to find Lee Fang asleep on his chest, at some point during the night he having put his arm around her in his sleep. He looked down at her and tried not to move, it the most peaceful she had looked since he had met her. Niner was driving, Dawson asleep in the passenger seat, they having liberated a vehicle after the attack on the train then renting a vehicle with one of Kane's fake ID's. They were now making good time across the Canadian Shield, a barren, rocky part of the vast country, and less than a day away from their reentry to Thorne's America as Niner had taken to calling it.

Niner flashed him a grin in the rearview mirror, his eyebrows jumping up and down suggestively and Kane smiled back, shaking his head. "You're a pig," he whispered.

"That's the way, uh huh uh huh, I like it, uh huh uh huh," sang Niner, executing a few disco moves from his perch behind the wheel.

The car jerked to the left as he accidentally hit the steering wheel. Niner immediately compensated but it woke everyone. Fang stirred and suddenly jerked upright as she realized where she was, looking at Kane shyly.

"Sorry."

Kane smiled. "No problem. I was asleep until two minutes ago so never even noticed."

Dawson stretched. "What the hell happened?"

"Our driver was channeling his inner Travolta and failed."

"Hey, BD's seen me on the dance floor. Tell him he's full of it, BD."

Dawson's head dropped to his left shoulder as he looked at Niner sideways. "Are you kidding me? You dance as white as I do."

Kane's phone vibrated in his pocket as he laughed, Niner defending him with his best Tony Manero impression, his Travolta impression better than his moves. He quickly read the update from Leroux.

"Apparently they're tearing apart CIA HQ but haven't discovered The Bunker yet. They don't know how long that's going to continue. Everything is still pointing to Fort Myer being the command center and Sherrie is still alive as far as they know. They want to know our ETA."

"We should be stateside by noon tomorrow. The rest of the guys hopefully a few hours ahead of us," replied Dawson, looking at the GPS. "I don't think it's a good idea to tell them though. They've definitely got a leak."

"Agreed."

"Tell them we're going radio silent. We can't risk any leaks if this is going to work."

Kane nodded, quickly sending a message with their new status back to Leroux. "I think it's time to put out the call." He handed his secure phone over to Dawson. "How much help can we expect?"

Dawson shook his head. "I don't know, but we don't have much time to waste. The longer this continues the tighter the lockdown will be. Right now they're still consolidating."

"Tomorrow night, then?"

Dawson nodded, typing away with his thumbs. "Can't think of a better time."

He tossed the phone back to Kane who looked at the messages that had just been posted on three different Twitter feeds by three different profiles.

2100

Myer

Bring the rain.

The Oval Office, The White House, Washington, DC

"What can I do for you, Mr. President?"

Jacob Starling had to admit he was slightly taken aback. To see a military uniform sitting behind the desk in the Oval Office was disturbing to say the least, and he could honestly say if he had seen it before he had handed over power, he never would have done so. The image was so un-American, so against everything he had been raised to believe in, he felt like he was in North Korea or China, not the District of Columbia.

It took him a moment to recover from the shock.

"This has gone far enough, General."

Thorne put his pen down, leaning back in his chair.

"What has gone far enough, Mr. President?"

Starling threw his hands up. "This! All of this!" He suddenly noticed a portrait of the General hanging on the wall to his right. He pointed at it. "*This!* This is all supposed to be temporary, but you've settled right in, haven't you?"

"And this bothers you?"

"Does it bother me? Of course it bothers me! I'm the President of the United States, and this is *my* office, not yours!"

"I beg to differ," replied Thorne, his voice irritatingly calm, his usual precise diction suddenly very annoying to Starling. "You ceded your authority to me, *begged* me to take power so that the tough decisions could be made, decisions *you* were unwilling to make." He spread his arms out, encompassing everything. "And now what do we have? Peace is being restored, attacks are down, deportations of non citizens, as per *your* and your predecessor's orders are being carried out rapidly. Crime is down and the deaths of innocent Muslims is dramatically down. Our allies are

239

supporting us and our enemies have made no moves, thanks to *your* nuclear decree, which they now know, with me in temporary command, will actually be carried out."

"*Temporary!* That's the key word here. Temporary." He again pointed at the portrait. "*That* is not temporary, that—" He stopped, his jaw dropping as he noticed that the flag to the right, over Thorne's left shoulder was no longer the Presidential flag, but the flag of the Chief of the Joint Chiefs of Staff—General Thorne's symbolic flag. He pointed at it. "Are you kidding me?"

Thorne glanced over his shoulder then back at Starling. "What would you have me do? Sit in this chair and pretend to be the President?"

Starling wasn't sure what to say, the twisted logic somehow making sense. Maybe he *was* overreacting, maybe he was seeing conspiracies where there were none. Everything he was watching on television matched what Thorne had just said. Crime *was* down. Fewer Muslims were dying at the hands of vigilantes. Those on expired visas were being deported and most importantly, terrorist attacks were down.

It was what he hadn't said that was important. Violating the territorial integrity of our neighbors, private security forces carrying out security sweeps and the military seizing of CIA Headquarters.

That was the final straw for him.

"And what about the CIA?"

"What about the CIA?"

"You know damned well what I'm talking about."

"The CIA has been breached, to what level I don't know. At the request of the Director of the CIA we secured the location and are assisting in vetting all of their employees. I anticipate we will have the mole or moles within twenty-four to forty-eight hours."

"I find it impossible to believe that Joel requested assistance."

"Mr. Wayne stepped down immediately upon martial law being declared. I have named a new Director of the CIA, acting of course until he can be vetted by Congress after the crisis is over. I can assure you, *he* requested our assistance."

Starling's heart was slamming in his chest, palpitations almost overwhelming him as he struggled to fight through the rage and terror consuming him. If the General were telling the truth about everything, or if he were lying, he couldn't tell.

And Starling could think of only one way to figure out which was the truth. He sucked in a deep breath and spoke the words that would forever settle his doubts, or confirm his worst fears.

"General Thorne, it is time that power be handed back to civilian authority. I request that you immediately step aside so I may resume my Presidency, and recall Congress."

General Thorne nodded, leaning forward and pressing the intercom button. The door opened behind Starling and two men in paramilitary uniforms, clearly part of the private security that he had been hearing about, entered. Thorne rounded his desk and stood in front of Starling.

"Mr. President. I am placing you under arrest on suspicion of sedition." He motioned to the guards. "Take him away, quietly."

Starling was immediately bookended by the two guards. "Come with us, sir."

Starling ignored them, his ears pounding with the reality of the situation. "It was you all along! *You* did this to our country, all so you could seize power!" Thorne looked down at him, his imposing frame leaning in slightly causing Starling to take an involuntary step back. He steeled himself, stepping forward and glaring at Thorne. "You're destroying your own country, and you call yourself a patriot?!"

"I *am* a patriot!" It was the first time Starling could recall hearing Thorne raise his voice. "Our country was in crisis long before you asked me to take over. Years of Presidents and Congressmen more concerned with getting reelected than doing what was right for our country. Too many politicians concerned with what the special interest groups might say rather than what the silent majority weren't saying. Too many people like you at the beck and call of the money that put you in office. One billion dollars to run for President! One billion! You aren't here for the people, you're here for the corporations and special interests. If you truly claim to represent the people, then bring in the damned campaign finance reform that the silent majority have been wanting for years. Corporations shouldn't be funding campaigns, individuals should be. And they shouldn't be allowed to donate millions. Cap it like England and Canada do. *Then* we'll see more honest politicians, not concerned with what their corporate masters are demanding, not concerned with what a special interest group with good funding is demanding. Christ, half the anti-pipeline lobbies in this country are funded by Middle Eastern oil! You've got a billionaire fighting pipelines because his railroad carries eighty percent of the oil those pipelines would carry instead, yet you listen to him despite the clear conflict of interest!

"No, you and your ilk sold out this country to the almighty dollar and self-interest long ago. *We the people* have taken it back. The Union will be restored, *by* the people and *for* the people, and when we're done, we'll once again be the country that my grandfather fought and died for in World War Two. Free and brave, a beacon once again for the world to aspire to, not some failed economy fighting other people's wars half-heartedly. We'll hammer our enemies into the ground, decisively and once only. We won't stop on the way to Baghdad like we did in Gulf War One. We won't only put barely a hundred thousand troops in a country like Iraq then wonder why we couldn't secure it. We won't try to nation build in countries like

Afghanistan, backwaters where the people aren't culturally evolved enough to know what it means let alone want it.

"If this were the America of fifty years ago we would have pounded Afghanistan back into the stone age then left, telling them that if they ever let another group like al-Qaeda or the Taliban do anything beyond their borders, we'd bomb them again. And if this were the America of fifty years ago, we'd have placed several thousand observers into Eastern Ukraine and dared the Russians to kill just one of them.

"We've become pussies. Not our men and women in uniform, but our leadership. Our military is willing to fight, is capable of fighting, but are so often hamstringed by ridiculous rules of engagement they literally have to take a bullet sometimes before they can even fire back.

"That time is over, Mr. President. We will purge our country of the Islamic threat, restore law and order, gain our energy independence, and engage our enemies with the full might of our armed forces. When our enemies once again tremble at our might, when our economy is restored, our corrupt institutions cleaned up, I will happily return power to the Speaker of the House. Until that time, things will remain as they are."

Starling stood stunned, not sure what to say. His worst fears had just been confirmed—a madman was at the helm of the most powerful arsenal in the world, and by the sounds of what he had just heard, there would be no reasoning with him.

"How long have you been planning this?"

Thorne returned to his desk, sitting down. "When the previous administration began firing generals for telling them the number of troops required to pacify Iraq was higher than they wanted to hear. We lost a lot of good men and women over there because of politicians who have no clue what war is. No soldier who has seen combat wants war. They would all gladly lay down their arms tomorrow if they could be assured their country and way of life would be safe. But that's not the world we live in. War is hell and war is bloody and innocent people die. That's why we try to avoid it unless it's absolutely necessary. But if you commit to war, then you have to commit fully. You can't do it half-assed. More of *our* people die then, which is inexcusable, intolerable. If we had sent in two-hundred-fifty thousand troops like Shinseki said, hundreds if not thousands of our fallen would be alive today." He pointed at Starling. "You ask how long I've been planning this? Since the day people like *you* betrayed this country so you could be reelected." He waved Starling away. "Take him, I'm done talking."

Starling was gripped by both arms and marched unceremoniously toward the door. He wrenched an arm free, spinning back toward the General.

"You said you'd give power back to the Speaker of the House. Why him and not me?"

Thorne looked up from the paper he was reading.

"Because, Mr. President, you didn't name a Vice-President to replace you, and you won't be around long enough to apply for the job."

DEATH TO AMERICA

Outside The Oval Office, The White House, Washington, DC

White House Press Secretary Timothy Humble pretended to check a text message but instead activated the video camera on his phone, holding it upside down in his hand, his palm hiding the device, his fingers splayed enough for the lens to not be obscured. He had heard the shouts from the Oval Office while sitting, waiting for what garbage he'd be told to spew to the media at the next press briefing. He had once loved his job, and had even been happy to continue in the role when the General requested it, but as things progressed he began to realize he was too often the public face of announcements that he simply didn't support, couldn't support.

And then he was forced to defend them as part of his job.

A job which General Thorne had refused to relieve him of. "The country is in crisis and it needs a familiar face to help steer it through these troubled waters."

And thus he had become this new military government's patsy, the public face delivering and justifying one civil liberties violation after another.

It made him sick.

But he went home at the end of the day, still a free man, admittedly feeling far safer now than a week ago. His kid had gone to school today for the first time since the crisis had begun and the stock markets were open and moving up for the first time in weeks.

Americans were beginning to feel safe again, those to blame apparently caught up in the Muslim net that had been tossed across the country.

What really disturbed him though was the fact he hadn't seen or heard from the President since power was handed over until a few minutes ago. He had apparently requested no contact and had been staying in the residence the entire time. Humble found that hard to believe. He had never really had much respect for Starling—Humble's President would always be Bridges. He found Starling to be an opportunist, his campaign to succeed Bridges already well underway.

And an opportunist didn't just shut himself up in his bedroom.

The voices were muffled, but the fact that at least one person was shouting was obvious, and if he knew Thorne, it wasn't him. When Starling had strode by him he had been shocked, barely returning the nod. It had made him wonder if this was the first time Starling had actually been out of the residence.

It also made him wonder if Starling had been sent for, or had requested the meeting with Thorne.

Suddenly the door opened again, the two guards who had entered only minutes before now escorting a grim, red faced Starling between them, their hands firmly gripping the President by the arms. Starling made eye contact with Humble but said nothing. Humble too kept his mouth shut, as did everyone, a stunned silence falling over the normally bustling office as their President, leader of the Free World only days before, was led away like a common criminal.

And Humble slowly turned his cellphone, he hoped keeping the President in the frame.

The phone buzzed on the secretary's desk and everyone jumped. She answered, then replied, "Yes, General," hanging up the phone. She looked at Humble, her face ashen. "He'll see you now."

Humble nodded and willed himself toward the door, his legs not wanting to cooperate for they were now existing in a new reality, a reality of horror and shock.

Where the rightful President of the United States had just apparently been arrested.

Which meant this was no temporary state of martial law.

It was a military coup d'état.

And he was the public face of it.

CNN Washington Bureau, Washington, DC

"Jack, you've got to see this!"

Jack Steinbeck looked up from his desk. The large black circles under his eyes were shared by many, the news fast and furious and the frustration levels increasing with each passing hour. Their military assigned Press Officer was vetting all their stories and it was getting more and more difficult to actually report on what was happening. Stories from around the world were fine, entertainment, sports, fluff pieces, but actual news about the roundups, the terrorist attacks, the security being imposed on the streets were limited to approved sound bites with little to no footage.

So he didn't really care what Nick Dyson had. If it was any type of scoop, it would never make it past the censors.

He was holding a memory stick in his hand, the door to Steinbeck's office already closed, followed soon by the horizontal blinds.

"What've you got?" he asked, no enthusiasm or energy available to make him sound like he even cared.

Dyson handed him the memory stick. "Watch this."

Steinbeck took it and was about to insert it into the USB slot on his computer when Dyson stopped him, shaking his head. "Not that one, it's networked. Use your laptop but put it in airplane mode first."

Steinbeck sighed, shifting slightly as he took the requested precautions, automatically turning off all communications capabilities of the laptop, essentially isolating it from the outside world. He inserted the USB key then opened the lone video file. A shaky upside down image appeared. "What the hell am I looking at?"

"I got it from Tim Humble just a few minutes ago."

"The White House Press Secretary?"

"You know another Tim Humble?"

Steinbeck ignored the jab—they were all testy, but it was soon forgotten as he watched the video of President Starling being led out by two uniformed private security.

"Is he under arrest?"

"Yes! For sedition!" Dyson's voice was now a harsh whisper and Steinbeck didn't blame him. They had no way of knowing who was listening in now or who was monitoring their computers, but he thanked God that Dyson had made him use the laptop and isolate it.

"How did he get it to you?"

"In person, a few minutes ago. He said that he saw Thorne immediately after and was told to tell the press that President Starling would be going to Camp David for the interim of the crisis with his family. When Tim questioned him about the apparent arrest, Thorne threatened him and said he'd have him arrested for sedition just like the President." Dyson lowered his voice even further. "Tim's terrified. He asked me if there was any way we could get his family to a safe house."

"Christ," muttered Steinbeck. "You realize what this means."

Dyson squatted, his voice barely a whisper. "That this has turned into a coup."

A shiver raced up Steinbeck's back at hearing his own thoughts vocalized. It was terrifying. The very thought of it made his stomach churn. He shoved his fingers into the bundle of nerves under his left wrist and massaged them firmly, the old Chinese pressure point trick having kept him from vomiting for decades. Today it would need to work harder than ever. He finally spoke, first double checking that nobody was looking in, finding Dyson had done a thorough job. "The public have no idea. Our latest polling shows they're almost ninety percent in favor of what's going on."

"But they don't know the truth. They'd never support this if they knew what was really going on."

"But what do we know? We know the President was apparently arrested but we have to take Tim's word for that. The video just shows him being led out. They could whitewash that and they'd shut us down within minutes."

"There's something else," said Dyson, looking around nervously. "I've been monitoring some of the, shall we say, questionable news sources."

"Today they're probably more reliable than us. What did you find?"

"Something's going on. There's apparently some secret message that's been sent to military personnel who are opposed to what's happening."

"What message?"

"I don't know the details, nobody does. If you're supposed to know, then you know where to look to find the details. It sounds like Special Ops soldiers around the country might be prepping for something. Something big."

"What do you know?"

"Tim told me that the CIA has been surrounded and completely cut off from the outside world. Troops are apparently searching it, Thorne claims they've got at least one mole inside and doesn't trust the CIA to find them because he doesn't know how high up it goes."

"Can we get some footage?"

"I can send Dan. He's a special kind of crazy. It will have to be cellphone footage, but if anyone can get it, he can."

"Okay, we're going to put together a burst package. We need to convey as much information to the American people as we can, as quickly as we can, with the most important stuff up front just in case we get cut off."

"What about our Press Officer? He's armed."

Steinbeck pulled open his bottom desk drawer halfway, revealing a Beretta. "You can never be too safe," he said as he closed the drawer.

"You're going to shoot him?" Dyson seemed shocked, his jaw dropping as he paled slightly.

"No, you idiot. The guy's just doing the job he was assigned. I can't see him being involved in any grand conspiracy. We'll just hold him at gunpoint then our shutdown will have to come from outside sources."

"What about the affiliates?"

"We'll just push the feed as part of a regular broadcast that they all use. As soon as we air I want every news outlet in the country hit with notification from us and a copy of the video with permission to rebroadcast, and I want it put out on all of our social media connections. We'll have one shot at this then I suspect we're going to prison for a very long time."

Dyson nodded. "I'll get Dan out right away." He stood up and pointed at the memory stick. "That's the only copy we've got."

Steinbeck quickly copied the video to his laptop, then handed the memory stick to Dyson. "Guard this with your life. I'll make a couple of copies and let you know where they're hidden. Don't tell anyone about anything."

"What do I tell Dan?"

"The truth. We heard a rumor about Langley and want some footage. Don't get caught and don't tell anyone. Loose lips sink ships."

Dyson stepped toward the door, his hand on the doorknob when Steinbeck stopped him. "What was the message that you found on the boards?"

Dyson paled slightly as he spoke the words.

"Bring the rain."

"The Bunker", CIA Headquarters, Langley, Virginia

"Sir, somebody just Tweeted that the President's been arrested."

Both Leroux and Morrison spun toward Sonya Tong. She pushed the Tweet to one of the main screens. "It went live about ten minutes ago from a new account. It's getting retweeted like crazy around the world by the looks of it. Not a lot within the US, at least not as much as you'd expect. But there's this weird phrase that keeps popping up."

"What is it?" asked Morrison.

"Bring the rain."

Leroux's eyebrows jumped. "How many times?"

"A few dozen in reply to this post. I'm running search algorithms now and I'm finding thousands of references all over the internet."

Morrison pursed his lips. "It's a pretty common phrase among our soldiers."

"These are all in the past twenty four hours, building rapidly."

Leroux's eyes narrowed. "Can you trace it back to the source?"

"The earliest reference is on Twitter from a new account with only the one post. I'm trying to access the Twitter servers now."

"How long?"

"A few hours probably, but once I'm in, we'll have everything."

Leroux was intrigued. "How are you trying to access them?"

Tong grinned. "I'm using the Chinese back door. I just need to find a router that has one."

Leroux smiled in appreciation. With most of the world's routers manufactured in China, the Chinese military was known to occasionally divert shipments and place their own tech inside. This was used to then access any number of civilian, military and government computer systems.

252

A panic a few years ago when this was discovered had sent the Pentagon and Washington scrambling to vet all their hardware, but civilian organizations were still very vulnerable.

It was just a matter of finding one of these routers which Tong was now doing.

"Good work," said Leroux, turning to Morrison. "This could be related to what Kane and Bravo Team are up to."

"I'm guessing it is. They mentioned a possibility of additional support. I have a feeling that this is a coordinated effort on their part to try and take action all at once." Morrison turned to Tong. "We need to figure out when they plan to get started. See if you can trace when the first message was sent and if any others from the same location were sent. We need to time our video evidence release to help them as much as possible."

"The video is ready, sir," replied Tong. "I can post it whenever you want. But if we're trying to get maximum exposure as quickly as possible, we might need to go bigger than my social network."

Morrison nodded. "I've got an idea on that." He pulled out his secure phone and looked up a contact. He snapped his fingers as if remembering something. "And somebody find out if the President actually has been arrested."

Unknown Location

"Where's my family?"

President Starling sat in what he would describe as a barracks room. Simple single bed with thin mattress and pillow shoved in the corner, a utilitarian night stand with a lamp bolted to the wall over the head of the bed, and an empty bookshelf and a desk with one hard metal chair. A single overhead light showed off the uniform grayness of the entire affair. A metal door with a small glass window with embedded wire mesh was now open, a private security "agent" standing in it with a tray of food in his hand, another behind him, weapon at the ready.

"There will be no communication with the prisoner," was the almost robotic response as the food was put on the desk and the door closed. A face appeared in the window then just as quickly disappeared, leaving him once again alone. The smell of what looked like from his bedside perch to be meatloaf with gravy and probably instant mashed potatoes and canned peas was sadly enticing.

He was starving.

He didn't know how long he had been here, but it had been hours. Many hours if the level of his hunger were any indication. He eyed the food and debated for a moment whether or not a hunger strike was in order, but with no press to even hear about it, he decided martyring himself to the silence of the room was pointless.

He rose and shoveled the food in his mouth, hoping it wasn't drugged.

Then again if it were, would that be such a bad thing?

His primary concern now was his family. He couldn't bring himself to think that these people would harm them, but then again, they had taken over the United States by murdering thousands for their cause. He wondered if his wife and kids were still at the residence or had they been moved with him. Or moved to an entirely different location.

One thing was certain—he had no clue where he was. The White House corridors had been cleared, very few staff seeing him, and most of those who had were either military or from this private security outfit. He had been led to the large underground garage and placed inside an unmarked car with blacked out windows, a hood put over his head.

All he knew was he wasn't far, the journey taking less than twenty minutes. He also knew he had crossed a bridge about halfway through. He was still in the DC area, but where was anybody's guess.

But he hadn't lost all hope. Not yet. He had faith in America. He had faith in his fellow Americans. He knew it was only a matter of time before the truth got out, before the people began to question their new leaders and the honest, patriotic American soldiers now enforcing that power began to question what they were doing.

It would take time.

Time that General Thorne certainly had implied he didn't have.

But again, he hadn't lost all hope.

Because he had seen the phone hidden in Humble's hand, the camera lens visible between his fingers. And judging from the look of fear on Humble's face, he was doing something dangerous.

Like filming the arrest of his President.

Which meant that video could soon be public, which might be enough for the public to rise up against their new oppressors.

For if there was one thing the American people loved, it was their President. Not necessarily the man, but the institution. And if they knew their current President had been arrested, they would then assume that their previous President had been assassinated by the same people, along with the congressional leaders assassinated at Capitol Hill.

No, it was just a matter of time before his country would be saved by its own citizens.

He just prayed he was around to see it.

A woman screamed nearby, her agony obvious.

And a little doubt crept into the confidence which had just been so strong.

DEATH TO AMERICA

Outside of Chevy Chase, Maryland

Senior Chief Chuck Skerritt pored over the plans for Fort Myer and the surrounding area. There were multiple points of entry that they could take advantage of, but they had an unknown number of men available to them. He currently sat with about a dozen of his fellow Navy SEALs and he knew many more were on their way. He had been in contact through encrypted phones with various other groups and the coordinated effort called for by a fellow brother in arms from the Delta Force, Command Sergeant Major Burt "Big Dog" Dawson was to begin at 2100 hours tonight at Fort Myer.

Beyond that he knew nothing.

What he did know was that Dawson was a top notch soldier, the best, and he had to believe that Fort Myer was the center of this current mess otherwise he would have named another location.

But he also knew command and control meant communications, which was why he and his team were reviewing every set of plans they could get their hands on. He and as many likeminded soldiers he could gather would assault Fort Myer if needed, but he was already coordinating with others to take out communications centers in and around Washington, DC. Their aim to disrupt all White House, Pentagon and Fort Myer communications simultaneously.

It was going to be a tough job, a nearly impossible job considering who they were going up against—their own fellow soldiers. But it was necessary. He just hoped they could keep military casualties to a minimum. He was hoping that many of the units would simply stand down. He had every intention of letting them know who was attacking them and making the offer. The grumblings among service members was growing, many if not most already uncomfortable with their new roll. He like many other Special

257

Forces had called bullshit on the new regime and went on vacation, most with the permission of their commanding officers, his own telling him a fifth column was needed outside of the new command structure just in case.

He and others like Dawson were that fifth column.

And soon they'd find out just how strong that column was.

"Got them!"

Skerritt turned to see Chip Turner enter the room waving a laptop in his hand. "Got what?"

"White House, Pentagon, Fort Myer. You name it. Blueprints showing all the fiber optic, copper, satellite, cellular, microwave—you name it, I've got it."

Skerritt's eyebrows shot up. "How the hell did you manage that?"

"I reached out to my buddy at the Pentagon. He pulled all the data, marched out of the building, handed it off to me then said he's picking up his family and heading into the mountains until he's heard things are sane again."

Skerritt's lips pursed as he nodded in appreciation. "A good man. Print out the plans for our three main targets. We'll split into six squads, one for each of the target's communications, one for each of the target's personnel. Preliminary intel seems to suggest an awful lot of private security, those Raven bastards we dealt with in Iraq. I don't want to be killing American soldiers unless absolutely necessary, but I won't hesitate to put these wannabes down and down hard. Agreed?"

"Agreed," said Turner, the rest nodding. "Let's just hope there's more than this"—he motioned to those gathered—"when we're ready to take action."

Skerritt smiled. "There will be. Trust me."

DEATH TO AMERICA

Akwesasne Reserve, New York

"Who the hell are you?"

Kane's shoulders sank as he realized they had been spotted coming ashore. The Akwesasne Reserve straddled the Canadian and US border and was an ideal way for smugglers and criminals to gain access to either country.

And today one CIA agent, one Chinese exile, and two Delta Force operators had taken advantage.

Kane decided to tell the truth. "I'm CIA, she's Chinese Special Forces, and they're Delta Force."

The old man lowered his shotgun. "What's your business here?"

"I'm sure you're aware of what's going on south of here."

The old man nodded, turning away from them and shuffling up the embankment toward what looked like a single-room cabin, a thin twirl of smoke rising from a stone chimney. "I'm Mohawk. I don't care what's going on down in your country." He paused, looking over his shoulder. "Are you American or Canadian?"

"American."

He nodded, continuing up the slope as they followed, their gear unloaded from the boat they had rented on the Canadian side, those operating it more than happy to take cold hard cash to fire them across the river in a cigarette boat. Kane had no doubt the boat, already halfway back across the river, was used nightly to smuggle cigarettes into Canada.

And worse.

But today the criminals had been of use, and assuming this man didn't turn them in, they just might get across the border safely, their op only hours away from starting.

259

"American? And a Chinese? Well, I'm not going to hold that against you. You can't help where you were born."

Niner looked back at Kane, grinning. "I like him," he whispered.

"You here to do something about that mess in Washington?"

"And if we were?"

"I'd give you a good proper meal and wish you well."

Kane eyed a shiny new Ford F-250 XL with crew cab. "What we could use is a good ride."

The old man stopped, looking over at the shiny new 2014 model. He reached in his pocket. "They gave me it to keep quiet. I don't even know how to drive." He tossed the keys to Dawson who happened to be closest. "Try to return it in one piece. With a few bullet holes in it if possible. That would make for some good stories around the campfire."

Kane laughed. "You're a good man, sir. We appreciate it."

The man batted his hand over his shoulder, already heading into his cabin. "Stew's already on the stove. Come get some before you leave."

Dawson climbed into the truck, starting it up and checking the fuel tank as they loaded their gear in the back. He gave the thumbs up.

"Shall we?" asked Kane, motioning toward the cabin.

"Absofrackinlutely," said Niner. "I'm starved."

Dawson turned off the truck, climbing down and following Niner. "Me too. Just don't ask what's in the stew."

Niner stopped, turning around. "What do you mean?"

Dawson nodded toward several small animal skins hanging from the front porch. "Do you see any cows around here?"

Niner shrugged. "I could eat the ass end of a moose right now I'm so hungry."

Kane winked at Fang. "You just might be."

"It looks good."

Jack Steinbeck looked at the length of the video. Five minutes almost exactly. Nick Dyson had come through, as had Dan their cameraman with disturbing footage of CIA Headquarters in Langley. It was completely surrounded with personnel being escorted out of the building in handcuffs, private security swarming the area. It appeared that military personnel were only outside the gates. It made him hope that when the shit hit the fan, whatever this 'bring the rain' initiative was, that the armed forces would stand down instead of fight.

It all depended on how it played out.

He couldn't see whoever was behind this initiative actually killing American soldiers unless it was absolutely necessary. He could see them killing the private security, they had been linked to almost every single atrocity across the country.

And there were thousands of them.

It was shocking that there could be what was essentially a paramilitary so large inside the country, hired by the government to replace the law and order apparatus normally provided by civilian authorities.

Terrifying.

"You've talked to Stan?"

Dyson nodded. "They're ready in the control room. We'll come in at two minutes to eight. You'll pull your weapon on our Press Officer. I'll cuff him with these"—he held up a pair of handcuffs with frilly pink fur—"and Stan will load the footage from the memory stick."

Steinbeck nodded toward the handcuffs. "Care to explain?"

"I'll take the secret to my damned grave. It was the only pair I could find."

Steinbeck started to laugh then stopped himself, realizing that if he gave into the nervous energy fueling him he might not be able to stop himself. He looked at his watch. "We better get going."

Dyson nodded and made the sign of the cross.

"I didn't know you were Catholic."

"I'm not. But it can't hurt, can it?"

Steinbeck shrugged as Dyson stepped into the hallway, Steinbeck saying a silent prayer, asking God to let him see tomorrow.

"The Bunker", CIA Headquarters, Langley, Virginia
7:57 PM EST

"I think they found us."

Leroux pointed at a screen showing various security feeds including one of the elevator entrance to The Bunker. The doors were opening, a team having apparently rappelled down, and the dull rumble of automatic weapons fire was felt through the flooring as their first line of defense opened fire.

Morrison looked at his watch. "It's almost eight." He turned to Tong. "You're sure that the three messages are linked?"

She nodded emphatically. "Absolutely sir. All three messages, the '2100', 'Myer' and 'Bring the Rain' messages were all sent from the same device from Canada. They are the first indicators of the message which sent off a cascade of follow on messages with the same phrase. The 2100 and Myer are never repeated, just the Bring the Rain. It's as if everyone involved knows where to look to get the other two parts."

"Okay, we're assuming the '2100' is nine o'clock tonight. We're positive the 'Myer' is Fort Myer, and we're pretty much positive Bring the Rain is the signal for everyone to begin whatever they're going to do at nine o'clock."

"We're assuming Eastern Standard Time?" asked Leroux. He shook his head. "It must be. Fort Myer local time."

"We have to assume that," said Morrison. "Now the question is what can we do to help?" He motioned toward the security feed showing smoke canisters being deployed by the attackers. "They'll have a hell of a time getting in here, but that's an assumption. Now that they've found us they might be able to find our links to the outside. I don't think we can risk waiting any longer."

"Yes, sir," said Tong. "I've got routines set up to flood Facebook, Twitter and several other social media sites, as well as use the Wireless Emergency Alerts system like you suggested to hit pretty much every cellphone in the country with the equivalent of an Amber Alert directing them to a link where they can watch the video."

"And the television networks?"

"I've accessed the Emergency Broadcast System," said Leroux. "Everyone in the country is going to see this. Just give the word."

"Sir!" interrupted Dillard. "You've got to see this!" He pointed at the central screen as CNN suddenly appeared, the audio fed through the Operations Center overhead speakers.

"Holy shit!" exclaimed Leroux.

CNN Washington Bureau, Washington, DC
8:00 PM EST

It had only taken seconds and Jack Steinbeck had to admit he remembered little of it. The footage was now playing, an equally shaky Stan Waters taking several stabs at inserting the memory stick while Nick Dyson handcuffed their Press Officer with the furry sex toy he still looked embarrassed about.

But none of that mattered now. They were rolling live, the Press Officer glaring at him, a gag stuffed in his mouth, his chair shoved into the corner. Steinbeck pointed at Dyson.

"Send the message."

Dyson hit the button, the message already queued, sending the footage and broadcast release to every news wire and network in the world. A grid of monitors showed all the other broadcast networks, and if everything went right, they would hopefully break into their newscasts with the loop now airing showing the President being led away, a red bar across the bottom reading "President Starling Arrested for Sedition!". The voiceover, done by him, cited their unnamed inside source, then showed CIA Headquarters being occupied.

An idea struck him.

He pointed to one of the interns who stood in shock, her face as pale as her blouse. "Go pull the fire alarm."

"Wh-what?"

"Pull the alarm. It will fill the stairwells with people and shutdown the elevators. Do it!"

She jumped then ran out, moments later the drone of the alarm sounding. To her credit she returned rather than join the evacuees. "Now

265

go lock all the doors. Get anybody who's willing to stay to help you barricade them."

She reached a new shade of pale, but nodded and left. "FOX just picked us up," said Dyson, pointing at one of the monitors.

He smiled as two more switched over. "ABC and the BBC now."

'BRING THE RAIN' flashed on the screen as text scrolled indicating the known crimes committed by the private security. Steinbeck had been careful to point everything at them and General Thorne, his aim to make the military units question their orders and hopefully stand down during whatever action might be taken.

"CBS and NBC," whispered Dyson. "And there's MSNBC."

"It's working," said Steinbeck as he collapsed in his chair, the video already on its second loop.

"They're here," said Pete, pointing to a camera they had set up in the main entrance. "Splicing it in now."

The screen split showing their loop on the left and live footage of the private security forces arriving at their broadcast center with 'CNN UNDER ATTACK!' emblazoned across the top of the screen.

"Under attack?" asked Steinbeck.

"All I could think of," replied Pete with a shrug of his shoulders. "It's true, isn't it?"

Steinbeck nodded slightly. "Unfortunately." The building wasn't high and they were only on the fourth floor. It wouldn't take long, even with the security team forced to use the stairwell. He pointed at the cameraman in the far corner. "You keep shooting for as long as you can. Once they're in the room step away from the camera and put your hands up. Move around the edge of the room. I want to let them try to figure out how to shut it off." He pointed at Pete. "Can you have everything go dark, but keep broadcasting?"

He smiled. "Absolutely."

The young intern burst into the room nearly giving Steinbeck a heart attack. "They're at the doors!" she cried, tears flowing down her face. "Oh my God! They're at the doors!"

Steinbeck rose, placing a hand on her shoulder. "Go to your desk and sit down. Put your hands up and do whatever they say."

She nodded, her entire body trembling as she went to the door. Then she did something Steinbeck hadn't expected. She closed then locked it, turning back to face the room. "I want to stay."

He smiled, understanding perfectly. This was history and she wanted to be a reporter. This was probably the biggest story to ever be told in his lifetime and he hoped there would never be one bigger. They were fighting back, doing what the press was supposed to do. It reminded him of the good old days when he was younger and reporters actually dug for information, reported the news rather than commented on it. He had missed it, had missed the feeling, and now that he remembered what it was like to get that scoop, to make a difference in the world, he regretted all those years wasted on sensationalism.

"There they are," said the cameraman, motioning with his head as he aimed the camera at the window. Steinbeck looked and saw half a dozen heavily armed men rushing toward the booth. He glanced at the grid of monitors and breathed a sigh of relief, every single monitor now showing their broadcast.

"It's time," he said, nodding to Pete. Pete hit several buttons and all the monitors went dark, the control boards dimming to a dull glow almost lost as Steinbeck flicked the switches turning all the overhead lights on.

Gunfire tore through the lock, the glass of the door shattering, the intern crying out as he grabbed her, pushing her behind him.

"Shutdown the broadcast immediately!" shouted the first to enter, a handgun held high, pointing directly at Steinbeck.

Steinbeck nodded toward the monitors. "Already done."

Three more men entered the room with submachine guns, what type Steinbeck had no clue, guns not his specialty. All he knew was they looked menacing and the men holding them looked trigger happy. The man who had spoken had a finger to his ear, obviously communicating with somebody.

His lip curled then he pistol whipped Steinbeck. He collapsed to the floor, the world fading as he fought to remain conscious. The intern's scream brought him back as she dropped behind him, grabbing him as she tried to pull him upright.

"Shut down the broadcast, now!"

Nobody said anything as Steinbeck struggled back to his feet. "Don't you realize what you're doing is wrong?" he said, his head throbbing. "Don't you realize that this is America? That civilian authority *must* be restored?"

"It's civilian authority that got us into this mess in the first place," replied the man, pressing a finger to his ear again. "What? We're on camera?" He looked and spotted the camera in the corner, rage smearing his face. "I'll take care of it." He stepped back, raising his weapon. "Open fire."

The last thing Steinbeck experienced beyond the searing pain of several gunshots were the struggles of the young intern, trapped under him when he collapsed, until she too was silenced by a single gunshot.

"Holy shit!"

It was Dillard who broke the silence, the only other sounds gasps and sobs, the room filled with the entire team, no one sleeping for the next shift. This was happening now, in the next few hours, and there would be no time for rest.

Leroux dropped into his chair, unable to believe what had just happened. An entire CNN crew murdered on the air, live. Now the domestic television sources were quickly changing to test signals or dead air, but the foreign sources were all playing the footage. He quickly fed some keywords into his computer and sucked in a deep breath.

"Sir, that broadcast is trending worldwide including the hashtag #bringtherain. Hundreds of thousands have already seen or read about what just happened. At that rate it will be millions in the next hour, tens of millions if not more before the nine o'clock deadline."

Morrison sat down himself, his expression solemn, the dull thuds of gunfire still felt through the floor panels from outside. He looked at Tong. "Can you add that broadcast to ours?"

"Doing it now, sir." They waiting in silence, nobody saying anything as they watched the foreign news broadcasts and the security footage of the battle raging just beyond the doors.

Tong nodded.

"Are you ready?" asked Morrison.

She nodded.

"Then do it."

She pressed a button, executing the prewritten program. "Done."

A status display showed the various steps being executed, her YouTube channel posting, Facebook, Twitter, email blast, with another display showing how many times the video was viewed and shared to the right. Next came the flooding of every feed they had been able to think of, foreign and domestic, and by the time it was sent, counters were already starting to roll on the initial blast. In the dozens at first, quickly in the hundreds, then things began to really roll. Within minutes tens of thousands had seen the footage with the pertinent points highlighted—that the Secret Service agent had been the killer and he had nodded either to General Thorne or his aide; that a CIA agent was being held hostage at a military installation and tortured; and that CIA Headquarters were being surrounded and searched by private security.

With "Bring the Rain" scrolling across the bottom of the screen the entire time.

"Wireless Emergency Alerts are next," said Tong softly as the counts continued to spiral upward. Suddenly cellphones around the room began to emit a strange tone. Leroux looked at his display, having never actually received an alert before.

Presidential Alert
You are being lied to. Turn on your television or radio now.
#bringtherain

"And now the Emergency Broadcast System."

Every domestic channel being monitored suddenly switched from test patters to the video they had just broadcast. Television stations wouldn't be able to override it, which meant the Press Officers were powerless to stop it. It would have to be shut down at the source and Leroux's team had caused enough havoc in the EBS security protocols that the only way they'd end up being able to stop it would be with explosives.

Unfortunately their enemy had plenty of those.

"Look at those numbers!" exclaimed Dillard, the counts now in the millions and the international broadcasters beginning to cover the story including the EBS feed on a loop.

A phone rang startling everyone. Morrison picked it up. "Go ahead...how long...fall back and surrender if necessary, our work here is done."

He hung up the phone and turned to the others, all staring at him with fear in their eyes. "They're almost through the outer doors. They estimate no more than an hour."

Tong let a cry slip as Dillard articulated what they were all thinking.

"And then we die."

Command Center, Fort Myer, Arlington, Virginia
8:18 PM EST

"Jesus Christ, stop the goddamned broadcast!"

Colonel Booker was red, beet red, his heart pounding in his ears as almost every network they were monitoring played a continuous loop that only those bastards at the CIA could have been able to push out. And every single station was still broadcasting, despite orders for the Press Officers to stop them.

"We can't, sir, they're using the Emergency Broadcast System."

"And how the hell did they get a text message to every one of our phones?"

"It's the new Wireless Emergency Alerts system, sir. It's been around for a few years, most of the newer phones are set to receive them. Presidential, emergency and Amber alerts are sent to everyone in the designated area. I've shut that down but it's too late, everyone in the nation with a turned on cellphone with this capability has received the message."

Booker pointed at the screens showing the main networks. "Christ Almighty! They've got footage of this installation! They've got *me* on camera!"

The screen flashed his name and vital statistics while footage of him with a bloodied Sherrie White played.

Booker collapsed in his chair, wiping the beads of sweat from his forehead through his close-cropped hair. Everything was falling apart. His dream, *their* dream of a strong, united country, once again the envy of the world where enemies trembled and people walked the streets with confidence, not worried whether or not their neighbor was a religious fanatic hell bent on killing them. The borders would be secured and

Fortress America would stand as a beacon to the world of how freedom and democracy could thrive in a world filled with hate.

But now the dream was crumbling.

All because of the damned CIA.

They had lost track of the Chinese defector and her CIA handler, their mole within the CIA cut off when this Chris Leroux character had gone into The Bunker. It had saved Leroux's life and also cut off their source of intel, The Bunker computers completely segregated from everything else. And Now Dylan Kane had escaped again from the Raven team sent to collect him and had somehow found friends that had helped them across the border to Canada and unbelievably shoot a Reaper UAV out of the sky.

They have to be Special Forces.

Reports from across the country were indicating Special Forces units had stood down just before the new orders were officially acknowledged as received, many of their commanders sending them on vacation, the excuse that these were trained killers not suitable for crowd control. They were right of course, you don't send Special Forces in to tame a crowd. You send them in to kill someone in the middle of that crowd.

"What the hell is this Bring the Rain thing?" he asked, all of the footage showing the same phrase over and over. He knew what it meant in military parlance—bring a shit storm of firepower down on a particular location—but for the CNN and CIA broadcasts to both be using it meant there was something else going on.

It was a code of some sort.

"I don't know, sir, but it's trending on Twitter like crazy. Millions of people are using the hashtag and our Google taps are showing massive activity."

"How many have seen those broadcasts?"

"Considering during a crisis about half the nation will watch TV news channels, and it was broadcast at eight pm, so primetime, I'd say easily half the country. And don't forget almost everybody has a cellphone and were told to turn on their TV's and radios. I'd be surprised if there's even ten percent of Americans who didn't see that broadcast."

"What about the troops?"

"Those on duty quite often still carry their cellphones, especially in a domestic deployment like this. Besides, their buddies not on duty definitely saw it."

"Show me the front gate."

Security footage of the front gate appeared and it confirmed Booker's worst fears. The soldiers manning the gate were no longer in their assigned positions, but huddled around looking at their cellphones.

"How many Raven personnel do we have here?"

"A little under two hundred, sir."

"Have them deployed to the perimeter." He sighed. "I'm going to talk to the President. Maybe I can *convince* him to record a broadcast to claim it's all lies."

He turned on his heel and headed for the President's cell.

And if he won't cooperate, there'll be blood on the streets.

Starting with his.

Days Inn, Arlington, Virginia
8:21 PM EST

Kane exchanged thumping hugs with the rest of the Bravo Team, several rooms having been rented by the early arrivals. Six of them were now jammed into the biggest of the rooms, and it wasn't big—at least not for five large men and one Chinese woman.

"Sorry we're late," apologized Dawson as he sat on a chair brought in from one of the adjoining rooms. "There were way more roadblocks than we were expecting. Where are the rest of the guys?"

"I wasn't sure if you were going to make it so I took the liberty of prepping," replied Master Sergeant Mike "Red" Belme, Dawson's second-in-command and best friend. "We've got the front and rear of the target under observation and sniper teams in position should you approve my plan." He paused, taking a more somber tone. "Did you see what happened at CNN?" Dawson shook his head. "They massacred them all for putting out a broadcast showing the President being arrested and the CIA HQ surrounded."

"They also scrolled a list of dozens of reported crimes committed by those Raven bastards," added Sergeant Leon "Atlas" James, his booming voice reverberating through the room.

"And they were flashing 'Bring the Rain' on the screen," finished Red.

Kane's eyebrows rose. "Really? I wonder if they knew what it meant."

"No idea, but chatter's picked up. And look." Red pointed at the television. "This has been running for almost fifteen minutes. It looks like the CIA hijacked the Emergency Broadcast System." The screen suddenly went black then a test signal replaced it. "Oh well, for about twenty minutes the American people were getting the truth for a change."

275

Dawson clapped his hands together. "Okay, we don't have much time. Status?"

Red took over, walking over to a table showing a map of the area. "The good news is this: Fort Myer was never designed to protect against serious incursions. The entire east side backs onto the Arlington National Cemetery. There isn't even a fence, just a knee wall then a parking lot."

"And the building we suspect is their HQ?"

"Not the official HQ." Red pointed at a large building. "Brucker Hall, it's been converted into their HQ and it's on the east side as well, just off the parking lots."

"That'll make things much easier," said Kane leaning in closer as he examined the map.

"Yup, but it's crawling with private security from what we can see."

"Raven?"

Red nodded. "Probably. Until a few minutes ago the rest of the base was secured by regular Army but Spock just reported that over one hundred Raven personnel just deployed."

"That could be a good thing," said Dawson. "It suggests Colonel Booker and his team no longer trust the reg forces to keep them secure. Chances are they're aware of the broadcasts and might be questioning their role in things."

"Could be," agreed Red. "I've deployed sniper teams here and here," he said, pointing to two locations on the map. "That should cover our rear. Chatter indicates we might get some help, but we can't be sure."

Dawson pursed his lips, turning to Kane. "What do you think?"

Kane drew his finger from the cemetery to Brucker Hall. "It's not far to cover and the aim is to get inside. Once in, there's nobody better than us. We kill everything in sight, take down their network and neutralize their command and control, then hold until people come to their senses."

Dawson's phone buzzed and he looked at the message. He smiled, holding it up for Kane to read.

6 Ps ready to assist. Bring the rain.

"Six platoons?"

"That's my guest. He's a SEAL buddy."

"You guys talk?"

"Usually while arm wrestling and drinking beer," said Niner, stretching his arm out as if it were sore. "Those boys are strong!"

"Can he be trusted?" asked Kane, already knowing the answer.

"Absolutely."

"Good." He looked at his watch. "Thirty minutes. Let's get in position and take back our country."

White House Situation Room, The White House, Washington, DC
8:28 PM EST

"Report!"

General Thorne's bark had everyone in the room jumping as he took his seat at the head of the table in the Situation Room. Displays across the far wall showed maps with green, yellow and red dots, more and more turning from green as he watched. Another bank of monitors to the right, normally showing civilian broadcasts, now all showed test signals.

"We've taken out the power supplies to the Emergency Broadcast System and destroyed the Wireless Emergency Alerts hardware. They won't be able to use either of those systems again. We should have regular broadcasts up within an hour as Raven personnel get into position. Broadcasters will learn from the example set at CNN."

Tony Logan, one of the seniors at Raven Defense Services and brother to the Secret Service Agent who had taken out the President was running things from the White House adeptly to this point. Between him and Booker at Fort Myer things had been running like clockwork until thirty-five minutes ago.

And Thorne wanted answers.

"Who did it?"

"The footage of the President looks like it was taken by Press Secretary Humble."

"Pick him up."

"We've already sent a team but they reported his house vacant. It looks like they left in a hurry with help."

"Help?"

"Both their cars were still there."

"Put out a BOLO on them."

"Already done, sir."

General Thorne watched as several of the networks suddenly came to life with regular entertainment programming. "And the rest of the footage?"

"CNN must have got hold of some footage of CIA HQ. Not really hard to do, sir. The CIA we know tapped our feeds at Fort Myer so that's how they got their footage, and Homeland had already supplied them with footage of the assassination before we took control."

"And what's happening at Langley?"

"Our forces have penetrated the first level of security at The Bunker and anticipate being through the second level within half an hour."

"Then?"

"Then, sir, they have to get through the secure doors of the control facility."

"How long will that take?"

"It could take hours, sir."

"We can't risk it. Pack the place with explosives. Blow the shit out of it."

"Yes, sir." Logan nodded toward one of his men who left to initiate the order.

"And the President?"

"Secure at Fort Myer, but Booker has just requested the family be sent there. He wants to use them to coerce Starling into recording a statement that we can broadcast denying what was just aired."

"Good idea. Too bad he'll never go for it."

"True, but worth a try. But we've got bigger issues." Logon motioned toward the screen with the dots.

"What am I looking at?"

"Green are military units still sending in regular reports, yellow are units that have questioned their orders, requesting clarification on what was just broadcast, and red are units that have either stood down, recalled their troops to base, or outright demanded the President's release."

"How many?"

"Dozens in the red already, and I think they're talking, General. It's growing dramatically, especially those requesting clarification. Those outright defying our orders are slow to grow, but they will the longer we delay."

"Solutions?"

"None that I can see. We could isolate base-to-base communications but they'll just use their cellphones. These guys all know each other—they talk."

Thorne frowned. He knew Logan was right. He was part of that apparatus. He could pick up his phone and call any number of commanding officers at these bases that he until a few days ago would have called friends. Now they weren't taking his calls.

The tide was turning.

All could be lost unless he acted boldly and swiftly.

"What about this 'Bring the Rain' thing?"

"We're not sure, sir. It's definitely a code of some sort and it's spreading like wildfire on the Internet, but most people seem to just be repeating it like a chant as opposed to knowing what it means."

"So it could be nothing?"

"I doubt it, sir. It's definitely something. Remember, the CIA used it, not just CNN. And the CIA package was slick, not tossed together, so there's no way they could have known CNN was going to use the same phrase."

Thorne shook his head in frustration. "It has to be related to the Special Forces guys going AWOL. They must be up to something."

"If they are, we may be in serious trouble, sir."

Thorne frowned, not liking what Logan had said, but forced to agree. There were many thousands of Special Forces in the country and if even just a fraction of them decided to get involved this conflict would quickly become bloody.

But he had spilled a lot of American blood already and was prepared to spill more should it become necessary. "What's the status on the internment camps?"

"Still secure with Raven personnel, but we just got a report of a group of civilians gathering at one outside San Diego demanding the prisoners be released."

Thorne pursed his lips and cursed as several more red dots appeared.

"I'm not going to turn our weapons on American citizens. How are the deportations going?"

"Extremely well, sir, but our schedule assumed we'd have at least twenty-four months to complete the task. We've barely managed to send a tenth of the visa people, let alone begin to repatriate over three million Muslims."

Thorne rose, his mind reeling at how quickly things had turned to shit.

"Our orders, sir?"

"Eliminate The Bunker at CIA, send a communique to all installations that the broadcast was faked and a statement will be forthcoming from the President himself."

"And if he won't cooperate."

"Get his double."

Logan laughed. "Good thinking."

"Declare an immediate curfew and arrest anyone who violates it." He paused. "And send extra units to Fort Myer. I want that place secure for as long as we can hold it." He pointed at the screen. "And I want every one of those still in green to report their commitment to the current lawful status then to deploy their men to take over positions abandoned by their counterparts."

"Yes, General!"

"Oh, and initiate three more attacks tonight and have the networks cover them. Just to remind the country how things were just a few days ago."

"Yes, sir!"

Thorne left the room and boarded the elevator to return to the main level. His mind raced as he tried to figure out a way to salvage what they had accomplished. He knew there were enough units loyal to him, men he had placed in their commands over the years for just such an occasion. They might not support what he was doing, his secret agenda, but they were loyal to him, and as long as they thought what he was doing was legal and supported by not only the government and the people, they would continue to execute their orders as long as they were lawful.

Raven would continue to handle the dirty stuff, and they numbered in the thousands.

If he could get Starling or his double to deliver a convincing enough speech on the networks tonight then they might be able to get things back on track. The elevator shuddered to a halt and he grabbed the wall, steadying himself. The lights flickered then went out, a dim red emergency light casting an eerie glow over the tiny car. He reached for the emergency panel when a sound above him caused him to look up.

He gasped as a figure dropped toward him, headfirst, arm extended with what looked like a Taser.

He was jerking on the floor before he could demand an explanation.

Near Fort Myer, Arlington, Virginia
8:44 PM EST

Senior Chief Chuck Skerritt law prone on an apartment building rooftop across from Fort Myer. He had two platoons worth of operators spread across the entire length of the base with sniper rifles at the ready and his targets were already picked.

Anybody wearing one of those cute little Raven Defense Services uniforms.

The standing orders were to not engage United States Military personnel, another platoon at ground level ready to provide cover fire should it be necessary and use rubber bullets should things really go to hell.

His men were to surrender to US Military personnel if it became necessary, not kill them.

But Raven was open season.

His phone sat in front of him, resting against a row of brick two courses high. The screen flashed a message. The final breach team was in place, the aim to take out all communications at once if possible, a platoon each assigned to the Pentagon, White House and Fort Myer.

All that was left now was to wait for 2100 hours.

And bring the rain.

Near the White House, Washington, DC
8:45 PM EST

"What the hell is going on?"

General Thorne couldn't see anything, a hood having been placed over his head before he had regained muscle control. He had been pulled up the elevator shaft by rope then carried and tossed into what he assumed was the back seat of a vehicle. He had been stunned again just before they cleared the main gates of the White House.

And they hadn't been stopped.

Which meant that whoever was doing this was well connected within the White House security apparatus. He knew it couldn't be his own men, they were loyal.

The missing Special Forces?

Now that was a definite possibility. They would have had the skills to execute his kidnapping, of that there was no doubt. Infiltrate the White House? Definitely.

They were the best.

But how were they able to simply drive off the White House property without security raising any questions?

Nobody had said a word since his capture, all of his protests and demands ignored. He could feel the vehicle picking up speed and they drove in silence for several minutes before slowing down and descending what he assumed was a ramp. The pitch changed and it sounded like they were now underground, perhaps in a parking garage.

The car stopped.

Doors opened and he was hauled roughly out of the car then marched forward, hands gripping each of his arms as he was guided through multiple turns until finally pushed into a chair, the hood ripped off his head.

And for the first time in his life, he felt fear.

Approaching Fort Myer, Arlington, Virginia
8:57 PM EST

"We're approaching Fort Myer now, sir. ETA twelve minutes."

Captain Mike Howards rode in the passenger seat of the lead Humvee, his convoy of reinforcements for Fort Myer stretching behind him about twenty vehicles strong. HQ had apparently received intel that a terrorist attack was imminent, perhaps on the cemetery itself, an attempt to desecrate the sacred remains that rested there.

And it pissed him off.

He was dispatched with a company of men to help secure the entire grounds with orders to shoot anyone who approached, civilian or otherwise, as it had been proven in previous attacks it was American citizens being coopted into this fight.

"It's better to kill them with one of our bullets then let them die by one of the terrorists' bombs," his CO had said.

He had asked about remote detonators and his CO had told him to make sure they took down any suspected terrorist before they could get close enough to harm military or government property. The thought sickened him, his anger not directed in any way at the victim, but at those cowards using them as pawns in their twisted religious war of domination.

He looked at his watch. *9:00PM.* He raised his radio to send in a status update when a burst of static erupted from it.

What the hell?

287

Utility Access Tunnel C4AR-7, Junction 12, Washington, DC
9:00 PM EST

"Execute."

Chief Winslow Pileggi turned away from the small bundle of explosives placed along the main wiring conduit that carried a good chunk of the Pentagon's external communications. He and the rest of his platoon were deployed in six tunnels that contained the fiber optic lines the Pentagon used for most of their communications to the outside world—not to mention their electrical feeds, the power requirements of the massive complex enormous.

He pushed the button on the detonator.

The explosion was rather small though the confined space did make its presence felt. The lighting in the access tunnel immediately went out, quickly replaced by dim emergency lighting. He waved away the dust and inspected his handiwork.

Nobody's getting that working again any time soon.

He turned and sprinted toward the exit before somebody arrived to ask questions he wasn't prepared to answer.

Arlington National Cemetery, Arlington, Virginia
9:00 PM EST

"Execute! Execute! Execute!"

Kane heard Dawson's whispered orders over his earpiece just as the power went down for the entire area. He flipped his night vision goggles down, his Glock 22 extended in front of him. Lee Fang was to his right, having insisted on joining them, her own Glock at the ready as the ten person team advanced, two sniper teams covering them along with hopefully several platoons of Navy SEALs nearby.

Emergency lighting kicked in showing Raven personnel scurrying about.

They continued to advance silently, so far unnoticed, through the sacred grounds, arriving at the knee wall unscathed.

Somebody shouted at his ten o'clock and gunfire erupted, the muzzle flash singling out the target. Kane hit the ground as did the others. Suddenly the shooter's body was skidding backward along the parking lot pavement, the loud report of a sniper rifle echoing a moment later.

All hell broke loose.

Gunfire belched from across the entire east side of the installation, the Raven personnel unloading their weapons into the darkness, aiming at nothing.

"Bravo Team, Bravo One, stay down," ordered Dawson over the comm. "Snipers, fire at will, over."

It was impressively terrifying. Kane had fired enough rounds from a sniper rifle to see the effect on the targets. It was one thing though to see that through a tiny scope, another to see it happening as little as ten yards away in living color.

Bodies began to skid back toward the buildings as the two Delta sniper teams eliminated Raven personnel. There were several military positions returning fire as well, but in a more disciplined manner, though he had to admit the Raven personnel weren't panicking, they simply didn't seem concerned about running out of ammo. But as their herd began to thin, some disarray was introduced as they scrambled to find cover, it taking almost a full minute to realize what was happening, eight of their numbers already down.

Kane cursed.

Several dozen Raven personnel emerged from their target building, Brucker Hall. As they spread out, their weapons blazing, Kane's heart leapt as the distinct pattern of the two coordinated Delta team's sniper rifles were suddenly joined by more, at least four or five additional weapons, the Raven personnel dropping like flies.

Kane pushed his earpiece in as Sergeant Will "Spock" Lightman radioed in from one of the sniper teams. "Bravo One, Bravo Five. We've got additional teams assisting, over."

"Roger that, Bravo Five. Keep them busy, out."

The Raven personnel were now taking cover from the snipers, their return fire minimal.

Kane heard Dawson's megaphone activate to his right. "We are United States Special Forces! All US military personnel, lay down your weapons! Our fight is not with you. If you do not comply within five seconds, you will be counted among the enemy. I repeat, we are United States Special Forces. All US military personnel, lay down your weapons!"

Kane looked at two of the military positions he could see from his location and the confusion was obvious, some of the men poking their heads up, one throwing his hands up.

Which seemed to create a wave as arms flew up everywhere, these men by no means cowards, but more likely relieved that they were under attack by their own as opposed to some terrorist group.

The sniper fire continued as targets of opportunity presented themselves, but the Raven personnel were now mostly behind cover, shielded from the deadly teams.

Which meant they weren't firing back.

Dawson signaled the advance.

Kane jumped to his feet, advancing quickly on a van he knew at least two of their opponents were hiding behind. He swung wide around the rear, firing two quick rounds, his first target dropping as the second spun. Kane fired another two rounds then dropped to a knee, looking for another target. More weapons fire around him, the disciplined quick and deliberate shooting of trained operators wasting little time and no ammo.

"United States Special Forces!" shouted Dawson to his right. Kane looked over to see Dawson and Niner advancing on one of the actual military positions, the men raising their hands even higher. Words were exchanged and the men jumped to their feet, their weapons in hand as they retreated into the cemetery then appeared to take up positions covering Delta Team-Bravo's six.

Fang fired twice, she tight to him, covering his rear as they advanced deeper into the parking lot. To Kane's left several more of the military positions were abandoned, the men taking the lead from their comrades, realizing who was actually in the right, they obviously having seen the broadcasts an hour ago.

Automatic weapons fire sounded in the distance and Kane had to assume that the SEALs teams and whoever else was here to assist had opened up another front, tying up he was certain a significant portion of the Raven personnel from redeploying to the east side.

He spotted a Raven uniform huddled under an SUV and lowered his weapon nearly to the ground, firing two rounds. The man cried out then was silent as Kane and Fang continued to advance toward the Brucker building. The gunfire on this end was dwindling now as Bravo Team swept from the left, eliminating any Raven personnel that remained, those who rose to flee immediately eliminated by snipers.

There were no orders to surrender here today.

These men had participated in the greatest criminal act in the history of their country, and all had been sentenced to death.

Kane recalled his promise to the USS Columbia's Captain. *"I intend to kill every damned last one of them."* He squeezed off another two rounds then reloaded, Fang firing as well.

The entire assault had taken less than five minutes and Niner was already rigging the main doors for Brucker Hall with explosives.

"We've got company," boomed Atlas. Kane spun to see eight men advancing in formation toward them but not firing.

"Friendlies on your six!" came a voice. "Navy SEALs!"

"Is that you, Chuck?" called Dawson.

One of the figures waved. "In the flesh, BD!"

Kane and the rest eased up slightly, turning their attention to their surroundings again as the new platoon arrived. "Sit rep?" asked Dawson as fist bumps were exchanged, everyone now hugging the windowless building wall.

"We've got the entire west side pinned down, about half the Raven posers eliminated, the military units standing down. Looks like they got the word they're playing for the wrong team. If we get their help we should be able to secure the entire facility in the next fifteen."

"Good," replied Dawson. "This is Booker's headquarters. We're going to breach now. Care to join us?"

Chuck Skerritt grinned. "With pleasure. Intel?"

"Limited. There's one CIA female hostage. Other than that we're assuming everyone's a target. If they're military, then they're in deep, so don't hesitate to shoot."

"Affirmative."

Skerritt moved his team to a set of doors farther down the front of the building, one of his men quickly rigging explosives. Dawson raised his hand, counting down with his fingers. "On Three, Two, One, Execute!"

Niner detonated the door, a simultaneous blast erupting from the SEAL position. Dawson took point with Niner, Red and Atlas breaking left as they entered, Kane and Fang right, Jimmy and Mickey covering the entrance. Emergency lighting lit the large drill area, dozens of government issue cubicles filling what was once used by the marching band to practice.

Gunfire erupted as shouts and screams from some of the cubicles had people running away or leaping up to fight. Kane squeczed off several rounds, taking down two Raven personnel who had burst from a hallway to the right. More shots, their double-taps distinctive, filled the hall as the squads advanced, clearing the cubicles. The process was swift and brutal, there no time for prisoners, no time to assess who might be surrendering, who might be pretending to surrender. They had one shot at saving their country, and this was it. Every single person in this room, regardless of uniform or gender, were traitors.

And they were going to die.

Fang and Kane advanced up one corridor of cubicles, clearing each one, occasionally pumping rounds into people fleeing as they heard the advance, others jumping out trying to fire, but to no avail.

Everyone dies today.

They reached the other side of the hall, joined by the other friendlies, the large room cleared. Dawson motioned to a set of doors to the left. "SEALs, you take left. We'll take right."

"See you on the other side," grinned Skerritt, leading his men off as Dawson and the others headed for a set of doors to the right. Niner pulled the door open, stepping aside.

They were greeted by a wall of bullets.

"Can you reach anyone?"

Colonel Booker was screaming at his team, but they were all useless.

As useless as all this equipment!

"I'm sorry, sir. Our backup communications are still up, but our primaries are down. And we can't reach the Pentagon or the White House. It looks like there was a coordinated effort to take down our comms."

"And they succeeded, apparently." Booker growled. "What's the ETA on that company of reinforcements?"

"They're still ten minutes out."

"Strength?"

"One hundred fifty men with Humvees, some heavy weaponry and a few armored vehicles. If they remain loyal we should be able to take back the base. I don't think we're under attack by that many."

"Maybe not many, but enough." He spun on his heel. "I'll be back."

He marched down the hall as the doors at the far end suddenly burst open. Raven personnel lining either side of the hall, tucked into doorways, opened fire. Smoke was popped by the enemy and he could see his men beginning to drop as well aimed rounds found their targets.

It reminded him of the opening of Star Wars, he half expecting to see Darth Vader's robed figure emerge through the fog.

He opened a door to his right, closing and locking it behind him.

"Good evening, Mr. President. I think it's time to die."

Dawson and Niner peered through the haze with their infrared goggles, picking off the blinded targets one by one. They advanced to the first set of doors, the doors already opened. Dawson found his room empty but heard Niner squeeze off several rounds then shout, "Clear!"

With the two of them now inside the hall, covered by their doorways, Atlas and Red were able to take position at the outer door and double the firepower now directed down the hall. The defenders quickly dropped, some throwing their weapons down and jumping up in surrender, others retreating.

All died.

Dawson advanced, kicking open the next door, this time with Niner covering him, Atlas and Red taking the right side, covered by the others. Dawson reached the third door and kicked it open. It contained a now dim large light on a stand and a single chair with a woman tied in it.

And even through his goggles he recognized her immediately from their meeting during the New Orleans crisis.

Sherrie White had finally fallen asleep.

And no one had woken her.

She had no idea how long she had remained that way before the sound of her door being kicked open woke her, but it was the most precious few minutes of sleep she could ever remember having.

But she awoke to confusion.

And hope.

Gunfire sounded in the hallway and a dark figure now stood before her, silhouetted by the emergency light behind them. The figure reached forward and she recoiled slightly.

A flashlight suddenly snapped on, highlighting the man's face and she erupted in tears, her shoulders heaving in relief as she recognized one of the Delta operators she had been teamed with previously.

"BD!" she cried as another figure appeared behind him.

"Sherrie!" cried the voice she immediately recognized as Dylan Kane, her beloved Chris' high school buddy and best friend. And the man responsible for getting the two of them together in the first place.

"Oh Dylan, BD, thank God you guys are here!"

Kane went behind her and cut the ties binding her wrists. "Can you walk?" he asked.

She tried but cried out in pain. "I can't," she said, shaking her head. "I think they might have broken my left leg."

A woman appeared behind them, Chinese. Sherrie didn't recognize her but the look she received told her at once this new arrival had been through what she had been through.

"I'll stay with her," said the woman. "You two continue clearing the building."

"Sherrie, this is Lee Fang. I trust her completely," said Kane as he gave her a quick kiss on the forehead.

"Chris? Is he okay?"

Kane frowned. "Last word I have is that they were holed up in The Bunker but were about to be breached."

Sherrie's eyes narrowed. "The Bunker?"

Kane smiled. "No time to explain." He rose and pointed at Sherrie, looking at Fang. "Guard her like she was my sister."

Fang nodded. "Done."

Sherrie sighed in relief, every muscle in her body relaxing for the first time in days.

And she fell asleep.

Kane took up position on one side of the next door, the rest of the hallway almost cleared by the others when the lights came back on, momentarily blinding them. Kane squeezed his eyes shut and threw up the night vision goggles. He looked at Dawson who nodded he was okay, then kicked open the door.

Dawson entered first, Glock raised high, breaking to the right as Kane went left, the room small, containing only a bed, nightstand and small desk with an empty food tray on it.

And one President of the United States, standing in the center with a gun pressed to his head.

"Colonel Booker, I order you to lower your weapon and surrender," said Dawson, his weapon aimed directly at the man's head, as was Kane's.

"Stand down! That's an order!" barked Booker. "You are in violation of military law instituted by the Military Stewardship Council!"

"Mr. President, I am Command Sergeant Major Dawson, Delta Force. What are your orders?"

"Kill him."

Kane squeezed the trigger at the same moment Dawson did. The shocked expression on Booker's face at the President's words would be something Kane would cherish for the rest of his life. Dawson's bullet went through the center of Booker's forehead, Kane's through the man's hand then into the gun grip, forcing the weapon away from the President's head just in case Booker's finger reflexively pulled the trigger.

It didn't.

Booker crumpled to the ground and President Starling nearly collapsed in shock. Dawson caught him before he fell then they both helped him to the bed.

"Sit down here, sir," said Kane as they lowered him to a sitting position. "Take a few moments to gather yourself. You're safe now."

"My family?"

"We don't know yet, sir. This seems to be their command and control center. We're hoping shutting it down will end this crisis. But we're going to need your help."

"Name it."

"We need to get you on the air right away," said Kane. "We need you to tell the country you're alive and back in control, for military units to stand down and return to base, and for all Raven personnel to be arrested immediately."

"Holy shit!" exclaimed Niner from the doorway. "Mr. President, sorry for interrupting, sir," he stammered, snapping out a quick salute. He turned to BD. "Ops Center secure. We managed to just shoot meat and not metal for a change." He grinned, then remembered whose company he was in. "Sorry, sir, I mean, Mr. President. Operational humor. It's twisted, I know." He turned back to Dawson. "Looks like their primary comms were taken down but they've got good backups. They can still communicate with the outside world but it looks like the Pentagon and White House are down."

"Can we send out a video signal?" asked Kane.

Niner shrugged. "They've got a camera with a nice backdrop set up in one corner. I'm guessing yes."

Kane turned to the President. "Are you ready?"

The man rose then fixed his tie, buttoning his suit. "How do I look?"

"All right, Mr. DeMille, he's ready for his close-up," said Niner in his best Gloria Swanson imitation. He shook his head. "I'm sorry, Mr. President, I just can't stop myself."

Starling chuckled, placing a hand on Niner's shoulder as they walked out of the room into the smoke filled hallway. "Son, never apologize for making an old man laugh. With the hell our country has been through these past few weeks, our sense of humor will be more important than ever."

They entered the Ops Center and Kane spotted the camera setup. "Anybody know how to work this stuff?"

Atlas stepped forward. "Allow me, Mr. President." He sat down on one of the stools, his massive frame almost looking as ridiculous as poor Ruben Studdard on an American Idol stool. He began pressing buttons then turned, nodding at the President who had already checked himself in a mirror and was standing behind the camera. "When you're ready, Mr. President."

Starling nodded and Atlas hit a button, the displays for the various networks switching showing their regular broadcasts as their own signal showed on a monitor with a flashing message.

Standby for a message from the President of the United States.

They waited and within a few seconds ABC had switched over, then several others, within less than two minutes they had all switched over.

"You're on in three, two, one, now," whispered Atlas, his voice impossibly low for a man his size, the display switching expertly to the President.

"My fellow Americans, good evening."

"The Bunker", CIA Headquarters, Langley, Virginia

"Are they doing what I think they're doing?"

Morrison nodded at Leroux's question. "I think so."

"Is that explosives?" asked Tong, their collective fear given voice. "Shouldn't we get out of here?"

"There's nowhere to go," replied Morrison. "These are strong doors, they might just hold, but in case they don't, when they're ready to detonate we'll all get on the opposite side of the room." He pointed at several tables holding terminals. "See if you can tip those over so we can use them as cover."

Dillard and several others jumped from their seats executing Morrison's orders as Leroux suddenly noticed the security feed from Fort Myer. "Look, sir!" He pointed excitedly at one of the feeds showing Sherrie's cell. She was still seated, but she was with an Asian woman and no longer bound.

"Sir!" Leroux turned to see Dillard pointing at the bank of screens on the left that showed the various news feeds. They were all switching over to the same signal then suddenly the President appeared.

Morrison jabbed a finger at the screens. "Let's hear that!" Leroux stepped over to a terminal and hit a few keys, the President's voice suddenly surrounding them. "Can you pipe that into the hallway so our guests can hear it?"

Leroux examined the console then nodded, hitting a button. The security feed showed the men stopping and looking up.

"—evening. This is your President speaking. I have been held captive by General Thorne's forces at Fort Myer in Arlington and have just been freed by loyal American soldiers. I assure my fellow Americans that for the moment I am safe, and if my family is

300

hearing this, I ask them not to worry. But the danger is not over. General Thorne's forces, mostly in the form of Raven Defense Services personnel, have staged the attacks our country has suffered over the past several weeks in an attempt to seize power. I repeat, these attacks were not carried out by our Muslim friends and neighbors but by General Thorne's forces.

"I know you will find it hard to believe that a coup d'état has actually occurred in our country, but it has. We have fought tyranny before and won, we have fought the unjust oppressor before and won. We did it over two hundred years ago, and I'm asking you to do it once more. Fight those who would take away your freedom in the name of security, fight those who would tear up our hard won Constitution, fight those who would dishonor the over one million who have died fighting in the past to preserve our way of life.

"It is time for all good Americans to rise up, to take to the streets, and to fight for what they know is right, and that is a country of the people, by the people, and for the people! We will not be held prisoner by the steel boot of a military dictatorship, nor will we be confined to our homes by fear of the unknown. Today we take back our freedom, take back our dignity and take back our country!

"I hereby order all United States Military personnel to stand down and return to their bases. I also order that all Raven Defense Services employees be immediately arrested. I am also ordering the immediate release of all those forced into internment camps and the immediate repatriation of any citizens who were deported illegally.

"I also am requesting that loyal members of the Secret Service and Capitol Hill Police retake the White House and Capitol Hill, and request that all members of Congress return to the Hill at once to rescind the recent decision to impose martial law. We were deceived, my fellow Americans, by General Thorne and his cohorts. I therefore order General Thorne's immediate arrest as well, along with any personnel who may have been assisting him.

"My friends, we have been through a grueling time and I ask you to endure just one more night. Take to the streets, demand them back, but remember, your military is not your enemy. The soldiers protecting you were following lawful orders; it was their

commander that was corrupt. Allow them to return to their bases unmolested. These are the same soldiers you loved and supported last week, and they deserve that same love and support tonight. They were deceived just as we all were.

"Make your feelings known, make your feelings heard. Take to the streets, peacefully. Demand those who won't stand down to do so, demand your law enforcement agencies arrest the Raven Defense personnel and free our fellow Americans who have been so horribly imprisoned.

"My fellow Americans, take back your country!"

The broadcast looped and as Leroux and the others watched, he glanced over at the security feed showing the hallway outside the blast doors. The Raven personnel were retreating to the elevator shaft. Morrison noticed as well.

"It looks like we've got a reprieve, ladies and gentlemen. Excellent work. Every one of you."

Tears of relief and joy flowed down many of the faces as Leroux turned his attention to the screen showing Sherrie and what he assumed was the Chinese woman Kane had been sent to collect.

"It looks like it's working," said Dillard, pointing at the feeds showing the main gates surrounding CIA Headquarters. Dozens of Raven personnel were being corralled by soldiers, CIA uniformed officers slowly taking over as they were freed and rearmed. As the soldiers secured the scene their heavy equipment began to roll out, and as their presence deescalated, Leroux felt his own heart rate begin to lower slightly.

We just might make it through this alive.

Approaching Fort Myer, Arlington, Virginia

Communications were still down as Captain Mike Howards' column made the final turn to Fort Myer. Sporadic gunfire flared and he realized they were going in hot. He stood up in his Humvee and motioned for the column to split, several platoons deploying to the rear, the rest to the front, the layout of the installation a narrow strip between the road they were on and the cemetery behind it.

Muzzle flashes from multiple positions burst from the defenders and the terrorists apparently on the rooftops lining the road. He pointed and several .50 caliber machineguns opened up, silencing the attackers' weapons. They rolled through the main gates, held open by private security, the military personnel he assumed would be assigned nowhere in sight.

And the gunfire from the enemy was curiously silent.

"Cease fire!" he ordered, listening. There were still the sounds of gunfire from the other side of the installation including what sounded like some serious firepower. *Sniper rifles?* He found it hard to believe that terrorists would have these types of weapons, but then again, they had apparently been using military grade explosives so anything was possible.

"Thank God you guys arrived," said one of the Raven men, approaching him and saluting.

Captain Howards didn't return the salute. *I don't salute civilians.* He had no time or respect for Raven personnel or their types. Too often he had met men like this in Iraq who were there for the money and the legal right to kill someone. True soldiers served their country, these men far too often served themselves. He knew they all weren't like that, some having put in their time honorably with the regular forces then going private to continue doing good work for good money.

But too many did it for the wrong reasons.

"Status?" he said, still eyeing the silent rooftops.

"We've been attacked from the front and rear, our HQ has gone silent."

"Where are the military personnel?"

The man shrugged. "Not sure, they retreated pretty quickly. Inexperienced maybe?"

Howards didn't buy that explanation, but the gunfire he continued to hear certainly confirmed that an attack was still underway.

"I'm unarmed!"

The voice came from the shadows across the street. Somebody was slowly walking toward them, his hands raised, something white held in his hand.

"Stay where you are or we *will* open fire!" shouted Howards, taking cover behind the hood of his Humvee. This was exactly what they were told to expect. Civilians coerced into becoming suicide bombers.

And this was the first.

The man stopped.

"My name is Senior Chief Sandy Jacob. I'm with SEAL Team Three. Have you seen the President's speech?"

Howards paused, not sure what to make of this new turn. The man might be an imposter, but there was something about his bearing that made him think he just could be who he claimed to be.

A single shot from his right had him ducking, the man spinning, dropping to the ground. Howards turned on the Raven employee who had fired. "Who the hell gave you permission to shoot?"

"I don't take my orders from you," sneered the man.

Suddenly a hole the size of a fist opened in the man's chest as he was shoved backward, into the ground, a single round from what was clearly a sniper rifle eliminating the offender.

Howards stood up, raising his hands. "Nobody shoot! We're going to check on your man!" He motioned for two of his team to check on the downed SEAL. He turned to those around him. "Does anybody know what speech he's talking about?" he shouted.

"I do!" yelled a voice. He turned toward the voice and saw a man hanging out his window from an apartment across the street. "We were lied to by your General Thorne. This whole things a scam!"

More windows started to open, people shouting similar things as his men dragged the body of the SEAL to the safety of Fort Myer. Howards knelt down beside him. "Is he okay?"

"Yes, sir. He's wearing a vest. Maybe some cracked ribs."

The man reached up and grabbed Howards by the arm. "Front pocket. Cellphone. Watch the speech."

Howards carefully, almost reluctantly reached into the pocket and pulled out the man's cellphone. The man pressed his thumb on the pad to unlock it, the video already queued up.

And Howards jaw dropped as he and his men listened.

The Oval Office, The White House, Washington, DC
The next day

President Starling shook the hand of the Supreme Court Justice, once again officially President of the United States, it having taken until morning to get a quorum together to rescind the previous idiocy they had implemented. His speech had worked, however. Military units across the country had immediately stood down, crowds had filled the streets in mostly peaceful protest, and FBI supported by local and military authorities had rounded up much of the Raven Defense Services personnel, many however having stripped out of their paramilitary uniforms and slipped off into the night.

They'd be found eventually.

Television stations were reporting the news again and though life was far from normal, people were in the streets again. He had actually heard laughter in the halls this morning, something that had been missing for too long.

Once word of the speech had spread, Capitol Hill and the White House were quickly taken back and though security was *very* heavy, they were all wearing the proper uniforms.

He pointed at Thorne's portrait on the wall. "Get that piece of shit out of here," he said.

One of the Delta operators who had help free him, Command Sergeant Major Dawson, motioned to one of his men Starling believed was named Niner. What the hell that meant, he didn't know, and he wasn't about to ask. Niner stepped over to the portrait and tore his fingers through the faux painting, tearing it in half, then shoving his arm up and around the frame, lifting it from the wall. He paused, looking at Starling.

"I'm sorry, Mr. President. You didn't want this preserved intact, did you?"

Starling chuckled. "No, Sergeant. I'd say burn it, but someday people will learn about this in history class and will want to see the portrait of the first military dictator in American history." He smiled. "And now your name will live on forever as the man who ripped it from the wall."

Niner winked at Dawson. "I always knew I'd be remembered."

Dawson rolled his eyes, looking at Starling. "Mr. President, he'll be impossible to live with now."

Starling laughed heartily as the door opened.

"Mr. President, they're ready for you now."

Starling nodded then shook the hands of the Bravo Team members that had helped save him. "It's too bad—what was his name, Agent White?—couldn't be here."

Niner lowered his voice. "He doesn't really exist."

Starling nodded, tapping his nose. "Of course he doesn't."

Dawson and the others saluted, Starling returning it then heading to meet the press, free once again.

Chris Leroux & Sherrie White Residence, Fairfax Towers, Falls Church, Virginia

Kane tapped on the door, it opening almost instantly, a beaming Leroux standing there to greet him.

"If I didn't know better I'd say you were expecting me."

Leroux gave him a hug, an uncharacteristic hug, Leroux not one for human contact from Kane's experience. Leroux didn't say anything, instead just holding on. Kane patted his friend's back. "It's good to see you too, buddy."

"Thanks for saving her," cracked Leroux's voice, and Kane knew his friend was crying, still hanging on so Kane wouldn't see his face. He decided to save him.

"You're welcome, buddy." He turned opposite Leroux's face, giving him a chance to break away and wipe his eyes. "I don't think you've met Miss Lee Fang."

Leroux smiled, his eyes red and shook Fang's hand. "I'm glad you're okay."

"I understand in no small part thanks to you."

Leroux shrugged, not one to take a compliment well. "I played a small part."

They stepped into the living area of the apartment to find Sherrie lying on the couch, her face swollen, bruises covering much of her body, her left leg in a cast. "Rough day at the office?" asked Kane.

She flipped him the bird, wincing. "That hurt, but it was worth it, asshole."

Kane roared in laughter as he and Fang sat down.

"Can I get you anything?" asked Leroux.

"Scotch for me. Glen Breton Ice, on the rocks."

Leroux frowned. "I'm not sure I have that."

Kane pointed toward the kitchen where Leroux kept the liquor. "Top shelf on the right, in the back."

Leroux's eyes narrowed as he stepped into the open concept kitchen, reaching into the back of the cupboard and producing a bottle. He held it up. "How the hell did this get here?"

Kane winked at Sherrie. "You guys are heavy sleepers."

Leroux poured Kane a glass, shaking his head. "Are we all allowed to partake in this smuggled scotch, or is this just for you."

Kane shrugged. "I guess I'll share for today. But if you guys finish it, replace it for the next time I'm here. I don't want to have to wait for you two to fall asleep before I can leave next time."

Leroux blushed and Sherrie laughed. "You're a perv!"

"Absolutely!"

"What's a perv?" asked Fang.

"If you spend enough time with him, you'll find out," said Sherrie, taking her scotch and wincing as she took a sip of the Glen Breton. "That's good!"

"Nothing but the best for me and my friends," said Kane. He looked at his watch. "Oh, I hope you don't have any friends at Kunlun, Fang."

She shrugged. "Not that I know of."

"Good. Your government would have just got their ten minute warning."

"Warning for what?"

"We've got half a dozen hypersonic weapons about to obliterate that complex. They're already in the air as we speak."

"What are those?" asked Sherrie.

"I could tell you, but I'd have to kill you," laughed Kane.

"Well, I can tell you," said Leroux. "Conventional Prompt Global Strike. They're an experimental hypersonic weapon that can reach a target anywhere in the world within sixty minutes. They're basically a massive warhead that uses explosives and kinetic energy to obliterate a target. Half a dozen of them should level the complex and destroy any F-35 parts that might be there. A rapid response without needing to use nukes."

"You're not worried about retaliation?" asked Fang.

Kane shook his head. "No. Langley sent them the footage I took from inside their complex and the President told them that if they reported anything other than an earthquake, there'd be hell to pay."

Sherrie sat up, yelping then waving off an ever attentive Leroux. "It's too bad you killed Booker. I wanted him for myself."

"Sorry, but I need all requests in at least fifteen minutes before my own kill opportunity. Besides, I think BD technically killed him."

"I'll thank him next time I see him."

"So what's going to happen to you?" asked Leroux, looking at Fang.

She shrugged. "I'm not sure. I can't go back to China. Your government has agreed to provide me with a new identity and a pension in thanks for trying to save President Bridges. I only regret that I wasn't able to."

"You did your best," said Kane. He turned to her. "If you're not doing anything, how about you join me in Costa Rica for a few days. I'm going for some R and R."

"R and R?"

"Rest and Relaxation," answered Sherrie.

"Nope, Rum and Rubdowns."

"Oy!" exclaimed Sherrie. "Be careful with this one, he'll break your heart."

Fang blushed noticeably, looking away and Kane smiled as he felt a warmth inside him at the thought this beautiful woman might actually like him. And what scared him was it wasn't just a sexual attraction.

There was an awkward pause for a moment when Leroux saved them all.

"I wonder what ever happened to General Thorne?"

Unknown Location

"You failed us, General."

The voice was disembodied, deep, the reverberation in the room as the man spoke adding an almost menacing quality. He had been held for hours, if not more. He was tired and sore and had been in this chair the entire time since being abducted. The moment the hood had been removed he had recognized the meeting place immediately. He had been here once before, four years ago, when he had first conceived of his plan.

A plan he had told almost no one of, yet somehow they knew.

They knew everything.

He had been picked up one night from the Pentagon, his regular driver apparently sick. But that wasn't the case, the driver activating some sort of knockout gas that had him out in seconds, unable to escape, the doors locked.

He had awoken in this very room, a large round table seating about a dozen men and women, all cloaked in the shadows, none of their faces visible to him.

They had called themselves The Assembly.

He had never heard of them but they were apparently powerful. Very powerful. And they claimed ancient, but he couldn't prove that. All his attempts to find out who they were had failed, and those attempts were few. A note on his wife's pillow one night had been succinct and terrifying.

'Stop asking questions.'

"Failure will not be tolerated. We told you that from the beginning." It was a woman's voice this time.

"But I didn't fail," he said, his mind reeling as he tried to figure out some way to get out of this alive. "I *did* gain power, I *did* implement the changes you wanted."

"Yet you are here."

"Send me back so I can continue."

"All was lost the moment you failed to contain the CNN broadcast. You should have shut down all news broadcasters as we ordered."

"But it would have raised suspicions!"

"Raised suspicions are always better than the unwelcome truth. If the broadcasters had been shut down, the American people would never have seen the footage of their President under arrest."

The woman's voice returned. "You should have killed him as we instructed you to."

Another voice. "If you had followed our instructions to the letter, we would still be in control of the country."

Thorne leaned forward. "But I thought you already were in control? You told me you controlled everything."

"We said no such thing!" yelled the woman, her voice sounding almost defensive, her control however quickly returning. "We influence everything over time, but sometimes we need to take direct action to protect our interests."

"And this is such a time," said the first man. "And you have failed us."

"But you were supposed to control the CIA!" cried Thorne.

"They reacted too quickly and their operative was simply too capable."

"Their analyst too," added the woman. "Perhaps it's time we put an end to his meddling."

"He has been looking into our affairs far too closely as of late," agreed the man, Thorne sitting back in his chair, wondering who they were talking about. The conversation was terrifyingly revealing, which could mean only one thing.

He wasn't going to be alive long enough for it to matter whether or not he heard it.

The conversation paused, then the first man spoke. "Your work for us is done, General Thorne."

"Wh-what does that mean?"

He felt something jab into his neck from behind then a sudden warmth spread through his body as things slowly turned to a fog.

"You are fortunate we kill our failed operatives humanely, General," said the woman. Her voice changed, as if no longer concerned with him as he felt his heart pound in his chest, slower and slower. "Now, what should we do about these problems?"

The first man spoke, the words fading into the background of white noise.

"Perhaps it's time to eliminate Agent Kane and Mr. Leroux."

THE END

ACKNOWLEDGEMENTS

For those of you who have read my books over the years, you know I am hugely pro-military. I love our troops and think they are the finest men and women our countries have to offer. This book should not be misinterpreted as being anti-military. As I was careful to try and illustrate, there were few actual military officers involved in the conspiracy. The military involved in securing the streets, rounding up the Muslim population and violating territorial integrity were doing so under lawful orders, or at least orders that were lawful at the time under martial law. Remember, the President and Congress had requested General Thorne take over, and the men and women under his command then began to secure their country from a threat only those few involved knew was from within. Private security was used for the truly heinous acts.

In no way should any of what was written be interpreted as anti-military, but should anyone have felt it was, I apologize for that wasn't the intent. Just as with any organization, there will always be bad apples, but as with most groups, one bad apple does *not* spoil the whole bunch.

Now a little fun anecdote. When my daughter was about five or six, her cousin, about a year younger, came to visit for a couple of days. It was a two hour drive one way to return her and the two girls were being a little rambunctious in the backseat. I was getting a little annoyed so I proposed the sleeping game. Within five minutes both were snoring away for the rest of the drive.

It's a miracle game that unfortunately doesn't work on teenagers.

And since I'm giving out free parenting tips, for those of you with young ones trying to learn to ride a bike, here's one that my late friend Paul Conway told me (it being passed on to him by another father). The keys to learning to ride a bike are balance and confidence. Remove the training wheels and remove the pedals. Have your kid sit on the bike and use their feet to propel the bike forward. If they begin to lose balance, they just lower their feet (since there's no pedals to put their feet on, they won't fall). As they learn to balance, they'll pick up more and more speed, and they'll gain confidence, getting over their fear of falling. When they're ready they'll ask for the pedals to be put back on.

My daughter had been on training wheels for months, too scared to have them come off. I came home after hearing this story, removed the training wheels and pedals, told her what to do, and left her in the driveway. Two hours later she asked for the pedals to be put on then promptly rode up and down the street for the next two hours.

Every single child that has used this technique (that I've heard about) has been biking within no more than a day or two, usually within hours.

Of course in these litigious times I am *not* suggesting you try this, in fact I discourage it wholeheartedly. I'm just telling you what worked for my child. If you do decide to try it, keep your lawyers on their leash should little Tommy still scrape a knee.

And that ends the parenting portion of my presentation.

As usual there are people to thank. Chief "Gramps" Michael and Fred Newton for their naval expertise, Brent Richards for weapons and tactics info, Joanne Sisetsky for some info on her hometown of Moose Jaw (yes, it's a real place!) and of course my dad for research. As always thanks to my wife, daughter, parents and friends for their continued support.

And to those who have not already done so, please visit my website at www.jrobertkennedy.com then sign up for the Insiders Club. You'll get emails about new book releases, new collections, sales, etc.

ABOUT THE AUTHOR

J. Robert Kennedy is the author of over one dozen international best sellers, including the smash hit James Acton Thrillers series, the first installment of which, The Protocol, has been on the best sellers list since its release, including a three month run at number one. In addition to the other novels from this series, Brass Monkey, Broken Dove, The Templar's Relic (also a number one best seller), Flags of Sin, The Arab Fall (also #1), The Circle of Eight (also #1) and The Venice Code (also #1), he has written the international best sellers Rogue Operator, Containment Failure, Cold Warriors, Depraved Difference, Tick Tock, The Redeemer and The Turned. Robert spends his time in Ontario, Canada with his family.

Visit Robert's website at www.jrobertkennedy.com for the latest news and contact information.

The Protocol

A James Acton Thriller, Book #1

For two thousand years the Triarii have protected us, influencing history from the crusades to the discovery of America. Descendent from the Roman Empire, they pervade every level of society, and are now in a race with our own government to retrieve an ancient artifact thought to have been lost forever.

Caught in the middle is archaeology professor James Acton, relentlessly hunted by the elite Delta Force, under orders to stop at nothing to possess what he has found, and the Triarii, equally determined to prevent the discovery from falling into the wrong hands.

With his students and friends dying around him, Acton flees to find the one person who might be able to help him, but little does he know he may actually be racing directly into the hands of an organization he knows nothing about...

Brass Monkey

A James Acton Thriller, Book #2

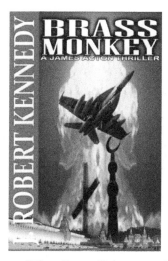

A nuclear missile, lost during the Cold War, is now in play--the most public spy swap in history, with a gorgeous agent the center of international attention, triggers the end-game of a corrupt Soviet Colonel's twenty five year plan. Pursued across the globe by the Russian authorities, including a brutal Spetsnaz unit, those involved will stop at nothing to deliver their weapon, and ensure their pay day, regardless of the terrifying consequences.

When Laura Palmer confronts a UNICEF group for trespassing on her Egyptian archaeological dig site, she unwittingly stumbles upon the ultimate weapons deal, and becomes entangled in an international conspiracy that sends her lover, archeology Professor James Acton, racing to Egypt with the most unlikely of allies, not only to rescue her, but to prevent the start of a holy war that could result in Islam and Christianity wiping each other out.

From the bestselling author of Depraved Difference and The Protocol comes Brass Monkey, a thriller international in scope, certain to offend some, and stimulate debate in others. Brass Monkey pulls no punches in confronting the conflict between two of the world's most powerful, and divergent, religions, and the terrifying possibilities the future may hold if left unchecked.

Broken Dove

A James Acton Thriller, Book #3

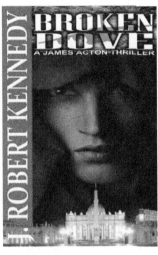

With the Triarii in control of the Roman Catholic Church, an organization founded by Saint Peter himself takes action, murdering one of the new Pope's operatives. Detective Chaney, called in by the Pope to investigate, disappears, and, to the horror of the Papal staff sent to inform His Holiness, they find him missing too, the only clue a secret chest, presented to each new pope on the eve of their election, since the beginning of the Church.

Interpol Agent Reading, determined to find his friend, calls Professors James Acton and Laura Palmer to Rome to examine the chest and its forbidden contents, but before they can arrive, they are intercepted by an organization older than the Church, demanding the professors retrieve an item stolen in ancient Judea in exchange for the lives of their friends.

All of your favorite characters from The Protocol return to solve the most infamous kidnapping in history, against the backdrop of a two thousand year old battle pitting ancient foes with diametrically opposed agendas.

From the internationally bestselling author of Depraved Difference and The Protocol comes Broken Dove, the third entry in the smash hit James Acton Thrillers series, where J. Robert Kennedy reveals a secret concealed by the Church for almost 1200 years, and a fascinating interpretation of what the real reason behind the denials might be.

The Templar's Relic

A James Acton Thriller, Book #4

THE CHURCH HELPED DESTROY THE TEMPLARS.
WILL A TWIST OF FATE LET THEM GET THEIR
REVENGE 700 YEARS LATER?

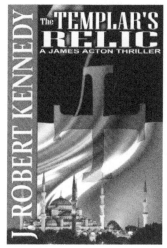

The Vault must be sealed, but a construction accident leads to a miraculous discovery--an ancient tomb containing four Templar Knights, long forgotten, on the grounds of the Vatican. Not knowing who they can trust, the Vatican requests Professors James Acton and Laura Palmer examine the find, but what they discover, a precious Islamic relic, lost during the Crusades, triggers a set of events that shake the entire world, pitting the two greatest religions against each other.

Join Professors James Acton and Laura Palmer, INTERPOL Agent Hugh Reading, Scotland Yard DI Martin Chaney, and the Delta Force Bravo Team as they race against time to defuse a worldwide crisis that could quickly devolve into all-out war.

At risk is nothing less than the Vatican itself, and the rock upon which it was built.

From J. Robert Kennedy, the author of six international bestsellers including Depraved Difference and The Protocol, comes The Templar's Relic, the fourth entry in the smash hit James Acton Thrillers series, where once again Kennedy takes history and twists it to his own ends, resulting in a heart pounding thrill ride filled with action, suspense, humor and heartbreak.

Flags of Sin

A James Acton Thriller, Book #5

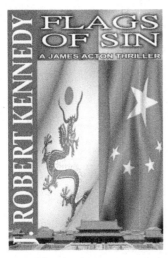

Archaeology Professor James Acton simply wants to get away from everything, and relax. A trip to China seems just the answer, and he and his fiancée, Professor Laura Palmer, are soon on a flight to Beijing.

But while boarding, they bump into an old friend, Delta Force Command Sergeant Major Burt Dawson, who surreptitiously delivers a message that they must meet the next day, for Dawson knows something they don't.

China is about to erupt into chaos.

Foreign tourists and diplomats are being targeted by unknown forces, and if they don't get out of China in time, they could be caught up in events no one had seen coming.

J. Robert Kennedy, the author of eight international best sellers, including the smash hit James Acton Thrillers, takes history once again and turns it on its head, sending his reluctant heroes James Acton and Laura Palmer into harm's way, to not only save themselves, but to try and save a country from a century old conspiracy it knew nothing about.

The Arab Fall

A James Acton Thriller, Book #6

THE GREATEST ARCHEOLOGICAL DISCOVERY SINCE KING TUT'S TOMB IS ABOUT TO BE DESTROYED!

The Arab Spring has happened and Egypt has yet to calm down, but with the dig site on the edge of the Nubian Desert, a thousand miles from the excitement, Professor Laura Palmer and her fiancé Professor James Acton return with a group of students, and two friends: Interpol Special Agent Hugh Reading, and Scotland Yard DI Martin Chaney.

But an accidental find by Chaney may lead to the greatest archaeological discovery since the tomb of King Tutankhamen, perhaps even greater. And when news of it spreads, it reaches the ears of a group hell-bent on the destruction of all idols and icons, their mere existence considered blasphemous to Islam.

As chaos hits the major cities of the world in a coordinated attack, unbeknownst to the professors, students and friends, they are about to be faced with one of the most difficult decisions of their lives. Stay and protect the greatest archaeological find of our times, or save themselves and their students from harm, leaving the find to be destroyed by fanatics determined to wipe it from the history books.

From J. Robert Kennedy, the author of eleven international bestsellers including Rogue Operator and The Protocol, comes The Arab Fall, the sixth entry in the smash hit James Acton Thrillers series, where Kennedy once again takes events from history and today's headlines, and twists them into a heart pounding adventure filled with humor and heartbreak, as one of their own is left severely wounded, fighting for their life.

The Circle of Eight

A James Acton Thriller, Book #7

ABANDONED BY THEIR GOVERNMENT, DELTA TEAM BRAVO FIGHTS TO NOT ONLY SAVE THEMSELVES AND THEIR FAMILIES, BUT HUMANITY AS WELL.

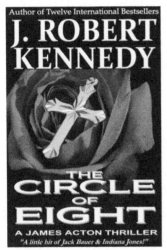

The Bravo Team is targeted by a madman after one of their own intervenes in a rape. Little do they know this internationally well-respected banker is also a senior member of an organization long thought extinct, whose stated goals for a reshaped world are not only terrifying, but with today's globalization, totally achievable.

As the Bravo Team fights for its very survival, they are suspended, left adrift without their support network. To save themselves and their families, markers are called in, former members volunteer their services, favors are asked for past services, and the expertise of two professors, James Acton and his fiancée Laura Palmer, is requested.

It is a race around the globe to save what remains of the Bravo Team, abandoned by their government, alone in their mission, with only their friends to rely upon, as an organization over six centuries old works in the background to destroy them and all who help them, as it moves forward with plans that could see the world population decimated in an attempt to recreate Eden.

In The Circle of Eight J. Robert Kennedy, author of over a dozen international best sellers, is at his best, weaving a tale spanning centuries and delivering a taut thriller that will keep you on the edge of your seat from page one until the breathtaking conclusion.

The Venice Code

A James Acton Thriller, Book #8

A SEVEN HUNDRED YEAR OLD MYSTERY IS ABOUT TO BE SOLVED.

BUT HOW MANY MUST DIE FIRST?

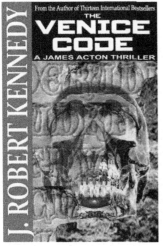

A former President's son is kidnapped in a brazen attack on the streets of Potomac by the very ancient organization that murdered his father, convinced he knows the location of an item stolen from them by the late president.

A close friend awakes from a coma with a message for archeology Professor James Acton from the same organization, sending him along with his fiancée Professor Laura Palmer on a quest to find an object only rumored to exist, while trying desperately to keep one step ahead of a foe hell-bent on possessing it.

And seven hundred years ago, the Mongol Empire threatens to fracture into civil war as the northern capital devolves into idol worship, the Khan sending in a trusted family to save the empire--two brothers and a son, Marco Polo, whose actions have ramifications that resonate to this day.

From J. Robert Kennedy, the author of fourteen international best sellers comes The Venice Code, the latest installment of the hit James Acton Thrillers series. Join James Acton and his friends, including Delta Team Bravo and CIA Special Agent Dylan Kane in their greatest adventure yet, an adventure seven hundred years in the making.

Pompeii's Ghosts

A James Acton Thriller, Book #9

POMPEII IS ABOUT TO CLAIM ITS FINAL VICTIMS—TWO THOUSAND YEARS LATER!

Two thousand years ago Roman Emperor Vespasian tries to preserve an empire by hiding a massive treasure in the quiet town of Pompeii should someone challenge his throne. Unbeknownst to him nature is about to unleash its wrath upon the Empire during which the best and worst of Rome's citizens will be revealed during a time when duty and honor were more than words, they were ideals worth dying for.

Professor James Acton has just arrived in Egypt to visit his fiancée Professor Laura Palmer at her dig site when a United Nations helicopter arrives carrying representatives with an urgent demand that they come to Eritrea to authenticate an odd find that threatens to start a war—an ancient Roman vessel with over one billion dollars of gold in its hold.

It is a massive amount of wealth found in the world's poorest region, and everyone wants it. Nobody can be trusted, not even closest friends or even family. Greed, lust and heroism are the orders of the day as the citizens of Pompeii try to survive nature's fury, and James Acton tries to survive man's greed while risking his own life to protect those around him.

Pompeii's Ghosts delivers the historical drama and modern day action that best selling author J. Robert Kennedy's fans have come to expect. Pompeii's Ghosts opens with a shocker that will keep you on the edge of your seat until the thrilling conclusion in a story torn from the headlines.

J. ROBERT KENNEDY

Amazon Burning

A James Acton Thriller, Book #10

IN THE DEPTHS OF THE AMAZON,
ONE OF THEIR OWN HAS BEEN TAKEN!

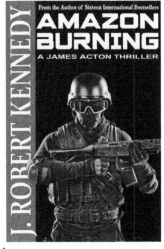

Days from any form of modern civilization, archeology Professor James Acton awakes to gunshots. Finding his wife missing, taken by a member of one of the uncontacted tribes, he and his friend INTERPOL Special Agent Hugh Reading try desperately to find her in the dark of the jungle, but quickly realize there is no hope without help.

And with help three days away, he knows the longer they wait, the farther away she'll be.

And the less hope there will be of ever finding the woman he loves.

Amazon Burning is the tenth installment of the James Acton Thrillers series in which the author of seventeen international bestsellers, J. Robert Kennedy, reunites James and his wife Laura Palmer with Hugh Reading, CIA Special Agent Dylan Kane, Delta Team-Bravo and others in a race against time to save one of their own, while behind the scenes a far darker, sinister force is at play, determined to keep its existence a secret from the world. The stakes are high, the action is full-throttle, and hearts will be broken as lives are changed forever in another James Acton adventure ripped from the headlines.

Rogue Operator

A Special Agent Dylan Kane Thriller, Book #1

TO SAVE THE COUNTRY HE LOVES, SPECIAL AGENT DYLAN KANE MIGHT HAVE TO BETRAY IT.

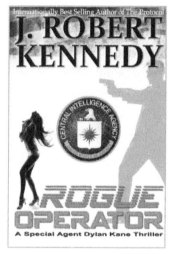

Three top secret research scientists are presumed dead in a boating accident, but the kidnapping of their families the same day raises questions the FBI and local police can't answer, leaving them waiting for a ransom demand that will never come.

Central Intelligence Agency Analyst Chris Leroux stumbles upon the story, and finds a phone conversation that was never supposed to happen. When he reports it to his boss, the National Clandestine Services Chief, he is uncharacteristically reprimanded for conducting an unauthorized investigation and told to leave it to the FBI.

But he can't let it go.

For he knows something the FBI doesn't.

One of the scientists is alive.

Chris makes a call to his childhood friend, CIA Special Agent Dylan Kane, leading to a race across the globe to stop a conspiracy reaching the highest levels of political and corporate America, that if not stopped, could lead to war with an enemy armed with a weapon far worse than anything in the American arsenal, with the potential to not only destroy the world, but consume it.

J. Robert Kennedy, the author of nine international best sellers, including the smash hit James Acton Thrillers, introduces Rogue Operator, the first installment of his newest series, The Special Agent Dylan Kane Thrillers, promising to bring all of the action and intrigue of the James Acton Thrillers with a hero who lives below the radar, waiting for his country to call when it most desperately needs him.

Containment Failure

A Special Agent Dylan Kane Thriller, Book #2

THE BLACK DEATH KILLED ALMOST HALF OF EUROPE'S POPULATION. THIS TIME BILLIONS ARE AT RISK.

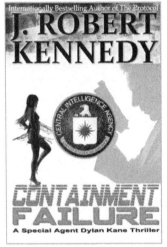

New Orleans has been quarantined, an unknown virus sweeping the city, killing one hundred percent of those infected. The Centers for Disease Control, desperate to find a cure, is approached by BioDyne Pharma who reveal a former employee has turned a cutting edge medical treatment capable of targeting specific genetic sequences into a weapon, and released it.

CIA Special Agent Dylan Kane has been given one guideline from his boss: consider yourself unleashed, leaving Kane and New Orleans Police Detective Isabelle Laprise battling to stay alive as an insidious disease and terrified mobs spread through the city while they desperately seek those behind the greatest crime ever perpetrated.

The stakes have never been higher as Kane battles to save not only his friends and the country he loves, but all of mankind.

In Containment Failure, eleven times internationally bestselling author J. Robert Kennedy delivers a terrifying tale of what could happen when science goes mad, with enough sorrow, heartbreak, laughs and passion to keep readers on the edge of their seats until the chilling conclusion.

Cold Warriors

A Special Agent Dylan Kane Thriller, Book #3

THE COUNTRY'S BEST HOPE IN DEFEATING A FORGOTTEN SOVIET WEAPON LIES WITH DYLAN KANE AND THE COLD WARRIORS WHO ORIGINALLY DISCOVERED IT.

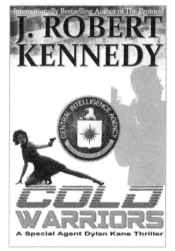

While in Chechnya CIA Special Agent Dylan Kane stumbles upon a meeting between a known Chechen drug lord and a retired General once responsible for the entire Soviet nuclear arsenal. Money is exchanged for a data stick and the resulting transmission begins a race across the globe to discover just what was sold, the only clue a reference to a top secret Soviet weapon called Crimson Rush.

Unknown to Kane, this isn't the first time America has faced this threat and he soon receives a mysterious message, relayed through his friend and CIA analyst Chris Leroux, arranging a meeting with perhaps the one man alive today who can help answer the questions the nation's entire intelligence apparatus is asking--the Cold Warrior who had discovered the threat the first time.

Over thirty years ago.

In Cold Warriors, the third installment of the hit Special Agent Dylan Kane Thrillers series, J. Robert Kennedy, the author of thirteen international bestsellers including The Protocol and Rogue Operator, weaves a tale spanning two generations and three continents with all the heart pounding, edge of your seat action his readers have come to expect. Take a journey back in time as the unsung heroes of a war forgotten try to protect our way of life against our greatest enemy, and see how their war never really ended, the horrors of decades ago still a very real threat today.

Death to America

A Special Agent Dylan Kane Thriller, Book #4

WHO DO YOU TRUST WHEN YOUR COUNTRY TURNS AGAINST ITSELF?

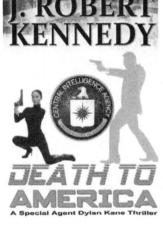

America is in crisis. Dozens of terrorist attacks have killed or injured thousands, and worse, every single attack appears to have been committed by an American citizen in the name of Islam.

A stolen experimental F-35 Lightning II is discovered by CIA Special Agent Dylan Kane in China, delivered by an American soldier reported dead years ago in exchange for a chilling promise.

Chinese Special Forces Officer Lee Fang overhears a conversation that sends her running for her life with information about a threat to America so great, it might be powerless to stop it.

And Chris Leroux is forced to watch as his girlfriend, Sherrie White, is tortured on camera, under orders to not interfere, her continued suffering providing intel too valuable to sacrifice.

From internationally bestselling author J. Robert Kennedy comes a disturbing action thriller that will have readers on the edge of their seat as they try to unravel the truth along with Kane, Leroux and Delta Team-Bravo as they question their own beliefs, their own government, and their own country.

The Turned

Zander Varga, Vampire Detective, Book #1

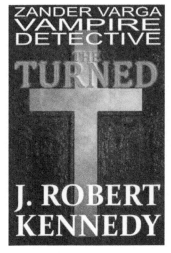

Zander has relived his wife's death at the hands of vampires every day for almost three hundred years, his perfect memory a curse of becoming one of The Turned—infecting him their final heinous act after her murder.

Nineteen year-old Sydney Winter knows Zander's secret, a secret preserved by the women in her family for four generations. But with her mother in a coma, she's thrust into the front lines, ahead of her time, to fight side-by-side with Zander.

And she wouldn't change a thing. She loves the excitement, she loves the danger. And she loves Zander. But it's a love that will have to go unrequited, because Zander has only one thing on his mind. And it's been the same thing for over two hundred years. Revenge.

But today, revenge will have to wait, because Zander Varga, Private Detective, has a new case. A woman's husband is missing. The police aren't interested. But Zander is. Something doesn't smell right, and he's determined to find out why.

From J. Robert Kennedy, the internationally bestselling author of The Protocol and Depraved Difference, comes his sixth novel, The Turned, a terrifying story that in true Kennedy fashion takes a completely new twist on the origin of vampires, tying it directly to a well-known moment in history. Told from the perspective of Zander Varga and his assistant, Sydney Winter, The Turned is loaded with action, humor, terror and a centuries long love that must eventually be let go.

Depraved Difference

A Detective Shakespeare Mystery, Book #1

WOULD YOU HELP, WOULD YOU RUN, OR WOULD YOU JUST WATCH?

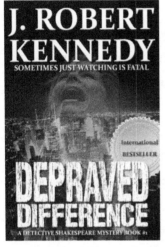

When a young woman is brutally assaulted by two men on the subway, her cries for help fall on the deaf ears of onlookers too terrified to get involved, her misery ended with the crushing stomp of a steel-toed boot. A cellphone video of her vicious murder, callously released on the Internet, its popularity a testament to today's depraved society, serves as a trigger, pulled a year later, for a killer.

Emailed a video documenting the final moments of a woman's life, entertainment reporter Aynslee Kai, rather than ask why the killer chose her to tell the story, decides to capitalize on the opportunity to further her career. Assigned to the case is Hayden Eldridge, a detective left to learn the ropes by a disgraced partner, and as videos continue to follow victims, he discovers they were all witnesses to the vicious subway murder a year earlier, proving sometimes just watching is fatal.

From the author of The Protocol and Brass Monkey, Depraved Difference is a fast-paced murder suspense novel with enough laughs, heartbreak, terror and twists to keep you on the edge of your seat, then knock you flat on the floor with an ending so shocking, you'll read it again just to pick up the clues.

Tick Tock

A Detective Shakespeare Mystery, Book #2

SOMETIMES HELL IS OTHER PEOPLE

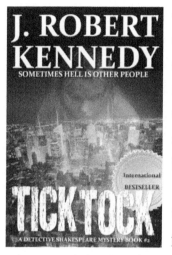

Crime Scene tech Frank Brata digs deep and finds the courage to ask his colleague, Sarah, out for coffee after work. Their good time turns into a nightmare when Frank wakes up the next morning covered in blood, with no recollection of what happened, and Sarah's body floating in the tub.

Billionaire Richard Tate is the toast of the town, loved by everyone but his wife. His plans for a romantic weekend with his mistress ends in disaster, waking the next morning to find her murdered, floating in the tub. After fleeing in a panic, he returns to find the hotel room spotless, and no sign of the body. An envelope found at the scene contains not the expected blackmail note, but something far more sinister.

Two murders, with the same MO, targeting both the average working man, and the richest of society, sets a rejuvenated Detective Shakespeare, and his new reluctant partner, Amber Trace, after a murderer whose motivations are a mystery, and who appears to be aided by the very people they would least expect—their own.

Tick Tock, Book #2 in the internationally bestselling Detective Shakespeare Mysteries series, picks up right where Depraved Difference left off, and asks a simple question: What would you do? What would you do if you couldn't prove your innocence, but knew you weren't capable of murder? Would you hide the very evidence that might clear you, or would you turn yourself in and trust the system to work?

The Redeemer

A Detective Shakespeare Mystery, Book #3

SOMETIMES LIFE GIVES MURDER A SECOND CHANCE

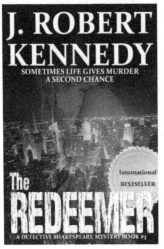

It was the case that destroyed Detective Justin Shakespeare's career, beginning a downward spiral of self-loathing and self-destruction lasting half a decade. And today things are only going to get worse. The Widow Rapist is free on a technicality, and it is up to Detective Shakespeare and his partner Amber Trace to find the evidence, five years cold, to put him back in prison before he strikes again.

But Shakespeare and Trace aren't alone in their desire for justice. The Seven are the survivors, avowed to not let the memories of their loved ones be forgotten. And with the release of the Widow Rapist, they are determined to take justice into their own hands, restoring balance to a flawed system.

At stake is a second chance, a chance at redemption, a chance to salvage a career destroyed, a reputation tarnished, and a life diminished.

A chance brought to Detective Shakespeare whether he wants it or not.

A chance brought to him by The Redeemer.

From J. Robert Kennedy, the author of seven international bestsellers including Depraved Difference and The Protocol, comes the third entry in the acclaimed Detective Shakespeare Mysteries series, The Redeemer, a dark tale exploring the psyches of the serial killer, the victim, and the police, as they all try to achieve the same goals.

Balance. And redemption.

Made in the USA
Monee, IL
01 December 2022

18984173R00204